# HIGHER GROUND

### THE WITCHES OF CANYON ROAD:
### BOOK SEVEN

## CHRISTINE POPE

Dark Valentine Press

This is a work of fiction. Names, characters, places, and incidents are either the product of the author's imagination or are used fictitiously. Any resemblance to actual events, places, organizations, or persons, whether living or dead, is entirely coincidental.

HIGHER GROUND

ISBN: 978-1-946435-25-5

Published by Dark Valentine Press

Cover design by Lou Harper

Print formatting by Indie Author Services

# 1

AVA CASTILLO STARED OUT HER KITCHEN window and sighed. Why exactly she was sighing on such a mild early summer day, with the flowers in the backyard finally showing all their riotous colors and a fresh, warm breeze blowing through the house, she really wasn't sure.

*You're just not used to having nothing to do,* she told herself, but despite the inner reassurance, she wasn't entirely certain that was the real problem.

All right, she supposed it was fairly normal to feel at loose ends less than a month after graduating from college…especially for someone who was a Castillo witch, and therefore didn't necessarily need to go out and look for a job right away. While most members of the Castillo clan actually did work full-time, if for no other reason than to make it seem as if they were normal, everyday civilians like the nonmagical people around them, it wasn't absolutely necessary, either. And although Ava had dutifully gotten a degree in English literature with a mind to go on and earn a teaching credential, when the time came to apply for a credential program, she realized she really didn't want to teach English.

She wanted…what, exactly?

A family someday, she supposed, when the time was right. At least, that was what her immediate family and the clan as a whole expected of her…not that she'd met anyone so far who seemed like a real prospect, or even appeared to be all that interested in making her a part of his life. Besides—although she probably wouldn't have the courage to tell anyone what she was thinking— settling down with the house and the picket fence sounded like such a tame existence, even though it was the one most witches and warlocks lived. Get married young, start a family, contribute to the clan. Who knew that being a witch could be so boring? It seemed very unfair to be blessed with magical talents and not, you know, be able to actually *do* anything with them.

Or possibly her restlessness stemmed from the knowledge that her big brother Tony had managed to get out and have an adventure, find true love with a witch from the de la Paz clan over in southern Arizona. Seeing her brother make his escape, get out of Santa Fe and start a new life in a whole new place, made Ava think that maybe there could be a bit more to existence than simply doing the same thing pretty much everyone in the Castillo family had done since time immemorial.

Of course, she had known better than to utter any of these heretical reflections aloud. Other clans might be a bit more freewheeling, but not the Castillos, who'd been here in Santa Fe for more than three centuries and were all too aware of the weight of history behind them. And although Ava had thought once or twice that it would be fun to use her singular magical gift of reading people's thoughts in a more public way— like setting herself up as a psychic—she knew that plan would never fly. The one underlying rule that all witches and warlocks followed was to do whatever they could to avoid public notice, to keep their magical talents secret so that no one in the outside world would ever be able to guess at their true natures.

She supposed that, as a matter of simple self-preservation, such a philosophy had its merits. But it sure made for a dull existence.

Shaking her head, she turned away from the window and went over to the refrigerator to refill her glass of iced tea. Maybe her current ennui also had something to do with this house. Yes, it had been super-generous of Tony to hand it over to her before he departed for Tucson with his…girl-friend? Fiancée? Ava wasn't exactly sure how she was supposed to view Cassandra Sandoval, except that obviously things were serious between her and Ava's older brother, even if the two of them hadn't set a wedding date or done anything quite so formal. Anyway, a big old Victorian house was probably the last thing Ava had been expecting to get as a graduation present, but here she was. The place was beautiful but stuffy, thanks to Victoria, the home's resident ghost, refusing to have anything but antiques inside her sanctum. At least the kitchen and bathrooms had been updated—Victoria had allowed that much in the way of improvements—but everything else looked pretty much like it must have back in the late 1880s when she'd still been alive. It was a little frustrat-ing, since Ava would have preferred to make the place more her own, but she also didn't think it was worth the ruckus any major changes would have caused.

She resolutely ignored the small bag of sugar inside the pantry and took her unsweetened iced tea with her to what had once been the sitting room and was now her TV room. Apparently, Victoria didn't have any problems with a television as long as it resided on an antique cabinet. Maybe it was silly to sit in here and watch TV when it was such a beautiful day outside, but what else was there to do? Reading, Ava's regular leisure time activity, didn't seem as appealing today as it usually did. She might have gone outside to spend some time working in the garden, except that Tony had also bequeathed his landscape team to her, so there wasn't much to do in the yard except enjoy the flowers.

*Just get a job,* she thought as she picked up the remote for the television. *Any job, as long as it gets you out of this big, gloomy house. Someone in the clan will give you something to do. Wasn't Cousin Eduardo saying the other day that he needed a hostess for one of his restaurants?*

Yes, she was pretty sure Eduardo could find something for her, although Ava knew if she took an entry-level job like that, her mother would probably inquire, in acid tones, why she'd bothered to get a bachelor's degree in the first place.

Sigh.

Just as Ava was about to click the power button on the remote, someone knocked at the front door. Frowning, she set down the clicker and wondered if she should ignore the knock—she wasn't expecting anyone, and so that meant the unwelcome caller was probably a solicitor of some sort. Since it was way too late in the year for Girl Scout cookies, she didn't see how it could be anyone she really wanted to see...not that she'd actually allow herself to consume a Girl Scout cookie after all the work she'd put in trying to lose weight the past couple of years.

Then the doorbell rang.

Obviously, whoever was out there wasn't one to give up easily. Ava permitted herself an eye roll but got up from the couch and went down the hallway to the front door. It had a beveled glass insert in its upper third, although she couldn't see much, only the dark silhouette of someone tall enough to blot out the light coming in through the glass.

Hoping she wasn't making a huge mistake, she unlocked the door and slowly opened it. The contrast of the bright sun outside against the dark hallway behind her made her blink, so for a moment, she couldn't exactly see who was standing on the front porch. Then her eyes adjusted, and she realized she was looking up at probably the most gorgeous man she'd ever seen in her life, with chiseled features and sooty black hair and dark eyes surrounded by a ring of fabulous lashes.

For a second, all she could do was stare at this apparition. But then she managed to say, "Can I help you?"

His expression was puzzled, as if he hadn't expected to see her standing there. "I very much hope so," he said, his English fluent but clearly accented. Mexican? Maybe, but she thought his accent sounded slightly different from that of the Mexican kids she'd gone to school with, even though she couldn't say exactly how. "This is 322 Hillside Avenue, is it not?"

"Yes," Ava replied slowly. For some reason, she felt reluctant to admit to such an obvious fact, despite the number being spelled out clearly in fancy tiles on the green-painted eaves just above them.

"Tony Castillo's house?"

Now she could only stare at the stranger, brows pulling together. "It *was* his house," she said. "I live here now."

"And you are…?"

Should she tell him? Ava hesitated for a few seconds, then gave an inner shrug. If the stranger thought Tony lived here, had his address, then they must have been acquainted in some way. With Tony, it was hard to know how they might have known each other, exactly, since her brother could strike up a conversation with almost anyone, anywhere. This godlike person could have met Tony at a party, at a bar downtown, a gallery opening…who knew?

"I'm his sister Ava," she said, figuring she might as well tell the unknown man the truth.

At once, the stranger smiled, and something in his posture seemed to relax, as though he'd feared she would be someone completely unknown to Tony, and therefore someone he had no reason to talk to.

"Hello, Ava," said the stranger. "My name is Gabriel Escobar."

She'd been caught by surprise, that was certain. The young woman's dark eyes widened, and he could see the way she took in a quick gulp of a breath. "'Gabriel Escobar'?" she repeated, as if she couldn't be quite certain of what she'd just heard him say. "But we thought—I mean, Tony said…." The sentence trailed off there, and she gave a quick shake of her head, obviously impatient with herself, with her current loss for words. "Why don't you come in?"

Gabriel could guess at the reason for her discomfiture. When her brother had last seen him, he had been surrounded by other Escobars intent on punishing him for helping Tony Castillo and the de la Paz witch who appeared to be his partner. No doubt, the Castillos had thought him dead all these months.

Well, he could forgive them for believing such a thing. There were times when he'd wished his brother Vicénte had killed him. That might have made things easier.

Ava led him down a dark, cool hallway and into a comfortable-looking room furnished with antiques and an improbably large television sitting on an old mahogany cabinet. A glass of untouched-looking iced tea sat on the table in front of the sofa.

Apparently noticing how he'd glanced at it, she said, "Would you like some iced tea?"

Since it was a warm day, and he'd walked here from the place where the Railrunner train had dropped him off in the Railyard district several miles from here, he nodded. "That would be very good. Thank you."

Her expression was still rather dazed, but she managed to smile. "I'll be back in a minute."

She went and he watched her go, thinking what a beautiful young woman she was. Although Gabriel supposed Tony Castillo had been good-looking enough, his was an angular sort of handsomeness, while Ava was all full lips and big, tip-tilted brown eyes, far lusher than he would have expected the Castillo warlock's sister to be.

This could be…interesting.

A few moments later, she returned with the promised glass of iced tea. After handing it to him, she sat down in the armchair to his left and gazed at him, her expression still perplexed. "I'm glad to see you're okay," Ava said, and her words had a ring of truth to them. She truly did seem relieved, although Gabriel wasn't sure why she felt it had been necessary to feel such concern about a stranger. Certainly not many in his own clan would have reacted the same way, had their roles been reversed. "Actually," she went on, "I was kind of angry with Tony for just leaving you there in El Salvador like that."

"There wasn't anything he could have done," Gabriel told her, which was nothing more than the truth. "I only just barely managed to send him and Cassandra away before they were over-whelmed as well."

Ava reached for her own glass of iced tea, but held it cradled between her two hands rather than raising it to her lips. "It still kind of boggles me that you were able to do that—send two people thousands of miles without batting an eye."

Gabriel supposed such a feat would seem rather fantastical to even a witch or a warlock. But teleportation—whether it involved sending himself or other people over vast distances—was only one of the many gifts that had come to him as the magic within him awakened not long after he entered his tenth year. What a feeling that had been, to begin to realize how powerful he was, that his talents soon far outstripped those of his half-brother, whom their father had made the Escobar clan's heir.

The memory of what had once been his made him realize how hollow he felt now.

"I am glad I was able to do such a thing for Tony and Cassandra," he said, hoping that the woman seated across from him hadn't detected any of his inner turmoil. "They were both very brave, to come to the heart of my clan's territory in order to recover the de la Paz grimoires."

"Or crazy," Ava remarked. "At least, that's what we all thought. I mean, I love my brother, but he's not exactly superhero material."

No, not really. But Tony Castillo had discovered a core of strength within himself when the crucial moment came, and that, in combination with Cassandra Sandoval's steely determination, had been enough to see the matter through. Despite everything that had happened afterward, Gabriel was still glad to know that the de la Paz grimoires were truly gone, burnt to ashes and no longer a threat to anyone.

"Possibly not a superhero, but a hero nonetheless," Gabriel said.

Ava didn't appear completely convinced, but she didn't protest. "But it all worked out, so I suppose whether he's a superhero or not doesn't really matter." Now she drank from her tumbler of iced tea, only a brief sip before she set the glass back down. When she looked back up at him, her expression was still puzzled. "How in the world did you get away from Pico Negro?"

"I didn't."

She blinked, obviously nonplussed by his reply. "What?"

Gabriel allowed himself a bitter smile. It was not so much of an indulgence, not after everything he had lost. "I could not get away. Normally, yes, my power to transport myself in the blink of an eye would have been enough for me to make my escape, but in my clan, there is a null—you know what a null is?"

"A witch or warlock who can suppress all magic around them," Ava said. "Or at least, that's how Tony explained it to me. So…that's what happened? The null from your clan came, and you were trapped?"

Succinct, if painful. He wouldn't allow himself to sigh, only replied, "Yes. My brother—the Escobar *primus*—was very angry with me. I believe he would have struck me down then and there if one of the elders had not stopped him."

"That was kind of them," Ava said, although her tone sounded a bit uncertain, as though she knew they hadn't been motivated by mere altruism.

"I fear kindness had little to do with their actions." Gabriel reached for his own iced tea and took a swallow. It was good, cold and not sweetened at all, but still mellow, not bitter. After wetting his dry throat, he went on, "No, it was more that the elders feared my brother would invoke the wrath of the gods if he committed kin-murder."

That remark made Ava's eyes widen again. "Wait, you're not…?" Her question trailed off, and she tapped her fingers against her jeans-clad knee. "Sorry," she went on. "I just kind of assumed that if you were from El Salvador, you must be Catholic, like us Castillos."

Had she put that bit about "us Castillos" in her comment to make him feel more at ease? Gabriel didn't know for sure, but he felt himself warming toward her anyway. "We are, at least nominally. But our clan also recognizes the gods who dwelled in that land before the conquistadors came. Anyway, it does not do to make them angry, and to kill someone of your own clan is taboo. Despite such a prohibition, I believe Vicénte would have killed me, except that the elders proposed an even worse punishment."

"Worse than death?" Ava said, looking skeptical. "I don't know…death is pretty final."

"True, and yet…." There were many times he had wished himself dead once he reawakened to himself and understood what they had done to him. But he would not say such a thing to Ava Castillo. He did not know her, even though she sat there with concern in her face, gazing at him with those beautiful dark eyes. Kind eyes. Such sympathy, for someone little more than a stranger. She must have a gentle heart, something almost as foreign to him as the land where he now found himself. He pulled in a breath, then continued. "You see, the elders of my clan wield terrible powers. They took me, and pulled the magic from within me, so that I am now no more than what you people call a civilian."

Shock registered on her face, along with a terrible sadness...and comprehension. "I'd say that was impossible, but I know our *prima's* parents did the same thing a long time ago to your...half-brother?"

Gabriel nodded. "Matías. Yes, he was my half-brother, although I never knew him. And of course it was when Angela McAllister and Connor Wilcox took Matías' powers away that my father swore his revenge. That was what made him leave Pico Negro and go to America, seeking vengeance."

For a few seconds, Ava was silent, absorbing what he had said. Perhaps this information was new to her, for of course, he had no idea how much Ava—or the rest of the Castillo clan, for that matter—knew about his father Joaquin. When she spoke, it was to ask a question he'd been dreading.

"What happened after they took your powers?"

Those were dark days, ones Gabriel would sooner forget. But he knew he needed to tell her the whole story, for he needed her to understand why he had come here to Santa Fe. "They stole my memory as well. I remember nothing after I stood there in my brother's home and heard the elders pronounce my punishment…and then enact it."

"Well, you must remember *something*," Ava said sensibly. "Or else you wouldn't have been able to tell me everything you've told me so far."

He nodded. "Gradually, my memories returned. Only after I had been taken from Pico Negro and left in Guatemala City, with a thousand dollars in my wallet and no I.D., no luggage, no nothing."

Gabriel paused, remembering how he had awakened in a hotel room in the capital city of El Salvador's neighboring country, blinking at his surroundings and wondering how in the world he had gotten there. Panic had lanced through him, even though his mind was still a fog. For days, he could recall nothing of his life, nothing of where he had come from. He had ordered room service and sent one of the bellboys out to fetch him a change of clothing and some toiletries, then sat there dully watching the television, hoping that something—*anything*—would jog his memory.

Then one day, he had awakened, and a single thought had slipped through his mind.

*I am Gabriel Escobar.*

But there had been nothing else to accompany that one moment of clarity, nothing to tell him exactly who Gabriel Escobar was, what his life had been before he awakened in this hotel room. However, he had also realized that if he stayed where he was, he very likely would not be able to recover anything of his past.

"That's terrible," Ava said, her tone emphatic.

He allowed himself to smile. "I suppose so. It would have been worse if they had given me no money. But a thousand dollars goes a long way in Guatemala. I left the hotel, bought myself some new clothes and false identification, and took a bus north to Mexico."

"Why there?"

Another good question, although one he had no true answer for. "I'm not sure. Something inside was telling me to head north, although at the time I didn't know why. Anyway, it seemed the best thing for me to do. I arrived in Mexico City and got a room at a hostel there, and hoped that something about the place would awaken my memories."

"Did it?" Ava asked.

"Unfortunately, no. But while I was wandering around the city, looking for anything that might help me remember something of my past, I met an Englishwoman—a photographer. She asked if I would be interested in modeling for her to earn some extra money. Since my funds were getting low, I agreed."

"So you worked for this woman for a while?"

"For almost five months, yes. It was easy work, although I will admit it made me feel rather foolish." That was something of an understatement. He had worn the clothes that Olivia asked him to wear, posed where she told him to pose. The entire time, he kept expecting her to shake her head and say no, that she had made a mistake and he actually had no aptitude for such a frivolous occupation. However, that didn't happen, because she seemed pleased with him and even introduced him to other photographers, made sure he had a portfolio he could show around. The money was good, enough for him to leave the hostel and get an apartment. It was not until one day when he was walking the city's streets in the spring and he glimpsed a dark-haired man with a beautiful redhead at his side that his memory suddenly came alive. He remembered Tony Castillo and Cassandra Sandoval, remembered how he had been born to a clan of witches and warlocks in El Salvador…how the elders of that clan had torn his powers from him in revenge for his perceived betrayal.

Ava's expression was thoughtful. She also didn't seem terribly surprised to hear that he had earned his keep all those months by working as a model. Was it because she thought him attractive enough to have that profession as his vocation?

He rather hoped so.

"But eventually your memories came back," she said.

"Yes. I realized that Mexico was not my home, and yet it certainly was not safe for me to return to El Salvador." Gabriel paused. Now that the time had come and he faced a Castillo witch in the flesh, he was suddenly uncertain as to how she would respond to the entire reason for his being here. And yet, after traveling all this way, he could not back down now. "I remembered how I had helped your brother and his woman. And I thought that possibly the Castillos might be able to offer me some assistance."

That comment earned him an uncertain smile. "I'm sure we'll do whatever we can. I doubt that our *prima* Miranda would turn you away, not after what you did for Tony and Cassandra. It might take some getting used to, but I think you'll like it here in Santa Fe."

While her words were encouraging, this was not all he wanted from the Castillos. He smiled back at Ava, and was glad to see the way her cheeks flushed and she glanced away for a second, as if not entirely certain of her reaction to him. "That is very generous, and I thank you. But that is not the only thing I was hoping you could help me with."

"Oh?" Ava said, now looking slightly disconcerted.

"No." Gabriel allowed himself a breath and then said, "I want you to help me get my powers back."

## 2

For a few painful seconds, all Ava could do was stare back at Gabriel, wondering if she just hadn't heard him correctly. How in the world was anyone in her clan supposed to help him recover the powers that had been taken from him? That they'd been stolen in the first place was just barely within the bounds of probability, since she knew the very same thing had happened to his half-brother, thanks to her *prima's* parents seeking their own justice for Matías Escobar's vicious crimes involving their clan members. But, as Ava had reflected on more than one occasion, it was a lot easier to destroy something than to rebuild it.

"Um, I don't think that's possible," she said, hating how blunt the words sounded. Then again, it would have been crueler to give him false hope, wouldn't it? Her tone gentle, she added, "No one in my clan has that kind of power."

Gabriel picked up his glass of iced tea and sipped from it. The whole time, though, his dark eyes were fixed on her face, as if he was doing his best to read something from her expression. "But it *is* possible," he replied, sounding unruffled. "Because my half-sister Renata summoned the power to restore Matías' magic after the McAllister *prima* and Wilcox *primus* took it away. Renata was a very powerful witch...but I think probably not as powerful as your Castillo *prima*."

Well, that might be true. Honestly, Ava couldn't think of anyone as powerful as Miranda, at least not in the Castillo clan. And actually, while Miranda's parents were amazingly talented, their true power came from the two of them working together. Individually, their daughter's gifts far outstripped theirs.

"Okay, maybe it's possible," Ava allowed. "But a while back when she and Tony were visiting Santa Fe, Cassandra told me something about this half-sister of yours and some of what happened back then—Renata used terrible dark magic to restore Matías' powers, right? I mean, people were killed."

"Yes, this is true," Gabriel said. Expression troubled, he added, "And I am not asking your *prima* to use such magic. I am only saying that these things are possible if the witch or warlock in question is strong enough."

That comment made Ava feel a little better. Not a lot, but at least he wasn't expecting the Castillos to abandon all their principles just to assist him. But still, she really didn't see how Miranda could help Gabriel. Her powers were extremely strong, true, but she didn't have much experience with using them, since they'd come to her so late in life, more than ten years after they should have appeared. How would she even go about hunting down the correct spell to use to help the Escobar warlock, if such a spell even existed? Most witches and warlocks used their powers by instinct; they didn't rely on charms and potions and other popular notions of how people might work magic. However, spell books existed because they helped witches focus their natural abilities to do something far beyond what they were able to accomplish on their own. That was why the stolen grimoires had been so dangerous. In the hands of the Escobars, they could have been used for all sorts of terrible things…

…like the spells Gabriel's half-sister had used, now more than twenty years ago. The Escobars must already have possessed their own spell books, or Renata wouldn't have been able to restore her brother Matías' powers. However, Ava was almost certain that the Castillos didn't have that kind of magical library. Records here and there for simple charms, possibly. Nothing on this scale, though.

"Miranda's magic really isn't like that," she said. "Or at least, it doesn't seem as if it is. I've never seen her use a spell. She just sort of…makes things happen."

"Well, then, she can try to make this thing happen," Gabriel responded, his tone reasonable. He tilted his head to regard Ava for a moment, and she sensed that she was blushing again and couldn't do a damn thing about it. There was something almost unsettling about being this close to someone so impossibly good-looking. Under his gaze, she suddenly felt plump and awkward again, although ruthlessly watching every single morsel that went into her mouth and forcing herself to walk almost everywhere had allowed her to lose those last fifteen stubborn pounds her senior year of college, after she'd dropped even more than that the year before.

"I-I suppose," she stammered, knowing how silly she sounded. "I mean, I can call Miranda and see what she has to say." Even as she made the offer, though, Ava could feel herself tense up. While it was true that only a couple of years separated the two women when it came to their actual ages, she couldn't help thinking of Miranda as in another class altogether, lofty in her role as the clan's *prima*—and much farther along in her life, with a husband and a baby and far more responsibilities than Ava had ever had to manage. She would have to steel herself to make that call…and not feel like some kind of impostor while doing so.

"I would very much appreciate it if you would," Gabriel said. A long pause, and then he added, his tone quiet but intense, "Your brother told me that your gift is reading minds. You can look into mine now, if you wish. You will be able to see that what I have told you is nothing more than the truth."

Oh, dear lord. That would be too awkward, even if he was giving her permission. Speaking far too quickly, she said, "Gabriel, I don't really need to do that."

He leaned forward, gaze fixed on her. "Actually, I think you do. Otherwise, how can you know that everything I have said is what really happened to me?"

Now it was Ava's turn to hesitate. She swallowed, knowing that if she continued to protest, he would think something was wrong. And while she knew her talent would allow her to see Gabriel's thoughts…and more…she wished she didn't have to do this. Her gift had always been difficult, a burden. Even though she'd told the others in her clan over and over again that she had to focus to see into their minds, that she didn't have the ability to sense every stray thought which might be bouncing around her, people still tended to look at her with suspicion, as if they wondered whether she was taking a surreptitious peek when they weren't paying attention.

"All right," she said at last. *God, I hope this isn't a huge mistake....*

His dark eyes suddenly seemed too piercing. "You take no joy in your gift, do you?"

For a guy with no magic, he sure seemed to see a lot. Ava managed a not very convincing laugh and replied, "Let's just say that it makes people uncomfortable."

"I suppose that's understandable." Now his mouth lifted slightly at the corners, not quite enough to be a smile, but sufficient to show he was a little amused. "But I've asked you to do this, so it is not the same."

He had a point. "Okay," she said. "You don't need to do anything. Just sit there, and I'll take a quick look."

His expression was calm. "I understand."

Did he? Although he'd once possessed what sounded like an astonishing array of magical talents, reading minds apparently hadn't been one of them. Not that it mattered. As she'd told him, this was going to be fast—just a quick peek to reassure herself that he was telling the truth. She guessed he had to be, since he knew far too many details about the Escobar clan that a civilian honestly couldn't, but it was still better to be safe.

Also, she realized then that she'd never felt the faint ping from him that she always got whenever she met a witch or warlock for the first time, that indefinable sensation which told her she was in the presence of someone like her. Gabriel felt like a civilian…but he sure didn't sound like one.

And, as he'd pointed out just a few minutes earlier, she had an easy way of discovering the truth.

There was always a brief moment of darkness, almost as if her talent had to find its way through the bone that protected the brain inside someone's head. Once that moment had passed, though, the images and words came fast. After more than ten years of doing this, Ava knew how to organize those images and syllables into easily recognizable thoughts, although she knew if she didn't stay focused, they could quickly morph into an onslaught of information and emotions that threatened to overwhelm her.

In Gabriel's mind, she saw herself—as someone far more beautiful than the girl who looked back at her from the mirror each morning—and the dark antiques that surrounded them in the room where they sat. She felt worry and antic-ipation and hope, saw crowded streets and bright, glaring sunlight and heard people speaking Spanish…saw Tony deliver a very respectable punch to the jaw of a tall, darkly handsome man she somehow knew was Gabriel's half-brother Vicénte. Saw the Escobar elders—a squat toad of a man and a tall, thin woman—glaring at Gabriel, saw the null standing off to one side, a good-looking man in his late twenties who appeared somehow guilty and miserable, as if he knew it was his fault that Gabriel had been caught.

Felt the pain that lanced through Gabriel's body as the elders murmured words in a language she'd never heard before, watched as he crumpled to the ground. Saw the world go black, and then his eyes open to a strange hotel room, plain but clean, with a television attached to one wall and dark patterned drapes at the window. A bus, more images of a place she knew must be Mexico City, with its tall buildings in a mixture of old and new and a dense haze that seemed to hang above the busy streets, and then a crowded airport, a big jet plane, the terminal at Albuquerque's Sunport.

She opened her eyes and saw Gabriel watching her, gaze expectant.

"You didn't tell me it hurt when they took your magic from you," she said, pity moving through her for what he had suffered.

His shoulders lifted. "If I had mentioned it, then you might have thought I was trying to play on your sympathies. Besides, for a long time, I didn't remember the incident at all. By the time those memories returned, the pain was distant enough that I could ignore it."

Ava wasn't sure she could be so casual about an incident that had clearly been excruciating, but if Gabriel didn't want to discuss it, then she'd let the matter go.

"But you saw," he went on. "So you know that I am telling you the truth."

She nodded. "Yes, that was obvious. And I am sorry. I know that Tony and Cassandra were worried about what had happened to you."

"It is not their fault. You know that I took the books in the first place."

Yes, Tony had told her about that part of the story, doing his best to paint Gabriel in a good light, since the theft of the grimoires had involved their mother getting knocked unconscious. True, Gabriel had been acting under duress at the time, fearing that Vicénte would hurt his own mother in some way if he didn't do as his older brother demanded, but still, there were probably some who would say that Gabriel had understood the risks when he agreed to help Tony and Cassandra get the de la Paz clan's grimoires back.

"I know," Ava said, "but there were extenuating circumstances involved."

Gabriel's English was obviously very good, but

that phrase seemed to puzzle him. His brows drew together. "I am not sure I understand."

"You were forced into taking the books, right? Because Vicénte was threatening your mother? I'd say that makes the situation not really your fault."

Now Gabriel relaxed against the back of his chair, clearly relieved she saw things that way. "I suppose so. But now, I am not going to worry about 'extenuating circumstances' or anything else. I only want to have my powers restored."

Curious, she asked, "What will you do if you somehow do get them back?"

This time, the smile he gave her was a genuine one. "Why, I will take revenge on my brother, of course."

As soon as the words left his lips, Gabriel realized that perhaps he had said the wrong thing. Ava didn't exactly recoil, but she did seem to withdraw slightly, the concerned expression she wore replaced by something almost ferociously blank, as though she was working very hard to not let any emotions show themselves on her face.

"I see you don't believe that is a noble cause," he said, and she looked as though she wanted to shake her head but stopped herself.

"I—well, I tend to think it's better to sit back

and let karma sort things out, but I've never had anyone do anything to me that's remotely close to what Vicénte and the elders did to you, so...." Nervous fingers played with a strand of long, dark hair, and she glanced down at the floor, as if she'd suddenly found something fascinating in the pattern of the intricate, well-worn Persian rug beneath their feet.

He had been honest with her because he'd already allowed her into his mind and saw no reason to dissemble when it came to his intentions, but it was possible he could have phrased things a bit more delicately. "You see," he went on, hoping he could make her understand, "it is not only what Vicénte did to me, but what he will continue to do as *primus* of the Escobar clan. He might not have all our father Joaquin's powers, but he is certainly as ruthless. For centuries, the clan has been ruled by men much like him, but Vicénte has a certain recklessness that worries me. He is not fit to hold such a position of power. He chafes at the isolation in which he must live, for even though his word is law and he has the finest house in the village, he can only think of what he might do if he were not so constrained. You understand?"

"I think so," Ava said slowly. Her fingers knotted together; for the first time, Gabriel saw that she wore on the middle finger of her right hand a gold ring with a fiery opal mounted in it, a ring that looked quite old. A family heirloom? Perhaps. "I assume it was Vicénte's idea to take the grimoires."

"Yes. He never revealed to me exactly how he heard of them in the first place, but he was very excited by the prospect of having them in his possession." Gabriel stopped himself there, deciding he did not need to relate in detail the arguments he and Vicénte had had regarding those books, how eventually Vicénte had resorted to extortion and threats because he knew there was no other way to coerce his more powerful brother into doing what he wanted done. "You see, if he'd had the books for any amount of time, had learned how to work the magic contained within them, then he would have been stronger than me. I am only one man, but he could have commanded armies of demons."

A visible shiver passed over Ava, and she gave a reluctant nod. "I can see how that would be a very bad thing. But...the books are destroyed, and you're safe here now. I don't know why you can't just leave it alone."

"If you had met my brother, you would not say such a thing." Gabriel reached for his iced tea and drank some more, for his throat was becoming dry. "He might have been thwarted when the books burned to nothing, true, but one setback will not stop him. Who knows what other valuable magical books or objects might be out there in the world to be taken, what prize he might set his sights on next? And also, even without the help of the grimoires, he is a very strong warlock. There are many strong witches and warlocks in the Escobar clan. If Vicénte decides he has had enough of hiding, then he will strike against the nonmagical people in the area, bend them to his will. The nearest village—San Matías—is already under his control, as it has been under the control of the Escobar clan for generations, but I doubt he will be content with so few followers for very much longer."

"He wouldn't really do something like that, would he?" Ava looked aghast; she swallowed, then reached for her own glass of tea and hastily drank some. "I mean, all of us witches and warlocks know that we can't let the civilians find out about us. We have magical powers, true, but we would be so outnumbered that it still wouldn't be any kind of a fair fight. If they wanted to get rid of us, they could."

"And would, if threatened." This was the same argument Gabriel had used with his brother, although Vicénte had not seemed terribly concerned. Most likely, he did not have any true concept of the world beyond the borders of El Salvador, or even the neighboring countries of

Guatemala and Honduras. He did not know—or seem interested in learning—how strong the civilians were, how large their armies were, what types of terrible weapons could be brought against witch-kind if it was decided they presented a large enough threat. His was an arrogance born of parochialism, of believing that the Escobar clan would be able to easily vanquish any possible foes.

"I can see why you want to stop him," Ava said, her expression more troubled than ever. Something about the vulnerability Gabriel saw in her face made him want to reach out and comfort her, but of course he could not do anything so bold, not when they had only met less than half an hour ago. He knew he should be glad that she was willing to listen to him at all. "But…even if you somehow got your powers back, do you really think you would be able to take on your entire clan?"

No, he was not quite that arrogant. He frowned, saying, "That was never my plan. It was my hope that I could persuade enough of them to realize our father Joaquin was mistaken in making him the heir, that I should have been the one to lead the Escobar clan. I was far too young when my father left for my powers to have begun to develop—I was barely two years old—and so he did what he thought best, which was to designate

Vicénte as his heir in the event anything happened to him."

"And he probably thought nothing would happen, and that he'd return to Pico Negro after putting Matías in place as the head of the Santiagos in Southern California," Ava remarked.

"Most likely. He did not have much sense of his own mortality, based on what I have heard other people say about him." Joaquin's pride wasn't entirely misplaced, for the Escobars had never seen a warlock like him before. Gabriel knew that even he, with all the talents he'd possessed before the elders had stolen them from him, could not have quite matched his father, since he did not have the null gift—or curse, depending on how one looked at it—and neither did he have Joaquin's dubious talent for coercing those around him and bending them to his will.

For a few seconds, Ava was quiet, fingers tapping against the side of her iced tea glass. Was she thinking how ludicrous it was for him to believe he could take control of his clan? After all, she had only her brother's testimony—and Gabriel's own recollection of the events in Pico Negro—to prove to her that he had the magical strength necessary to become the leader of the Escobars. Indeed, although he would not admit it to her, not when he was trying desperately to enlist her help and the help of her *prima,* he could not be entirely sure whether he would sway the members of his family or not. They were used to following Vicénte, although if he led them in a direction that invited outside scrutiny and very possibly persecution, they might cast aside their blind obedience in the interest of self-preservation.

But still, Gabriel knew he had to try, even if the odds seemed daunting. Vicénte's ambitions could not be allowed to go unchecked.

Ava deliberately put her glass back down on its coaster, then looked up, her gaze meeting his directly. Although he could see the way her finely arched brows pulled together, her pretty mouth was set, almost resolute.

"All right," she said. "I'll call Miranda."

## 3

THIS HAD TO BE CRAZY, DIDN'T IT? HAD SHE really agreed to help Gabriel Escobar recover his stolen magical powers? After all, the guy had just walked into her house barely a half hour earlier. What evidence did she have that would allow her to even trust him, except the memories he'd let her see?

But the thing was, those memories were enough. People could try to cover up the things that had happened to them, or at the very least attempt to make themselves look better, but Ava knew memories didn't lie, not when they were accessed in such a way. She'd seen the elders take away Gabriel's powers, had experienced his confusion and fear when he awoke in that strange hotel room...had felt the despair that coursed through his mind and spirit when he finally remembered who he was and what had been taken from him. Knowing all that, could she honestly refuse to help him?

Not really. Maybe there were people in the world—or even in her own clan—who could have hardened their hearts and told him that his misfortune was none of their concern, but Ava knew she wasn't that person. Not the Ava Castillo who'd rescued more strays than she could count, who'd volunteered at the animal shelter in the summer as a caretaker and animal cuddler.

No, it seemed Gabriel was another one of her strays, and she had to do what she could to help him get his powers back. As for the rest...well, she had no idea whether his ultimate goal of taking the leadership of the Escobar clan away from his dangerous brother was at all feasible, but that was for Gabriel to decide. The assistance he'd given Tony and Cassandra meant that the Castillos needed to do whatever was required to get his magic restored. Her clan owed him a debt.

Ava had excused herself to come into the kitchen, where the house still had an old-fashioned land line. She hardly ever used it, but it provided a good reason for her to come in here where she could speak to Miranda at least semi-privately, rather than pick up her cell phone from where she'd set it down on the coffee table and make the phone call in the TV room right in front of Gabriel.

Miranda's phone rang…and rang… and Ava wondered whether the *prima* was out, or maybe just busy with the baby. After all, little Ginny wasn't even six months old yet.

But then Ava heard Miranda's voice through the phone's speaker, sounding out of breath. "Hello?"

"Hi, Miranda," Ava said, even as she realized that the *prima* probably wouldn't recognize her voice. They'd only met once or twice, after all. Miranda had spent a lot more time around Tony, since Ava had been down in Albuquerque going to college while all that mess with Simon Escobar was happening, now more than a year and a half ago. "Um, this is Ava…Tony's sister."

"Oh, hi, Ava," Miranda replied, sounding justifiably mystified to be contacted by someone she'd probably exchanged ten words with, if even that much. "What can I do for you?"

"Well, I've had kind of a situation come up."

"A 'situation'?" the *prima* echoed, her tone sharpening. "What kind of situation?"

"Nothing dangerous," Ava said hastily. What with all the craziness that had occurred in the Castillo clan ever since she'd come here from northern Arizona, she could see why Miranda might be easily spooked, but the current situation didn't warrant that kind of alarm. Or at least, Ava hoped it didn't. "But it's kind of crazy. I just had Gabriel Escobar show up on my doorstep...literally...and he—"

The *prima* cut in at once. "Wait...*who?*"

"Gabriel Escobar. You know, the guy who helped Tony and Cassandra down in El Salvador."

"I know who he is. I just...." A pause, and then Miranda said, "I just suppose I wasn't expecting to hear that he'd shown up in Santa Fe."

"Well, he came here looking for Tony. I wasn't really expecting Gabriel to appear like this, either." There was an understatement. She was still coming to terms with the reality that the man they'd all thought was dead had somehow appeared at her house. However, Ava took a breath and forged ahead. "But he's in kind of tight spot and is asking for our help. Is it okay if we come over so we can talk to you in person?"

"I—" Miranda broke off, as if she'd begun to say something and then thought better of it. "Sure. You want to come now?"

"Yes, if that's okay."

"It's fine. Ginny has a pediatrician's appointment at four, but that's hours from now. I assume this won't take that long?"

Good question. Ava didn't think so, but then, she had no idea whether Gabriel would expect Miranda to try to restore his powers on the spot.

Maybe, but even if he insisted, such a thing didn't seem very feasible. Miranda would need some time to prepare for a magical feat of that magnitude, wouldn't she?

"No, it shouldn't take long," Ava replied, figuring she could always backtrack if necessary. Better to get their foot in the door, so to speak, and then see what happened. "We'll be over in about five or ten minutes."

"All right. See you then."

Miranda ended the call, and Ava replaced the old-fashioned phone's handset in its cradle. Actually, now that she'd committed to this course of action, she felt almost relieved. Now all they had to do was go and state their case. After that, it would be up to the *prima* what happened next.

When she returned to the TV room, Gabriel was still sitting in his chair, the glass of iced tea she'd gotten him now almost gone. He looked up at her expectantly, and once again she had to fight to keep herself from flushing. It was crazy to have that kind of reaction to him, wasn't it? All right, she'd never met a guy as good-looking as he was, but still, this wasn't seventh grade.

To cover her discomfiture, she said hastily, "Miranda is okay with seeing you. We need to head over to her house now."

The relief in his expression was obvious. "That is…wonderful. Thank you, Ava."

*Don't thank me yet,* she thought. *I have no idea what Miranda is going to say to you.*

However, she managed a smile and said, "It's no problem. Come with me—it's faster to get to the garage through the kitchen."

He put down his nearly empty glass of iced tea and rose from the chair, then followed her as she led him through the back door to the detached garage, which faced out onto an alleyway. As they went, she sent him a questioning glance over one shoulder.

"I just realized…if you came to Santa Fe all the way from Mexico City, don't you have any luggage?"

A shrug. "Yes, but I stopped on the way over here and got a room at one of the hotels downtown. It seemed the wise thing to do. Anyway, my luggage is there."

Well, that was convenient. Ava realized that at the back of her mind, there had been the nagging worry of what to do with Gabriel if Miranda agreed to help and he needed to remain in Santa Fe for an extended period, but if he'd already found a place to stay, then that awkwardness was handled. She supposed if he'd been working as a male model for the past four or five months, he probably had a decent amount of cash on him, which also would make things easier.

They got in her Honda CR-V—a present

from Tony, who she knew had felt guilty about all the money he'd inherited from their grandfather when all she'd gotten was a few pieces of jewelry— and she let the car back itself out of the garage. Miranda's address was already programmed into the navigation system, just because it made sense to have the *prima's* home as one of its set destinations. The house wasn't really that far away, and under different circumstances, Ava might have walked, but she didn't know whether Gabriel's impatience would allow for a leisurely stroll through Santa Fe's historic district.

Five minutes later, they pulled up to the large hacienda-style house that had been home to the Castillo clan's *primas* for several hundred years. Although Gabriel didn't say anything as he got out of the car and walked with Ava along the path that led to the front entrance, she could tell by the faint nod he made that he was impressed by the property. She had to admit that it was pretty imposing, if a bit heavy and gloomy for her taste. But roses were blooming everywhere in the expansive gardens, and hollyhocks had just begun to flaunt their colors in the beds along the side of the house, so the effect was more cheerful than the place itself might have otherwise allowed.

Miranda opened the door almost as soon as Ava put her finger on the doorbell. She looked casual enough in her elbow-sleeved blouse and faded jeans, her wavy dark hair falling over her shoulders. Ava had to tamp down a stab of envy; it didn't seem fair that someone who'd had a baby less than six months earlier could manage to be so slender.

For a second, Miranda's green eyes appraised Gabriel, and then she smiled at him and said, "Hello, Gabriel. I'm Miranda Castillo, the clan's *prima*."

"I am very honored to meet you," he said gravely, causing her to purse her lips and give him another piercing look, as though she was trying to decide whether he was being completely serious or whether he was mocking her in some way. Of course, Ava knew he was serious, and she guessed that some of the formality of his speech had probably come from learning English from books rather than having conversations with actual English speakers, but she supposed she could see how Miranda might have been slightly put off by the way he spoke.

However, the *prima* apparently decided to let it pass, because she said, "It's very nice to meet you. Please, come inside."

They followed her through the foyer, which was made cheerful by a large yellow vase full of roses from the garden, and on into the living room. The space used to feel much darker and heavier than it did now; Ava noticed that Miranda had replaced the thick velvet drapes at the tall windows with filmy, semi-sheer linen curtains, and there were more flowers here, roses and lilies and tall stalks of iris.

"Go ahead and sit down. Rafe took Ginny for a little outing in the park down the street. We can talk privately," Miranda said, so Ava took a seat on the couch, with Gabriel next to her. Not too close, but enough for her to be acutely aware of his presence, the way the muscles in his arms strained against the dark T-shirt he wore as he clasped his hands on one knee, or the scruff of dark hair on his cheeks and chin, not heavy enough to be a true beard or even to obscure the strong, clean lines of his jaw. He smelled good, too, of something fresh and a little citrusy.

She took a breath and told herself to concentrate on why they were here...which would have been a lot easier if he weren't so distracting.

"Thank you for seeing me," Gabriel said. "I know my presence here must be something of a surprise."

"That's an understatement." Miranda pushed up the sleeves of the pale green blouse she wore, then crossed her arms. "But I'm glad to see that you're all right. You did a lot to help Tony and Cassandra, and that's not the sort of thing any of us will forget."

Something about Gabriel seemed to relax as

he heard those words. Maybe he'd been worried about what kind of reception he was going to get, but from the way Miranda was talking, it seemed obvious to Ava that her *prima* wasn't going to ignore how he'd put himself in harm's way to make sure a Castillo warlock and a de la Paz witch made it safely out of Escobar territory.

"I am glad to hear that," he said. "So let me explain what happened next."

He launched into the same story he'd told Ava, just the simple facts, with no embellishment or dramatic pauses to determine whether he was eliciting the correct sympathetic response from his audience. When he came to the end of it, he gave a simple lift of his shoulders.

"And that is why I have come to you, Miranda. It was my hope that a *prima* of your vast gifts might be able to restore what was taken from me."

For a second or two, she only stared back at him, as though she wasn't quite sure of what he was asking…or maybe simply didn't want to acknowledge it. Then she offered him a rueful smile and said, "I think you may have overestimated my abilities."

"I am not so sure of that," he returned. "After all, you defeated my half-brother Simon. That could not have been an easy feat."

Her expression turned grim for a moment. "No, it wasn't. But I also had help."

She stopped there. Ava had a feeling she wasn't going to explain how the demon lord Loc had swooped in to provide his own unique assistance, probably because said demon lord was now happily living with Miranda's sister-in-law. For all her outward friendliness toward Gabriel, the *prima* probably wasn't quite ready to reveal that the Castillo witch family could now claim Loc as one of their own.

"Still," Gabriel said, "it seems clear enough that your gifts rival those of the most powerful in my own clan. And if my clan elders could take my magic away, why could you not return it?"

"Because…." Miranda spread her hands wide, a helpless sort of gesture, and looked over at Ava, as if asking for her help. About all Ava could do was offer a small lift of her shoulders. She'd already said as much to Gabriel, but clearly, he needed to hear it from the horse's mouth, so to speak. When Ava remained silent, Miranda pulled in a breath and continued. "Because I wouldn't have the foggiest idea even where to start."

"Where did you start when all your gifts began to awake?" he asked, tone almost pleading. "Your talents just sprang from nowhere?"

"That's what it felt like," she said. "But it was more like Simon…woke them up."

"How?"

That was a part of the story Ava had wanted to know as well. Of course, she'd heard that supposedly Miranda didn't have any powers, had never shown any signs of being anything more than a *nunca*—someone born to witch-kind but lacking in magic—until she came here to Santa Fe. Then her talents had emerged with ferocious intensity. Ava had heard that much, but no one had ever really come out and explained precisely why her magic had come alive here and not back in northern Arizona where she came from.

"It was your half-brother Simon," Miranda informed Gabriel then, sounding somehow rueful and annoyed at the same time. "He told me he just knew that I had to have powers, which was why he arranged a fake 'coincidental' meeting on the train when I was traveling here. He wore an amulet with some kind of herbs in it, a mixture he said would wake up my powers if they really did exist. And obviously, that's exactly what happened."

"What kind of herbs?" Gabriel asked, dark eyes narrowing.

The *prima* gave a helpless shrug. "I don't know. He didn't say."

"But the knowledge must exist someplace. We only have to figure out where Simon got that information."

On the surface, this suggestion sounded promising. Only…. Ava hated to squelch the growing enthusiasm in Gabriel's expression, but she felt compelled to say, "Is it really the same thing, though? I mean, these supposed 'herbs' only woke up a gift that Miranda already had. In your case, Gabriel, the real problem is that your powers have been taken away. How can you wake up something that isn't even there?"

At once, his face fell, and she hated herself for having to be the voice of reason, one that destroyed even his minor hope. However, Miranda nodded, looking resigned.

"You're right," she admitted. "We're talking about two completely different situations here."

Gabriel clenched his fists on the knees of his faded jeans. "But do we know that for sure? It's possible that the elders only blocked my magic rather than taking it away entirely."

Again, Ava hated to be the one to shed cold water on yet another theory, but she felt compelled to speak, to point out something she'd noticed almost as soon as she realized who he was…and what he was supposed to be. "I'd say maybe that was true…except that when I met you, I didn't get that same twinge I feel whenever I meet a witch or warlock for the first time. I wouldn't have even known you were a warlock if you hadn't told me who you were."

"I hadn't thought of that," he said, and although the disappointment in his face and tone was clear, he didn't look angry with her for stating something so obvious. "I suppose if you couldn't sense that I was a warlock, it must mean I'm not really one anymore."

She wished she could give him a reassuring hug, because he sure looked like he needed one. But that would have been going way over the line with someone she'd only just met. Instead, she said quickly, "You were born a warlock, Gabriel. You *are* a warlock. You're just…working through a problem right now."

His eyes met hers, and a little tingle went through her, one entirely different from the sort she would have felt while sensing his warlock nature…if it had still existed. Ava reminded herself that Miranda was perched right there on the couch a few feet away, and sitting here and getting all gooey over an Escobar warlock probably wasn't a very good idea.

"Yes, that's a good way to look at it," Miranda said, voice brisk. Had she noticed the way Gabriel seemed to make Ava melt inside whenever he glanced at her?

Hopefully not.

"And I suppose I can try something," the *prima* went on. She smoothed her hands over the legs of her jeans and stood up. "Although I can't really forgive Simon for the things he did to me, to this clan, I also can't deny that he taught me new ways of thinking about my magic, of working with it. A lot of what he showed me was simply ways to look within and communicate with it, for lack of a better term. So let me do that."

"Yes, of course," Gabriel said, a hopeful light returning to his dark eyes. "What do you need me to do?"

"Nothing," Miranda replied. "Just sit quietly where you are."

He nodded and she closed her eyes, while Ava held herself still, hardly daring to breathe in case the faintest sound might interrupt whatever it was Miranda intended to do. It certainly didn't look very impressive—she only stood there a few feet away from Gabriel, hands raised slightly, eyes closed. Her lips moved, but Ava couldn't hear what she was saying.

A faint golden glow began to form between her palms, shimmering with individual sparks of light that looked like fireflies. They danced around one another, then moved toward Gabriel, encircling him, drifting around his head and down onto his shoulders and chest. After a moment or two, they disappeared, and Miranda opened her eyes.

"Anything?" she asked.

Gabriel reached out with one hand, as if to

summon some magic of his own. Whatever he'd intended to do, however, it didn't seem to work, because Ava couldn't see anything move or change in the room around them.

He let out a discouraged sigh. "Nothing at all. I only meant to move the vase on that table over there a few inches, but I couldn't manage even that simple task."

"Well, damn," Miranda said. She tucked a strand of dark brown hair behind her ear and rocked back on her heels slightly, as if doing so would somehow help her analyze what had just gone wrong. "I thought if I sent some of my own magic out toward you, it would connect with the dormant magic inside you and somehow bring it forth, wake it up. But obviously, that didn't work."

"Thank you for trying," Gabriel responded, clearly trying to be polite even though his disappointment was almost a physical thing, it was so palpable. "I had hoped for a better outcome, but even I realized the chances were not that good."

She shook her head. "I'm not giving up that easily. But this is something we're probably going to need some outside help with. I wonder if you should talk to Loc."

"Who is Loc?" Gabriel asked, even as Ava stared at her *prima* in surprise. She hadn't thought Miranda would voluntarily offer any information about the Castillos' resident demon lord, not when there were still many members of the clan who still had no idea about his true identity and thought he was nothing more than the Spanish artist he was pretending to be.

Miranda's full mouth curved into a half-smile. "Loc is…Loc is a member of this clan, but he's not a Castillo. He's something else entirely."

That reply only made Gabriel frown in puzzlement, even as he sent a pleading look in Ava's direction, as if asking her to explain the situation before he became even more confused.

"Loc's, um…he's a demon lord," Ava said, hoping the statement sounded a little less crazy to Gabriel than it did to her. "It's a long story, but basically, he's stuck on this plane, although with all his powers intact. So that's why he might be able to help you even when Miranda can't."

At once, Gabriel's face brightened. "Yes, I can see how his otherworldly powers might be useful in this situation. You really think he would help me?"

"Well, as long as he forgives you for being Simon Escobar's half-brother," Miranda observed dryly. "I mean, it's Simon's fault that Loc is here."

"But it worked out for the best in the end, didn't it?" Ava asked. As far as she'd been able to tell, the exiled demon lord seemed perfectly happy to be here with Cat Castillo, Miranda's sister-in-law. "I mean, he wouldn't go back where he came from even if he could, right?"

"No, he wouldn't," Miranda said. "You're right about that. Anyway, let me give them a call, see if he and Cat are at home and can talk to you."

Gabriel nodded, and Miranda got up and went into the kitchen, where Ava knew there was also an old-fashioned land line, just like in her own house. That phone and its associated number were sacrosanct in the clan, since both had been in use since the early 1980s. Right then, she guessed that Miranda was using the phone for the same reason Ava had used hers—to give herself some privacy while making the call.

"This Loc," Gabriel said in an undertone. "He is very powerful, yes?"

"Very," Ava replied. "He defeated a horrible dark warlock in New Orleans without breaking a sweat...or at least, that's what I heard. That all happened while I was still down in Albuquerque at college, so I missed the whole thing."

The Escobar warlock was quiet for a moment, apparently pondering what she'd just said. A faint frown settled on his handsome features, and then he said, "If he is so strong, I'm surprised you didn't suggest that we go see him first."

Well, doing so might have been the logical course of action, except that Ava hadn't been sure whether Miranda would be on board with divulging Loc's true identity to someone they'd just met. Should she tell Gabriel the truth, or would he be offended?

However, he didn't seem like the type of person to easily take offense, so she told him, "Well, Loc's identity isn't common knowledge in the clan. I know about him because my brother Tony knows about him, but Miranda and Rafe made it pretty clear that they didn't want Loc's true nature to be a subject of clan gossip. I didn't know whether it would be okay to tell you about him."

"But your *prima* apparently had no issue with telling me," Gabriel remarked, and Ava gave an apologetic shrug.

"True, but I didn't know for sure she would. Anyway, that was her decision to make."

Their conversation was halted by Miranda's return. She came back into the living room, looking pleased, which told Ava that the planned meeting could go ahead.

"Cat and Loc are fine with you going out there to see them," the *prima* said. "They're easy to find—just head north on Highway 84 and then got off at the exit for Highway 103, the one that's the start of the high road to Taos. The vineyard is on the left about half a mile off the highway. The old Luna Rio signs are still out on the roadside, so that makes it even easier."

"Thank you for reaching out to them," Gabriel said.

Now Miranda smiled, a smile that was tinged with relief. Was she happy there might be another solution to Gabriel's problem, or just glad that she'd found an easy way to foist him off on someone else?

Ava chose to think it was the former. She couldn't admit to knowing the *prima* very well, but everything Miranda had done so far seemed to show that she had the best interests of the clan at heart...and maybe that also went for stray former warlocks who had washed up on their shores, so to speak.

"It's no problem," she said. "I hope Loc can help you."

"And we'll head out right now," Ava put in, already getting up from the couch. "That's about a twenty-minute drive, right?"

"Around there," Miranda replied. "Good luck."

Gabriel followed Ava back out to her car, and she programmed the turn-off for Highway 103 into the nav. After that, she'd take over manually.

"All right," she said, flashing a quick smile at Gabriel as she fastened her seatbelt. "Let's go see what Loc can do for you."

## 4

GABRIEL WATCHED THE LANDSCAPE PASS BY outside the car windows and found himself wondering why anyone would settle in such a dry, arid place. True, the mountains off to the right were quite majestic, and the hillsides weren't completely bare, but covered by a variety of scrubby evergreen trees he didn't immediately recognize. Even so, everything looked very brown, very bare compared to the lush rainforest that surrounded the hidden village of Pico Negro, the only place he had ever known…until his powers were stripped from him and he was sent into exile.

In a way, he supposed he had banishment in common with the demon lord he was going to see. Clearly, Loc had been summoned to this plane and then had no choice but to remain once Simon had been killed. The Castillos did not practice that sort of dark magic, and so he doubted any of them possessed the necessary talent and skill to send Loc back whence he came.

Although, Gabriel thought, as Ava turned off the main highway and onto a country road bordered in majestic trees with shimmering green leaves, then again onto a private lane that wound through lush vineyards, it seemed as though this Loc had found a good place to land. Certainly, the immediate surroundings were far lovelier than the barren landscape Gabriel had viewed on the way here seemed to indicate.

That impression was only reinforced as the two of them got out of the car and walked toward a large house built of mellow stone, with ivy climbing up the walls and tall, arched windows. It was a very impressive place, utterly different in style from the sprawling hacienda of the *prima's* home, and yet just as stately.

Ava had only begun to reach for the doorbell button set in the wall next to the front door when it opened, and a lovely young woman probably a few years older than his companion looked out at the two of them. There was a faint family resemblance in the delicate nose and wide dark eyes, but this woman's face was more heart-shaped, where Ava's was a smooth oval.

"Hi, Ava," the woman said, then glanced past

her to Gabriel. "And you must be Gabriel. Come in."

"Cat, thank you so much for letting us come over like this—" Ava began, but Cat Castillo only shook her head.

"It's no bother. We were done in the vineyard for the day anyway. Since it's so nice out, I thought we'd sit on the patio. This way."

Yes, it was a fine day, the air mild but not hot at all, with a brisk westerly breeze blowing. Gabriel had to admit that there was something about the air here, not heavy like in his native El Salvador, but fresh and wild, the kind of air that spoke of possibilities.

He hoped he would find some of those possibilities here at this lovely, secluded villa.

They walked through the house, which was large and beautifully furnished, with a fireplace of stacked stone and elegant landscape paintings on the parchment-colored walls, and out onto an intimate little patio with ivy-festooned walls and a wrought-iron dining set off to one side. Sitting at the round table was a striking man with shoulder-length black hair that moved in the breeze. In front of him was a pitcher of iced tea and several glasses.

And as the man looked up at the newcomers and Gabriel met his gaze, he realized this was no man at all, but Loc, the demon lord. How the members of the Castillo family had not been able to recognize him for something other, Gabriel didn't know for sure, but it seemed obvious enough to him. There was an impression of immense power about this person, something banked down so that it might be hidden, but still there nonetheless.

When he spoke, however, his words were prosaic enough, if not exactly friendly. "So you are the Escobar warlock."

Gabriel could feel Ava stiffen slightly where she stood next to him, but he was determined not to take offense. "I am an Escobar, true," he replied. "I am not sure whether I can still be called a warlock, however."

"Loc, be nice," Cat said, her rebuke accompanied by a half-smile that took a good deal of the sting out of the comment. "He had nothing to do with anything Simon did."

"That much is true," Gabriel said. "Considering that I did not even know of my half-brother's existence until fairly recently."

The demon lord appeared to relent, because he remarked, "I suppose that does put a different complexion on things. Please, sit down."

Ava sent Gabriel the slightest of sideways glances, as if she was still worried about how he might react to his less than enthusiastic reception by Loc. However, he wanted to make sure this meeting went well, and so he pulled out one of the chairs for her and waited for her to sit down, then took a seat for himself as Cat went around to the other side of the table and sat next to her companion.

"Iced tea?" she asked, sounding a bit strained.

"Yes, thank you," Gabriel said politely, even as he wondered whether the Castillos ever drank anything else.

A minute was spent in pouring the tea for the newcomers and herself, and then Cat set the pitcher back down. From across the table, Loc was watching him with a speculative gleam in his night-dark eyes.

"You say you were born a warlock, and yet I can sense nothing of magic from you."

"Because it is gone," Gabriel said bluntly. "The elders of my village burned it out of me in retribution for the assistance I gave to a member of the Castillo clan. But surely Miranda already told you this."

"She told us some of it," Cat put in. "Not everything. I suppose Loc thought he might be able to pick up something we regular witches and warlocks couldn't."

"It is an interesting conundrum, that's for certain," Loc remarked. He picked up his iced tea and took a sip. Although Gabriel had only just met him, he got the impression that the demon lord would also have preferred something to drink that was a little stronger than iced tea. "I have been told that such a thing is possible, but I have to confess that I'm surprised by the...thoroughness...of what they did to you."

Oh, yes, they had been very thorough. Once his memories had returned and he understood who he was, what he had once been, he had found himself wondering whether he was even truly himself anymore. After all, a witch or warlock's magic went to the very core of their being, was something that defined them as forever separate from those who had not been blessed with such gifts. When that magic was taken away, did it mean he was even still Gabriel Escobar, or some strange, stunted creature who would forever be on the outside of the wondrous world he had once taken for granted?

About all he could do was lift his shoulders. He would certainly not confess such doubts to Loc, who might look human and yet was clearly anything but a mortal. If he had defeated a powerful dark warlock, as Ava had said, then it seemed obvious enough that he had lost nothing of his powers by being confined to this plane of existence.

"I fear it is very possible," he said, then sipped at his own iced tea, deciding it was better to leave the matter there and let Loc determine what he wanted to do.

"Can you help him?" Cat inquired, her expression anxious.

"I don't know," Loc replied, and frowned slightly. "But you know I like a good challenge."

He got up from his chair and came around the table to the spot where Gabriel sat. It was not an entirely comfortable position to be in, with the demon lord looming over him, although he had done nothing remotely threatening. Gabriel supposed some of his current discomfort was due to the knowledge that his powers truly were gone, that he would in no way be able to adequately protect himself from any attack Loc might mount. Of course, he understood that Loc intended to help him, not hurt him, but at some deep, instinctual level, it felt terrible to know that the magical talents he'd wielded with such careless abandon were unavailable to him, perhaps gone forever.

Because of this, it was impossible to prevent himself from flinching when Loc's hands descended and the demon lord's fingers wrapped around his head, as though to probe through the hard bone of his skull down to the brain within. Sitting next to him, Ava looked surprised as well; clearly, she hadn't expected Loc to make this kind of direct contact. Her mouth parted, but if she had intended to voice some kind of protest, she thought better of it and instead settled back in her chair, full mouth compressed and dark eyes worried.

Loc's strong fingers tightened, and Gabriel forced himself to remain still and let the demon lord do his work, no matter how uncomfortable it might be.

"I can't feel the slightest hint of any magic," Loc said, his voice calm, almost musing. "I have sent my powers within, but there is no whisper of any kind of magical talent, not even the faintest stirring of something that might be a remnant of what your clan's elders took from you. This is why no other witches or warlocks can sense an answering call when they are near you, because there is nothing to call out to them."

"There has to be something you can do," Ava said. Her voice was pleading...as was her expression as she looked up at Loc. "Your powers aren't like ours. You can do so much more with them...can't you?"

The demon lord's shoulders lifted, but Gabriel could tell that he was uneasy, as if he did not much like having to admit that this was one instance where his talents had failed him. However, when he spoke, he sounded calm enough, almost resigned.

"I have used my magic to destroy...to protect,

on certain occasions." His gaze strayed to Cat, and the corners of his mouth lifted slightly as he gazed at her. Had he used his powers to shield her from harm? Ava hadn't provided any details of Loc's conflict with the dark warlock he'd defeated, and yet Gabriel guessed that Ava's beautiful cousin must have been involved in some way. "But it is not the sort of magic that can make something out of nothing. It might look that way to some people, because I can summon objects as the whim takes me, but all I really do is bring something to me that already exists. To give you magic when you currently have none…that is an entirely different matter."

"I see," Gabriel said carefully. There really wasn't any other way to reply. Protests would do little to help him and might only anger the demon lord, who had already shown he had little use for Escobar warlocks, even ones who currently lacked any magical gifts. "Well, thank you for trying."

Ava shifted in her chair and stared up at Loc, the set of her chin seeming to indicate that she was not quite as ready to accept defeat. "Maybe you can't help him directly. But you come from a place outside this world. You know things that regular witches and warlocks don't. Don't you know of anyone…anything…that might be able to help?"

"I am afraid not," Loc said. To his credit, he

did appear genuinely sorry to have to say such a thing to her. "In the place I came from, I was supreme. There were no others with powers that rivaled mine. I can't reach out for help because there is no one to reach out to. Do you understand?"

Her gaze slid toward Gabriel for a few seconds, but her chin remained lifted. "All right, maybe not exactly where you came from. But... somewhere else? Somewhere outside your world... your plane...whatever it was?"

"You are talking about very dangerous magic," Loc said. He paused for a moment, something cold and terrible in his black eyes. Once again, Gabriel had the impression of someone, some*thing*, entirely other, even though he wore the face of a handsome man in his twenties...even though the gaze he sent toward the woman who was his companion was warm and loving. The demon lord might have taken up residence in this world and found his own attachments here, but his current circumstances couldn't change what he once was. Not completely.

"As dangerous as the magic that brought you here?" Cat asked, looking more curious than troubled. "Because it didn't seem to rebound too badly on Simon."

"Only at the end, when he realized it did not do to have made me his enemy," Loc responded. Still, he let out a breath, his expression much more troubled now…and more human. "But you are right. Simon only failed to bind me because Miranda interfered with his spells. Otherwise, I would have been his slave, and he would have been free to do as he wished."

"I know it's dangerous magic," Ava said. Now there was a glint of hope in her big brown eyes, although Gabriel feared that hope might be unfounded. "But as long as we're careful—"

"It doesn't matter," Loc cut in. Even though he'd interrupted her, his tone was kindlier than Gabriel had expected. "The spells Simon used were the ones contained in the grimoires he stole from the de la Paz clan…and those grimoires have all been destroyed, have they not?"

"Yes," Gabriel said, hoping he didn't sound too defeated. Had he helped to rid the world of the only thing that might have helped him out of his current predicament? Even if that proved to be the case, he couldn't say he regretted their destruction. Vicénte would have done terrible things with those spell books. Better to be deprived of magic for the rest of his life than to have such spells in the Escobar *primus's* possession. "They all burned to ash."

Even Cat appeared to slump visibly at this latest wrinkle. Her fingers tapped against the side

of her glass, which glistened faintly with conden-
sation. "So…that's it?"

"Possibly," Loc said. He lifted his head, as if he
heard something on the wind…or perhaps he was
merely looking away from the rest of them so he
might gather his thoughts. "At least, the current
situation does present something of a dead end."

Ava, who had been sitting up straight,
slumped against the back of her iron patio chair,
arms crossed. "I find it hard to believe that the de
la Paz clan is the only one in the world that has
those kinds of books."

"Probably not," Loc responded. His tone was
mild, though, and Gabriel had the impression
that the demon lord was doing his best not to lose
his patience. "But I can tell you that I spent many
months wandering this world, trying to find
someone who could send me back to the plane
where I'd come from. In all that time, I encoun-
tered no one who possessed the talents I required,
no one who came anywhere close to being strong
enough. I suppose it is possible they were hiding
grimoires that could have been of use, but most of
the time, those who practiced the darker arts were
all too glad to reveal themselves to me, since they
believed that by helping me, I would in turn be of
assistance to them once I was restored to my
realm."

That story sounded plausible enough. Anyone

who was willing to walk the dark paths would certainly not scruple at reaching out to the demon lord for favors in return for their help. If Loc had already scoured this world and found no one whose gifts were sufficient to help him, then it seemed as though there wasn't much chance of Gabriel locating anyone—or anything—that could provide the assistance he required.

"It does sound as though you've already put in the work," he said, and the demon lord nodded.

"I have. I wish I had better news for you. But I also would not want you to waste your time on a search that would ultimately prove fruitless."

Just as this little venture had turned out to be. However, Gabriel would not say such a thing out loud. They had only been trying to help him, these Castillos...and he included Loc in that number, because, whatever else he might be, it seemed clear enough that the demon lord viewed himself as a member of this witch clan.

"I knew the chances weren't very high," he said, then made himself swallow some of his iced tea. The cool liquid helped relieve some of the dryness in his throat, but he found himself wishing more than ever that the glass contained something much stronger than tea. If he could not get his powers back, at least he could blunt the edges of his loss with something worth drinking. He pulled in a breath, then went on, "And I have taken up enough of your time. We'll leave you to enjoy the rest of your afternoon."

Even as he began to rise from his chair, Cat protested, "You don't have to run off like this. Stay and relax for a while."

To Gabriel's relief, Ava came to his aid, saying, "No, it's better if we go. Gabriel probably wants to get back to his hotel and rest a bit."

"Yes, exactly," he said, glad that she'd given him such an easy excuse for making his escape. "I have been traveling since dawn today."

"Then we won't keep you," Loc put in. "Let them go, Cat."

She subsided, leaning against the back of her chair. "Okay. But Loc and I will talk about this some more. If we can think of anything, we'll let you know."

"Thank you," Gabriel responded. At least he sounded grateful, although he knew in his heart of hearts that neither Cat nor Loc would be able to offer any sort of solution to his dilemma.

No, this was his own problem...and he would have to solve it.

The two of them walked Ava and Gabriel to the front door. Silently, Ava headed over to the spot where she'd parked her small SUV. Neither of them spoke until they'd left the vineyard grounds and were traveling down the narrow country road that led back to the main highway.

"I'm sorry," she said at last.

Gabriel lifted his shoulders. "There is nothing for you to be sorry about. You tried. Loc tried. It's no one's fault that you couldn't help me."

"Still." Her fingers tapped on the steering wheel; he noticed that she'd engaged the vehicle's auto-drive computer as soon as they were back on the road but had kept her hands close to the wheel. A quick sideways glance, and she added, "You really just want me to take you back to your hotel?"

"It seems the best course of action." Although he hadn't intended to say anything else, he found himself blurting out, "Then again, I think I would like a drink."

A quick smile touched her lips. "That's understandable. You're staying at the La Fonda, right?"

He nodded.

"Well, they have a very nice bar right there in the hotel. We can go there. Sound good?"

It sounded better than good. Gabriel noticed that Ava's eyes were fixed on the road again, even though, with the car doing the driving, she really didn't need to pay that kind of attention to their route. Was she second-guessing her decision to have a drink with him?

He hoped not. Even though he had first approached her in error, thinking that Tony Castillo still lived in the gray Victorian house on

Hillside Avenue, now Gabriel found himself glad that Ava had been there instead. He'd only been in her company for a few hours, and yet he knew he enjoyed being around her. She'd thrown herself whole-heartedly into helping him with his quest, and he knew he would be always grateful to her for that, even if nothing came of it.

And although he wished that this matter could be wrapped up quickly, he couldn't help thinking that the alternative might not be so bad…not if he could keep Ava at his side as he continued his search.

## 5

AT LEAST THERE WEREN'T ANY CASTILLO cousins haunting the bar at the La Fonda Hotel. Ava had already confirmed this by casting a surreptitious glance around the place as the hostess—luckily, a civilian—seated her and Gabriel at a table around the corner, near the little stage where they had live entertainment on the weekends. But it was a weekday afternoon, barely three o'clock, and so the bar was empty except for several older couples, obviously tourists, and a loud group of women at the bar's one large table...women who were probably on their third or fourth margarita, by the sound of it. While they were annoying, they didn't pay any attention to Ava or Gabriel, except for a few of them giving him an admiring glance before they returned to their drinks.

If he'd noticed how raucous they were being, he didn't give any sign of it. He picked up the small menu the hostess had placed in front of him and scanned the offerings. Since he didn't ask for any help, Ava assumed that he could read English just as well as he could speak it.

She only gave the menu a cursory glance, since she already knew that she wanted a prickly pear margarita. Her companion seemed to note the way she ignored the bill of fare, because he asked, "You've been here often?"

"Not that often," she replied. "The hotel is owned by civilians, and we Castillos tend to hang out in places owned by clan members. My cousin Eduardo has five restaurants, which makes it pretty easy."

"Your clan is very prosperous, isn't it?"

From anyone else, that sort of question could have been viewed as digging to see how rich her family was, but she didn't see anything except simple curiosity in Gabriel's expression. Or at least, Ava was fairly sure that was all she could detect; she didn't want to peer at him too closely, since that would have been way too awkward. It was hard enough just sitting across the table from him. Of course, this wasn't a date or anything like it, but still....

"We do okay," she said, hedging, then relented and went on, "but that's easy enough to do when a family has been living in one place for hundreds of years."

He nodded but didn't appear inclined to pursue the subject, since he only said, "Are you hungry? Possibly we should order some food with our drinks."

Actually, she was hungry, since she hadn't really eaten a proper lunch. "Um…sure. Whatever you like." Impulsively, she added, "It's on me."

He raised an inquiring eyebrow, dark eyes puzzled. "What is on you?"

"I just meant that I'll pay for it," she said, hoping she hadn't blushed. Well, at least it was fairly dim inside the bar. "My treat."

At once, he shook his head. "No, I would not ask you to do that. It was my idea to have a drink."

"But you're a guest in Castillo territory."

"More of an interloper, I think."

"No," she told him. The last thing she wanted him to think was that he was unwelcome in Santa Fe…or anywhere in her clan's territory, for that matter. "You're not. You came here looking for help. Like I told you earlier, you made sure my brother and Cassandra were safe. You sacrificed your magic to do that. You really think I'm going to make you pay for your own drinks?"

Her question made him grin, then shake his head. Something about his smile, about that flash of white teeth, made another flush go through her, one that didn't have anything to do with embarrassment.

It would have been so much easier to relax around him if he weren't so good-looking....

To her relief, a waiter came by right then and took their order—a prickly pear margarita for her and a regular margarita on the rocks for Gabriel, along with some street tacos and nachos. Ava knew she probably didn't want to think about all the calories this "snack" might contain and tried to reassure herself by thinking she'd have a salad for dinner to try to rebalance things a bit. God knows she always had plenty of organic baby spinach and romaine lettuce in the house.

The waiter had brought some water over, so Ava reached for her glass and took a sip. Since she really didn't know what to say, she found herself blurting, "How long are you staying here at the hotel?"

Luckily, it didn't seem as though Gabriel found anything all that strange about her question. "I got the room for three nights," he replied. "I suppose I thought if I didn't make any progress in that amount of time, then there wouldn't be much point to remaining here any longer."

"That makes sense." Well, she supposed it did on the surface, but at the same time, she hated the thought of him leaving Santa Fe with his quest forever unfulfilled. The two of them just had to figure out a way to keep that from happening.

Something that looked almost like a flicker of disappointment crossed Gabriel's face. Was he sorry that she hadn't said something to urge him to stay longer?

No, she was flattering herself.

Speaking more quickly than she'd intended, she went on, "So what will you do after that? Go back to Mexico?"

He didn't reply right away, because the waiter returned with their drinks right then and told them the food would be out in a few more minutes. Gabriel reached for his margarita, swirled the straw in it for a moment, and said, "I suppose so. I hadn't really thought that far...probably because I wanted to believe that I would find some way to succeed."

"You will," Ava told him. The words had slipped out easily enough, although she didn't know whether she truly believed them. Loc had put up some pretty convincing arguments for why Gabriel's quest appeared to be doomed from the start. She lifted her own drink and took a sip. Yes, that was just about perfect—strong enough for her to feel it, but not so strong that the tequila overwhelmed the sweet-sharp taste of the prickly pear syrup.

Gabriel shook his head before allowing

himself a swallow of margarita. "You sound very confident."

"I suppose so." She put her drink down on the table, ignoring the urge to take a long pull through the straw. "It's just…a lot of crazy things have happened in this clan in the past year or so. I guess I've learned that it's better to never say never."

For a moment, he didn't respond. Was he analyzing the idiom she'd used, or just trying to decide whether she truly believed what she'd said or whether she was blowing the proverbial sunshine up his ass? He let out a breath, but it wasn't exactly a sigh…more like a way of releasing some of the tension she'd noticed in the set of his broad shoulders.

"I want to believe you," he said. "But right now, I can't think of a way to make this happen."

"Neither can I," she replied frankly. Another sip of margarita, and she found herself beginning to relax a little as well. "That doesn't mean it won't. There has to be an angle we haven't thought of yet, something we're overlooking."

"Possibly." He drank some more as well and looked as though he'd intended to continue their discussion, but the waiter came back with their tacos and nachos right then. Another silence fell as they both transferred some food to their individual plates. Gabriel appeared somewhat bemused by the nachos—maybe they really were an American invention? Ava honestly didn't know —but he took a bite, chewed, then seemed to nod to himself, as if approving of the flavor combination even though it wasn't truly authentic. "That is, Loc says he traveled the world looking for someone who could help him, but even a being as powerful as he couldn't have possibly visited every place where witches and warlocks lived. I suppose it's possible there's someone he might have overlooked."

"Exactly," Ava responded, glad that Gabriel wasn't ready to give up without a fight. "Also, the books that Simon stole from the de la Paz clan were burned, but it's not as though he took *all* of them. I know that for a fact because Cassandra told me the *prima* of her clan built a library attached to her house so all the de la Paz books could be kept safely in one place."

For a second or two, his face seemed to brighten. But then he shook his head and said, "I never knew my half-brother…and after hearing about what he tried to do to this clan, I'm glad of that. But he was cunning and single-minded, and so of course he would leave behind the books that were of no use to him, if for no other reason than their presence would make it that much harder to notice that a few volumes were missing. I'm sure the de la Paz clan has a very fine library…but I'm also sure it contains nothing that would be of any help to me. Simon would have taken the grimoires which held the knowledge he required, and it's those books that are now lost forever."

Ava supposed she should have thought of that. After all, even though she'd never actually seen the books, she'd known her mother had hidden them in the house, in a closet in the family room that contained a safe. While key locks didn't pose any problem for witches and warlocks, combination locks were an entirely different matter. Ava's mother had thought the extra layer of protection —in addition to all the wards Miranda had set— would be enough to protect the dangerous contents of that safe. She'd been proven horribly wrong, but even so, that safe hadn't been large enough to hold more than a couple of dozen books at the very most. It made perfect sense that Simon had only cherry-picked the most valuable volumes from the de la Paz collection.

Dejected, she picked up a carnitas street taco from her plate and took a bite. It was very good, but the savory food didn't do much to fill the hollow feeling in the pit of her stomach, a sensation that had everything to do with the apparent hopelessness of their situation and nothing at all with the hunger pangs she'd experienced just a few minutes earlier.

Gabriel ate as well, punctuating bites with

swallows from his margarita. In fact, at the rate he was going, he'd need to order another one pretty soon.

*Might as well,* Ava thought as she allowed herself a modest sip from her own drink. *It's not like he has anywhere he needs to go except upstairs to his hotel room. If anyone deserves to get drunk, it's him.*

She wasn't exactly sure what she'd do if he did end up wasted. Guide him to the elevator and tell him she'd call him the next day?

Probably. Going up to his room when he was drunk sounded like a recipe for disaster.

However, when the waiter came by, eyed the level of liquid in Gabriel's glass, and asked if he'd like another, he shook his head.

"No, one is fine," he replied. "But thank you for asking."

The surprise must have been obvious on her face, because as soon as the waiter had left, Gabriel asked, "You thought I intended to get drunk?"

"Well…not exactly," she said, hedging. As his brows began to lift, she added hastily, "I mean, after everything you've been through, I don't think anyone would blame you for wanting to have a few drinks to erase it all."

"I drank quite a bit in Mexico City," he responded, surprising her once again…this time with his frankness. "For a time, all I wanted to do was numb myself, to pretend that my life wasn't what it had turned out to be. But I realized I was doing myself no favors. It's one thing to drink to be social and something very different to use it as a drug."

"I'm sorry," she said, and he tilted his head to one side, eyes narrowing slightly.

"Why are you sorry?"

"About…just about everything you've been through, and all because you helped my brother. If the universe was fair at all, then your brother would be the one stripped of his powers and you'd be doing your best to make a kinder, gentler Escobar clan." Was that the right thing to say? Ava didn't know for sure, but it sounded better than confessing she felt pity for him.

No, pity wasn't the right word. More like she felt righteously indignant on his behalf, that someone who'd been trying to do something good had been punished so severely for his actions.

Now Gabriel smiled and settled back slightly in his chair. "Well, I learned a long time ago that there is very little fairness to this world…or rather, we have to make such fairness for ourselves, since the universe does not seem inclined to provide it. I'll find a path through this, one way or another."

What, really, could she say to that? Except…. "I hope so. And I hope I can help."

The warmth in his eyes as he gazed at her from across the table was unmistakable. "You already have."

They had to stop there, because the hostess seated another couple at the table next to theirs, and so it would be pretty much impossible to continue a conversation that touched on so many sensitive subjects. Instead, Ava talked about Santa Fe, about some of the places Gabriel might want to see while he was in town, making it sound as though he was only a tourist here on a brief visit, someone who'd want to visit Loretto Chapel and the museum and other local sights before he moved on to the next town on his itinerary. He picked up on her cues right away and played along, and the couple next to them didn't show any signs of wanting to eavesdrop on their conversation.

Eventually, though, they were done with their drinks and food, and Ava grabbed the bill and handed over her credit card before Gabriel could even see what the total had been. He sent her a rueful look.

"You will have to let me return the favor sometime."

"Maybe," she allowed, and to her relief, he didn't push it, but just smiled to himself as he gave a small shake of his head.

They left the bar, and she walked him over to the elevator.

"I'll call you tomorrow morning," she said after he pressed the button.

"I don't have a phone."

For a second or two, she stared at him, nonplussed. How had he managed to get along all this time without a phone? Or maybe he'd had one in Mexico City but had left it behind for some reason? She shrugged and replied, "That's okay. I'll just call the hotel and ask for your room. Are you staying under your name?"

"No," he said. "My Mexican identification says I am Ramón Hernandez."

Probably a good idea. Of course, Ava had no idea whether the Escobars had even bothered to track Gabriel after they dumped him in Honduras, or whether they'd completely washed their hands of him once they'd determined he no longer presented any kind of a threat. Even so, she thought it was probably wise for him to have taken on an assumed name.

"Ramón Hernandez," she repeated. "Got it."

"I look forward to hearing from you."

There wasn't much she could do except smile in reply, then offer a hasty goodbye and head toward the stairwell that led to the parking garage. She certainly didn't know him well enough to give him a hug, so an awkward retreat seemed like the best idea.

After she got in her car, though, she sort of wished she'd had the courage to hug him after all. He looked like he could have used one.

But the moment was past, and there wasn't much she could do about the oversight now. Probably just as well, she reflected as she waved her credit card at the reader next to the parking garage exit. Her phone beeped, indicating that the charge had been successfully applied to her account.

It wasn't far from the hotel to her house, although the place felt weirdly empty as she came in through the kitchen. Was it only that Gabriel had been here a few hours ago, but now she had no idea whether he'd ever be back?

Maybe. Or maybe she was just thinking she should have come up with a reason to hang out with him at the hotel for a while longer, even though Ava had a feeling that any such attempt would have seemed way too transparent. She wouldn't lie to herself…she knew she liked being around him, even as she wished she could have helped him more. It seemed that the more they tried to find a solution to his predicament, the more they came up with reasons for why such a thing was impossible.

She realized she should probably call Tony and let him know that Gabriel was okay. While her brother had been busy enough in Tucson, getting settled in his new life with Cassandra, acclimating to his new hometown and the clan he'd sort of adopted, Ava had a feeling Tony would be annoyed with her if she didn't let him know right away that the man they'd all thought was dead had miraculously survived his encounter with the Escobar clan elders.

After pouring herself a glass of water—the margarita and spicy food had made her thirsty— she went into the living room, got out her phone, and settled down on the couch.

"Call Tony," she said, and her phone instantly connected.

Three rings, and she worried that maybe her brother was off doing something fun and therefore not disposed to pick up his phone. This really wasn't the sort of information she wanted to leave in a voicemail, but she supposed that was what she would do if necessary.

However, he picked up just before the phone could ring a fourth time. "Hey, Ava. What's up?"

He sounded breezy and casual and relaxed, just as he always did. Honestly, if she hadn't seen in Gabriel's memories the way Tony had clocked Vicénte Escobar on the chin, she wouldn't have believed her brother capable of that kind of violence.

"Hey, Tony," she replied, knowing she didn't

sound half as nonchalant as he did. "Guess who showed up on my doorstep, thinking it was still your house?"

Still unconcerned, he said, "I have no idea."

"Gabriel Escobar."

"*What?*"

Okay, that response hadn't sounded nearly as relaxed. She grinned to herself. "You heard me. Gabriel Escobar."

"He's all right?"

Good question. "Um, physically he's fine."

"What's that supposed to mean?"

"Well, the Escobar elders didn't exactly hurt him, but they stripped him of his powers, just like Miranda's parents did to Matías Escobar more than twenty years ago."

"Holy shit. But otherwise he's okay?"

"Yes, he's fine." *Damn, is he fine.* However, Ava knew better than to utter that particular observation aloud. Like most big brothers, Tony really didn't want to acknowledge that his little sister might date and have romantic relationships. Then again, since she'd had exactly two real "dates" in her entire existence, she supposed her brother could be forgiven for ignoring that part of his sister's life. Taking a breath, she went on, "I guess the Escobars thought it was enough of a punishment to take his powers away. For a long time, he didn't even know who he was. He's been living in Mexico for the past six months or so."

"So what's he doing in Santa Fe?"

"He was hoping we could help him."

"Help him what?"

"Get his powers back."

Judging by the silence that followed this response, Ava guessed her brother was nonplussed. After a long pause, he said, "What did you tell him?"

"I took him to see Miranda. She couldn't help him. Then we went to see Loc, but he couldn't do anything, either. Now we're trying to figure out what to do next."

"Doesn't sound like there's much you can do."

That depressing observation did seem to be an apt description of their current situation, but Ava knew neither she nor Gabriel was about to give up that easily. "We'll figure something out," she said.

"'We'?" Tony repeated, now sounding somewhat ominous.

"Yes, Gabriel and me. There has to be some sort of solution neither one of us has thought of yet."

"Where is he now?"

"He's staying at the La Fonda," she replied, knowing she sounded tetchy and not much caring. The question might have been innocent enough on the surface, but she had a feeling that

Tony had asked because he wanted to make sure Gabriel wasn't crashing in the spare bedroom. Never mind that Cassandra had done the very same thing when she was stranded here in Santa Fe. Ava knew her brother wouldn't see anything similar in their situations.

"Oh." Another pause, and then Tony said, "Have you told Mom and Dad?"

"No," Ava returned, again experiencing a flash of irritation. "Why do I need to tell them anything? This doesn't involve them."

"Well, except for the part where Gabriel knocked Mom out cold with his magic when he took the grimoires."

"I thought you said he apologized for that."

"He did, but—"

"But nothing," Ava cut in. "Like I said, this doesn't involve our parents. Miranda knows that Gabriel is here in Castillo territory, and if the *prima* is cool with him being around, then that's all that matters, right?"

"Okay," Tony said. Now he sounded a bit defensive, which meant he was probably on the retreat. "I didn't mean to make a big deal about it. I just thought that maybe you could use their help. This is a pretty big problem that Gabriel's dropped into your lap."

Yes, it was, but she realized she didn't mind. Helping the Escobar warlock had given her a sense of purpose she knew she'd been seriously lacking. Of course, she would never come out and admit such a thing to Tony...although she realized he'd been dealing with a similar sense of ennui when Cassandra Sandoval came into his life...but Ava knew she wasn't going to let this go.

"Honestly, what could Mom and Dad even do?" she asked, hoping she sounded reasonable and logical. "Neither of them has the kind of talents that would be at all useful in this situation. And, in case you'd forgotten, I'm an adult and can make my own decisions."

"You're twenty-two," he pointed out.

"I vote, drink, pay taxes," she said. "I'm an adult."

He chuckled then. "All right, all right. I get it."

Thank God. Ava had just been about to remind him that Cassandra was only a year older than she was, and never in a million years would Tony have tried to insinuate that his girlfriend wasn't a grown woman capable of making her own decisions.

"Good," she said. "I just thought you should know that Gabriel was okay. I know that both you and Cass still were worried about him."

"Yes, we were." Tony was quiet for a second or two, then said, "I honestly never thought he'd make it out of there alive. I wanted to believe that

Vicénte Escobar wouldn't stoop so low as to kill his own brother, but I saw the guy in action. Evil, just like all the other Escobars."

"Most of the Escobars," Ava corrected him. "Gabriel isn't like that."

"No, he isn't." Another pause, and her brother went on, "It must be rough for him, having to live without magic. I can't even imagine what that must be like. I mean, I'm not the world's most powerful warlock by any stretch of the imagination, and even I don't want to think about having to live without my powers. And Gabriel was so strong…."

The words trailed off there, but Ava knew what Tony meant. To an ordinary witch or warlock, suddenly losing their magical talent would be like losing a limb. For someone like Gabriel, who'd commanded what sounded like a dizzying array of powers, it must have been like being struck deaf, mute, and blind all at once.

Or worse.

"He's doing okay, though," she said quickly. "I mean, obviously he wants to do whatever he can to restore his powers, but he seems to be coping all right. But then, he's had some time to come to terms with what happened to him. I'm sure it was a lot harder right after it happened."

"True. So, what's your plan?"

"'Plan'?" Ava repeated with a shaky laugh. "I

don't have a plan yet. That is, I thought maybe I had one, but since we struck out with both Miranda and Loc, it's back to the drawing board. But I'll come up with something…or Gabriel will."

"I hope so. But…I hope you know what you're doing."

*You and me both.* "Oh, sure," she said, her tone light. "I've got this."

Tony didn't reply right away, which told her he saw right through her act but wasn't going to call her on it. "Okay. If you need any help, though—"

"I'll call." Ava knew she wouldn't, though. Tony and Cassandra had made a pretty effective team as they hunted down the stolen grimoires—probably more effective than even they had thought they would be—but this was an entirely different circumstance, one that called for a different set of skills. She doubted her brother or his girlfriend could really do that much to help Gabriel.

Unfortunately, Ava had a feeling she probably couldn't do all that much, either.

But she had to try.

## 6

GABRIEL LAY AWAKE IN HIS HOTEL BED, staring up at the ceiling. He didn't bother to roll over and look at the clock...he knew it would tell him that only a few minutes had passed since the last time he'd glanced at it. Then, it had been four-thirty, far too early to even think about getting up. And while he understood that he should be trying to get as much sleep as possible, since he had no idea what this new day would bring, he also knew that sleep was proving to be just as elusive as his lost magical powers.

At least he knew the best way to deal with sleeplessness was to remain in bed, to close his eyes and try to rest even if sleep itself eluded him. His eyelids slipped shut, but instead of a calm, soothing darkness, he saw Ava's lovely, earnest face, saw the bright flash of her smile and the warmth in her big brown eyes. No matter what he did, she remained there, seemingly imprinted on the back of his eyelids like the glow of the sun after he'd had glanced up at it by accident.

Why she had made such an impression on him, he wasn't sure. In his time in Mexico City, he had met many beautiful women, had even embarked on a few romances, although he'd inwardly known those relationships were doomed from the start. They had been based on physical attraction and nothing more. It was as though he had known deep inside that he would never give his heart to any woman who wasn't a witch.

Possibly a laughable restriction, given that he now had no powers of his own, nothing he could offer a woman from a witch clan. Back in Pico Negro, he hadn't dallied with any of the women in his village, had traveled to San Salvador on those occasions when he knew his body needed some kind of physical release. Each time, he had told himself he slept with civilian women simply because he would not treat an Escobar witch so casually, but now he knew the reason was more that there had been no one of interest among the distant cousins who could have been a viable match, no one who touched his spirit in any true way. Inwardly, he'd wondered if that indifference was because he had inherited something of his late father's cold heart, then set the concern aside, since he'd had many more important matters to worry about.

Now, however, he began to understand why he had been so aloof, his heart never engaged.

It was because he had not yet met Ava Castillo.

She was beautiful, of course, but he also found himself drawn to her spirit, to her obvious sincerity and compassion. Even after they had met with disappointment the day before, she had refused to give up. While he found himself doubting that she would produce the miracle he needed...more because it didn't exist than for lack of trying...he wondered if she might surprise him. After all, his mere reaction to her had been rather eye-opening.

But whatever he might think of her—whatever hopes he might hide within his heart, so he wouldn't make a fool of himself the next time he was around her—he knew he needed to remain focused on the problem at hand. The only way he would ever be a fitting match for her was if he somehow managed to regain his powers, and so that was what he needed to concentrate on for the moment. If he became himself again...if he had something to offer...that would be the time to learn whether she shared any of his feelings.

His eyes opened, and he stared once more at the blank white plaster of the ceiling, even as he wanted to shake his head at his foolishness. He had met Ava less than twenty-four hours earlier. It was mad to be thinking these things.

And yet…and yet he could not quite stop himself.

With a sigh, he turned over on his side—away from the hated clock—and closed his eyes once again.

Ava rinsed out her coffee mug and glanced for what felt like the hundredth time at the clock on the microwave. Nine forty-eight. She'd showered and dressed and eaten breakfast, brushed her teeth and put on her makeup. Not too much, although she invested more time than usual in the application of those cosmetics, knowing she wanted to look as good as she could in front of Gabriel, even as she chided herself for caring about something so frivolous when she knew he probably wasn't paying any attention to her appearance. Why should he? With all the important things he had occupying his mind, she doubted she was taking up too much space in there.

Despite all her morning preparations, despite dutifully checking her email and watching the local news and doing anything else she could think of to kill some time, it still wasn't ten o'clock yet. While she had a feeling that Gabriel was probably already awake, she couldn't know for sure. Her mother had drummed into her the etiquette of never calling before ten in the morning unless it was an emergency, and that was why Ava hesitated now.

*It's only ten more minutes,* she told herself. *Go sit on the back porch in the sun and try to get your head together.*

So she went outside and sat down on one of the Adirondack chairs on the porch, letting herself breathe in the mild air—scented with warm grass and roses and lilacs—and allowing the sun to touch the bare skin of her arms. That did feel good, actually. While she didn't quite close her eyes, she let her lids slip down a little, shielding herself from some of the glare.

Although she couldn't exactly call what she was doing meditating, she let her breathing slow and become more rhythmic, allowed her mind to become still and calm. It was at times like these when she was sometimes struck by inspiration. Or maybe it was more that some of the everyday clutter and clamor in her brain quieted down for a bit, allowing thoughts that were previously obscured to stand out in sharp relief. She recalled her and Gabriel's meetings with Miranda, with Loc and Cat. She thought of all the possibilities that had been broached, then promptly shot down.

None of that seemed very helpful, but for some reason, her mind kept circling back to Cat and Loc. Why, Ava wasn't sure, but there had to be a reason why the unlikely couple remained at the forefront of her thoughts.

Not the two of them specifically, she realized. What they'd gone through together.

Who'd they defeated.

Her eyes opened then, and Ava blinked at the bright backyard, at the color that seemed to leap at her from the flowerbeds, yellow and purple and brilliant scarlet.

Cat and Loc had beaten Nicholas Toulouse, a dark warlock in New Orleans. Ava hadn't gotten the whole story, but it sounded as though Toulouse had managed to unnaturally prolong his life with some kind of very black magic. He'd wanted to work with Loc because he needed Loc to get the de la Paz grimoires for him, even though he already had a substantial magical library.

A magical library....

What had happened to it? The warlock was dead at Loc's hands, had apparently shivered into bone dust as his unnatural life left him, but the Dubois clan must have gone in and cleared out the house Nicholas Toulouse had occupied, just as the Castillos here in Santa Fe had packed up all of Simon Escobar's belongings after his death.

Maybe that library had contained the very spell she and Gabriel were looking for.

Excited, Ava pushed herself out of the Adirondack chair and hurried into the kitchen, then picked up her phone from where she'd left it on the kitchen counter. All right, it was still three minutes until ten, but such a small difference hardly mattered now.

She found the listing for the La Fonda hotel, entered the number, and then asked for Ramón Hernandez's room. A minute later, she heard Gabriel's voice, already oddly familiar to her.

"Yes?"

"Gabriel, it's Ava. I just had an amazing idea."

She hadn't told him over the phone what her idea precisely was, only that she'd thought of something and needed to come over to the hotel right away. Gabriel was certainly amenable to this suggestion, since he'd already found himself looking forward to seeing her again this morning. Possibly he anticipated their meeting far too much, but he would analyze those feelings later on, when he had time. Now he had hope again, even as he was forced to admit to himself that her suggestion might be something of a long shot.

They'd gotten coffee and some pastries from a bakery near the Plaza downtown and now sat on one of the benches there, enjoying the sunshine and the mild breeze. Yes, there were plenty of people here, but they all seemed occupied with their own activities and obviously were not inclined to eavesdrop. That was probably why Ava had suggested that they come here, rather than have a late breakfast at the La Fonda's restaurant. There, it would have been much more difficult to keep their conversation between just the two of them.

And besides—his current lack of powers notwithstanding—Gabriel couldn't think of any place he would rather be than on this bench with Ava Castillo seated next to him, the light wind playing with the dark waves of her luxurious hair, the brilliant sunshine showing how smooth and perfect her warm-toned skin truly was.

"Do you truly think the Dubois *prima* would let us come to her territory to look at Toulouse's books?" he asked.

From the slight frown which pulled at Ava's finely arched brows, he guessed that a similar concern had already crossed her mind. However, she sounded blithe enough as she replied, "I don't see why she would say no. After all, Loc did

Estelle Dubois a huge favor—he got rid of the dark warlock who killed her husband and was playing footsie with her younger daughter."

"'Footsie'?" Gabriel repeated, not entirely sure what Ava had meant by that. It didn't sound like the sort of activity he could imagine a dark warlock engaging in.

"Oh," Ava said, and sudden color touched her cheeks, a flush that couldn't entirely be blamed on the bright sun beating down on them. "I just meant that it sounded as if they were in some kind of weird relationship."

"I see," Gabriel said carefully, deciding he'd better leave it at that. Why the Dubois *prima's* daughter would have gone to be with the very man who'd murdered her father, he had no idea, but he supposed this Nicholas Toulouse might have been endowed with some of the same mind-control powers that Gabriel's own father had once possessed. At any rate, he could tell the topic made Ava uncomfortable, so he saw no need to pursue it. "Well, if Loc did that sort of favor for Estelle Dubois, then I can see why she might be more open to your request."

Ava nodded, obviously relieved that he hadn't asked any more questions about Toulouse and the *prima's* daughter. "That's what I was thinking. Of course, Miranda is going to have to do the actual asking, because this is the sort of thing that has to be handled *prima* to *prima,* if you know what I mean. A nobody like me can't just go and ask the *prima* of a neighboring clan if she can drop in for a visit."

"You are not a nobody," Gabriel said, his tone a bit more severe than he'd intended.

Luckily, Ava didn't seem to notice, only shot him a smile and then shook her head. "I didn't mean it that way. But it's always been tradition that the *prima* of one clan talks to the *prima* of another when it comes to asking for permission for something like this. Otherwise, I can see how it might turn into a free-for-all."

"Do members of the Castillo clan ask permission when going to McAllister or Wilcox lands?" he asked, genuinely curious.

"Not exactly, but that's different. I think Miranda still sort of lets her parents know when someone wants to travel into northern Arizona, but I don't think there's really much 'permission' involved, if you know what I mean." Ava sipped from her cappuccino. Gabriel glimpsed the tiniest hint of the tip of her tongue licking away the foam, and a small thrill went through him. He really shouldn't be staring at her so closely, and certainly not allowing his body to react to something so innocuous as her licking some of her drink's foam off her lips.

Then again, he supposed he should be glad

that he was noticing such things at all. After his magic was stolen from him, months had passed before he found himself at all interested in women again, even though there had been plenty who'd shown an interest long before that. Not Olivia, the photographer who had found him on the streets of Mexico City—she was only attracted to other women—but many others. Eventually, he had rediscovered that side of himself again, although he had indulged his body only, not his heart. There had been no one who made him feel the way that Ava Castillo did.

But now she was speaking again, and he made himself focus on her words, rather than the delicious shape of her mouth.

"Anyway, I doubt Estelle Dubois will say no to us coming there, not when she would still have Nicholas Toulouse to deal with if it weren't for Loc and Cat."

Gabriel broke off a piece of his croissant and chewed it slowly, considering. Then he said, "Even taking into account as grateful as you think she might be, aren't you worried that the Dubois *prima* might not wish for us to see the dark warlock's library?"

"We-ell...." Ava hesitated for a moment, then sipped some more of her cappuccino. "I guess I was thinking that maybe we wouldn't ask for that particular favor up front."

"So you would go to New Orleans under false pretenses?" He wasn't sure he liked the sound of that.

"Not exactly." She set down her drink and took a bite of her own croissant. "More like…we need to talk to her about Nicholas Toulouse, but it's the sort of sensitive subject that needs to be discussed in person. Something like that. She'll understand. From what I can tell, it wouldn't be the first time a *prima* made a request like that."

No, probably not. Gabriel was still getting used to the way the witch clans here in the United States interacted with one another, because the Escobars had done their best to either absorb or eradicate any clans in the countries that bordered El Salvador. However, the U.S. was vast, and back when these witch families had first settled here, they had most likely thought there would be plenty of room for everyone to have all the land they required. Anyway, he knew he needed to let Ava take the lead in this, since she understood how it all worked while he was still finding his way.

"And how do you plan to explain me?" he asked quietly.

"'Explain' you?" Ava echoed, obviously not comprehending.

"Does the Dubois clan know of what my half-brother did here in Santa Fe?"

"Well, yes, but—"

"Then you can see why I might be concerned that they wouldn't be open to helping someone whose last name is Escobar."

"Oh." She slumped against the back of the bench, pretty features suddenly troubled. For a moment, she didn't say anything else, only pursed her mouth slightly, as though she was working through the problem in her mind. Then she appeared to brighten and said, "Honestly? I don't think that's going to be as much of a problem as you think it might. Miranda will tell Estelle Dubois about what you did for Tony and Cassandra down in El Salvador...and what happened to you afterward. She'll know that you're not a typical Escobar."

Even though that last statement had been intended to reassure him, Gabriel still couldn't help but wince internally. He had been raised to be proud of his family name, to be proud of the powerful magic that had passed down through generations of Escobar *primuses* to him. Unfortunately, if one looked at the situation in an objective manner, it was only too easy to realize that the men of the Escobar line had not done all that much to make one proud. They used their powers to control and to dominate, to ensure that no one ever questioned their preeminence. Certainly there was no one here in New Mexico—or

Arizona or California, for that matter—who would say a word in defense of the Escobar clan.

To tell the truth, Gabriel himself had no such words, either. After all, one of the main reasons he wanted his powers back was to confront Vicénte, to tell him that this needed to end here, that the cycle of darkness and domination could not continue past their generation. His brother had no children yet, but Gabriel knew that Vicénte had already begun thinking about replacing the wife he had lost in childbed. It was only a matter of time before there was another heir to the Escobar clan's *primus*. And while Gabriel did not think he would hesitate to stop his brother by any means necessary, he knew he couldn't be so ruthless when confronting an innocent child. There were some who might say that even a child's blood was sullied by his father's cruelty, but he knew he could not allow himself to believe such a thing. If all Escobar blood was marred by the same evil, then he was also tainted.

But he had stood up to Vicénte, had made sure the grimoires were burned to dust and no longer a threat to anyone. Surely doing such a thing was proof enough that he was not truly Joaquin Escobar's son, that he would rule the clan in a much different way.

Of course, Gabriel knew he had many obstacles to overcome first. If he could not restore his powers somehow, then he would be like a child bringing a butter knife to a gunfight. He could not possibly hope to prevail against Vicénte unless he was himself again.

And that meant letting the Castillo *prima* reach out to the leader of the Dubois clan to make this simple request. It also meant swallowing his pride and not worrying whether those Louisiana witches might look down on him because of where he came from, who his father was. In the end, it was his own actions that would define him, no matter what anyone else might think.

"You're right, of course," he said, facing Ava's anxious gaze and doing his best to offer her what he hoped was a reassuring smile. "Go ahead and call Miranda and explain to her what we are hoping to do…and we will see what happens after that."

## 7

AVA WATCHED AS THE PLANE DESCENDED toward the airport in New Orleans—or rather, far outside the city, since they would still have a good thirty-minute cab ride into town. Next to her, Gabriel looked calm enough, but there was something about the tightness in his jaw that told her he would be all too glad when this flight was over.

Actually, she was sort of surprised that she'd gotten him on the plane at all. Sure, he wanted to meet with Estelle Dubois, clearly hoped she would be able to provide him with something that might actually work to restore his powers…but he'd also argued with Ava about flying here and had tried to convince her that they could drive or take the train. When she'd reasonably pointed out that a road trip would take several days and a train ride almost as long—and that they'd also have to get the permission of the Montoya and Calhoun *primas* to take such a journey, since they'd be passing through their territories—he'd still tried to argue that it would be safer.

"'Safer'?" Ava had echoed, not sure what in the world he was talking about. "You have a much bigger chance of getting into an accident in a car —even a self-driving one—than you do when you're flying in a commercial jet. Plus, it's so much faster."

Of course, she hadn't added that she didn't really want to drive the thousand miles or so to New Orleans. She did fine around town and going back and forth between Santa Fe and Albuquerque, but she'd never undertaken the kind of road trip Gabriel was suggesting, and she really didn't want to. And that didn't even take into account the awkwardness of the two of them being cooped up in a car alone for hours and hours each day. It wasn't that she didn't like being around him...more the exact opposite. She wasn't sure she couldn't trust herself to not blurt out something that would reveal her feelings for him, or at least what she thought her feelings for him might be. Honestly, it could just be overwhelming physical attraction and nothing more, although she honestly didn't think so. There was something about Gabriel that drew her to him, a kind of connection she'd never felt with anyone else.

In the end, he'd given up pushing for a road trip, although Ava had kept wondering why he was so hesitant to fly. He'd told her when they first met that he'd taken the train to get to Santa Fe, so clearly this wasn't a particular objection to flying to New Orleans.

Now, as their Delta jet glided down toward the airport, she thought once again how much better it was to take a nice, quick plane ride of a few hours and get it over with. Yes, she and Gabriel would be sharing an Airbnb in the French Quarter, but the flat had two bedrooms and two bathrooms, so the situation wasn't quite as fraught as it might have been. It wasn't as if they had to share a bedroom or something.

*Too bad,* her traitorous brain told her, and she forced herself to focus on something more important, like what was going to happen after their plane touched down.

They were going directly from the airport to Estelle Dubois' home on Marais Street, so they would have a little time before facing the sleeping arrangements. Thank God the Dubois *prima* had been fine with their visit, although Miranda had reported that she seemed a little mystified by the secrecy surrounding the request.

"But she didn't say no, and that's the important thing," Miranda added. For a second, her startling green eyes had narrowed, and Ava worried that the *prima* might ask whether she really knew what she was doing, or whether she'd talked to her parents about her plans. But then Miranda seemed to shrug off any misgivings she might have had, and instead just inquired whether Ava needed any help with the travel arrangements.

Luckily, she hadn't. She had the Airbnb picked out and the flight selected, so once she got the green light, she quickly plugged her personal details and payment information into the various websites where she was ordering tickets and such, and got everything handled in less than five minutes. And only a few hours later, she and Gabriel were on this Delta flight, leaving New Mexico behind.

It felt strange to realize she was no longer in Castillo territory. Her entire life, she'd been sheltered in the knowledge that she was part of a powerful witch clan and that there was really very little she needed to fear. True, Simon Escobar's actions had shaken some of that serenity, but since she'd been safely away in Albuquerque during all that mess, she hadn't been touched by any of it, except to experience a deep relief afterward that Rafe and Tony—and so many others—had managed to survive the ordeal. They had lost Genoveva, but it could have been much, much worse.

A line of cabs waited at the curb outside their

terminal. To her surprise, Ava realized the vehicles weren't self-driving, but had actual human beings behind the wheel.

"No automated cabs in the French Quarter," the cabbie—a handsome black man in his late thirties—told the two of them as he stepped forward to take her one overnight bag and Gabriel's single duffle, then deposit them in the trunk of his older-model sedan. "Local ordinance."

"Oh," Ava responded, knowing she sounded slightly foolish but not sure what else she could have said.

"Go ahead and get in," the cabbie said. "Where you going?"

"Fifteen twenty Marais Street," she told him, glad that she'd memorized Estelle Dubois' address and didn't have to pause to double-check the notes she'd made on her phone.

"Got it."

He walked around to the driver's side and got in, so she and Gabriel went ahead and climbed into the back seat. Belatedly, she realized that maybe one of them should have taken the passenger seat up front so this wouldn't feel quite so much like they were being chauffeured around, but there wasn't much they could do about it now.

Soon enough, she forgot about the awkwardness of being crammed in the back seat of the cab next to Gabriel, because she was gazing out the window at the utterly alien nature of their surroundings, the rivers with their calm, slow-moving brown water, the wide-limbed oak trees with their eerie hanging curtains of gray-green Spanish moss. The landscape was so unlike anything she'd ever seen in New Mexico that it felt more as though she'd traveled to an entirely different country rather than simply flying two states over from the place where she'd been born.

Gabriel also seemed mesmerized, because he stared outside as well, dark eyes wondering as he took in the countryside. When he spoke, his tone was hushed, as if he didn't want the driver to over-hear him. "How far have we traveled to get here?"

"About a thousand miles, give or take," Ava replied.

"I have never seen a place like this," he said. "I have read about New Orleans, but the pictures did not quite tell the whole story."

"It's a huge change from New Mexico," she agreed, figuring that was a safe enough comment to make.

"Or El Salvador," Gabriel added. "We have our rainforests there, but they look nothing like this."

She supposed not. Tony hadn't talked much about what El Salvador was like, so although she'd also done a bit of research just out of curiosity, she still didn't have much of a sense of the place. "People call Santa Fe 'the city different,'" she remarked, "but I think we're going to find out that New Orleans might also fit that description."

Which proved to be the case. Ava couldn't help gawking a bit at the cemeteries they drove past, full of stone sarcophagi and crypts rather than regular graves because of the area's high water table. Equally foreign to her eyes were the brick buildings of the French Quarter with their shutters and wrought-iron, lacy-looking balconies. A little over a half hour after they'd left the airport, the driver stopped in front of an imposing—and intimidating—town house, tall and narrow, its green-painted shutters seeming to hide their own secrets.

Which of course they were. This was the Dubois *prima's* house, after all.

The two of them got out of the cab, Ava pausing to let the driver scan her credit card to pay for the trip. The total was a bit mind-boggling, and much more than she'd been anticipating, but she refused to let the amount throw her off. She smiled at the cabbie and thanked him…and then paused on the sidewalk, really feeling for the first time the heat and the heavy weight of the damp air that surrounded them.

Her expression must have changed—and not

for the better—because Gabriel grinned at her. "You feel that air?"

"Yes. It's horrible."

He chuckled. "Horrible? No, it feels alive, more like the air of my homeland. New Mexico is dry, dry as a bone. I wonder that you can breathe there without choking on the dust."

"I guess it's just what you're used to," she replied lightly, thinking that this was definitely not the time to get into an argument about the relative merits of their native climates. "Anyway, do you want to ring the doorbell, or should I?"

"I'll do it," he said, then stepped past her to touch the button in the brass plate next to the front door.

A moment later, the door opened, and a pretty blonde woman in her middle or late twenties looked out at them. A flash of recognition as she appeared to sense that one of the strangers standing in front of her was another witch, and she smiled.

"Are you Ava Castillo?"

"Yes, and this is Gabriel Escobar."

For a second, the Dubois witch's smile wavered, but then she nodded and said, "Welcome to New Orleans. I'm Martine Calhoun, Estelle's daughter and her *prima*-in-waiting. I'll take you to her."

"Thank you so much," Ava replied, relief

washing through her as she realized there wasn't going to be any problem about Gabriel. Yes, it was obvious that Martine hadn't been thrilled to come face to face with an Escobar warlock…but it was equally obvious that she had no intention of turning them away.

They followed the Dubois witch through a grand foyer with a chilly black-and-white marble floor and down a hallway with a high ceiling ornamented in fine plasterwork. A number of crystal chandeliers placed at regular intervals hung from that ceiling. The house was very formal, just as grand in its own way as the sprawling hacienda-style home where the Castillo *primas* lived. Right then, Ava was glad that she'd put on a dress and some pretty ballet-style flats, and that Gabriel wore a dress shirt with his jeans. Of course, he was so gorgeous that it probably didn't matter too much what he was wearing, but still….

Martine paused at an open doorway and said, "*Maman?* They're here."

"Bring them in."

The woman's voice was soft, with a gentle Southern drawl, but for all that, it had an element of steel to it. That was the voice of a woman who was used to being in charge.

*Well, of course she is,* Ava thought as Martine stepped aside so they could enter the room. *She's the Dubois* prima.

The resemblance between the two women was strong, both of them blonde and blue-eyed, with graceful, well-proportioned features. However, Estelle Dubois wore her hair up in an impeccable French twist, while Martine's blonde locks lay loose on her shoulders. The *prima* sat on a chair upholstered in rose-colored antique satin, back so straight, it was impossible to imagine her lounging casually on a sofa. A book sat on the marble-topped table next to her, but Ava couldn't see the title.

"Welcome to New Orleans," Estelle said, rising gracefully from her chair. The cream-colored skirt she wore looked like linen, but it didn't show a single wrinkle. Maybe even linen knew to be on its best behavior around this clan's *prima.* "I'm Estelle Dubois." She extended a hand.

"Thank you so much for seeing us," Ava said. "I'm Ava Castillo, and this is Gabriel Escobar."

Estelle's sharp blue gaze moved toward Gabriel and took him in with a single sweeping glance. Whether she was impressed or not was difficult to tell, since her expression didn't change a bit. When she spoke, her tone was almost musing. "I have to say, when Miranda called me, I almost said no. After all our troubles last year, I was not very eager to have an Escobar warlock in our territory."

"That is understandable," Gabriel said. "I am grateful that you changed your mind."

"Well, Miranda helped to change it. But please—sit down."

The *prima* gestured toward a couch covered with striped satin in cream and the same deep rose shade as the chair where she'd been sitting. The barest of nods in the direction of her daughter, and Martine excused herself and left the room, closing the double doors behind her.

"Some iced tea?" Estelle inquired, gesturing toward a pitcher and set of glasses that rested on a silver tray atop a table of inlaid maple. "It's quite a warm day."

There was an understatement. Ava thought she could still feel her hair sticking to the back of her neck, even though she'd only been outside for a few minutes. Thank God the house was blessedly cool; obviously, a state-of-the-art air conditioning system was working overtime in the background.

"Thank you," she said, then reached for one of the glasses and took a sip. The sweetness of the tea was unexpected, but somehow she managed to swallow it without blinking. She'd heard about Southern "sweet tea" but had never had any before this.

*I'm surprised they're not all diabetic,* she

thought, but made herself sip again from the tea before she set it back down on the tray.

Beside her, she could feel Gabriel stiffen at his first taste of the sweet tea, but, just like her, he gamely forced some down. However, he continued to hold on to the glass rather than put it back on the tray.

"Now," Estelle said, apparently ready to move on to the meat of the conversation once the niceties had been attended to. "What was so secret that you had to come here and speak to me about it in person, rather than handle this on the phone?"

Ava exchanged a quick, sidelong glance with Gabriel, and he gave her a very small nod. They'd already discussed how to approach the situation and had decided that it was probably better to let her do most of the talking, but she was still glad of the way he'd subtly confirmed what they'd agreed upon.

"Miranda told you how Gabriel helped my brother and his girlfriend down in El Salvador?"

"Yes," Estelle replied. She drank some of her own tea and shifted slightly backward, although she still didn't come anywhere close to touching the back of her chair. After crossing her slim legs, she added, "Very commendable, Mr. Escobar, to take on your own clan like that."

His shoulders lifted slightly. Ava could tell he

hadn't been expecting the praise and wasn't sure how to respond. "It was the right thing to do, given the situation."

"But because of what he did," Ava went on, thinking it was better not to get too sidetracked, "his clan elders stripped his powers from him."

Comprehension flared in Estelle's clear blue eyes. "Ah. Now I understand why I could not tell that he was a warlock. I thought it was just another Escobar trick."

Gabriel shifted slightly at that remark, but, to Ava's relief, he remained silent. She pulled in a breath and said in carefully neutral tones, "That actually is something Simon Escobar could do— hide his warlock nature. But Gabriel doesn't need to do that because right now he has nothing to hide."

"That was quite a revenge your clan elders inflicted on you," Estelle observed. "I am sorry to hear it."

Once again, he shrugged. Ava said, "He hoped that Miranda might be able to help him. She couldn't do anything, though…and neither could Loc."

The Dubois *prima* appeared almost startled by that revelation, although her expression smoothed itself quickly enough. "Really? I was under the assumption that Loc's powers were quite vast."

"They are," Ava replied. "But they aren't up to

handling something like this, apparently. We were thinking, though, that since this involved a kind of magic that isn't commonly used, that's been mostly forbidden for generations, maybe there might be something in Nicholas Toulouse's library that could help us. According to Loc, he was a big collector of books of dark magic."

"He was," Estelle said, her nostrils flaring slightly with distaste. "And we did find a large collection of books in his house after his death."

That comment made hope surge in Ava, and she sent a quick glance over at Gabriel. He didn't smile, but his expression grew eager, intent, and he shifted where he sat on the satin-covered sofa, fingers grasping the knees of his Levi's.

"Did you catalogue those books?" he asked. "Do you know what was in them?"

At once, Estelle shook her head, something that looked almost like pity flickering across her elegant features. "I'm afraid you misunderstand me. We found those books, true, but as soon as we were able to ascertain what was inside them, we burned the entire lot. That sort of knowledge is too dangerous to keep around, especially in troubled times like these, with dark warlocks and witches coming out of the woodwork."

Oh, no. Ava wished she could reach out and take Gabriel's hand, give it a reassuring squeeze, but she'd never shared even that kind of small intimacy with him and wasn't about to start now. Not in front of the Dubois *prima,* at least. But she could still sense the way his entire body stiffened with shock, even as he sat up a little straighter.

"You what?" he said.

"I'm sorry," she replied, although there wasn't much indication in her tone that she really felt all that sorry for him. "We just couldn't take the risk. We knew how Nicholas Toulouse had tried to get Loc to retrieve the stolen de la Paz grimoires and were worried that our own clan might become a target if word got out that we had Toulouse's library in our possession. Even locking the books away didn't seem safe enough, and so I made the decision that they should be destroyed."

Although Ava understood why the Dubois clan had burned the grimoires—after all, Gabriel and Tony and Cassandra had done the exact same thing to the stolen de la Paz spell books—she couldn't quite hold back a flash of anger. There could have been valuable information in those books, something that might have helped Gabriel. Now they were back to square one, with pretty much nothing to show for their efforts.

"I'm sorry," Estelle said again, this time looking a little more sympathetic. "We did what we thought best. If Miranda had given me a bit more information about what was actually going on, I could have told her that there was no point in your coming here. I'm afraid you've made this journey for nothing."

"It's all right," Gabriel told her. He sounded far more relaxed than Ava thought she would have been in a similar situation. "And I would not say it has been for nothing—I've always wanted to see New Orleans. We will be on our way, then, so we might get some exploring done before nightfall."

The *prima* looked relieved, clearly glad that he didn't seem inclined to press her for further assistance. "Oh, New Orleans will still be lively after sundown, no worries about that. But you will be able to see more of the architecture while the sun is still out." She rose from her chair then, and Ava got up as well, with Gabriel following suit after he put his barely tasted glass of sweet tea down on the antique silver tray. It seemed obvious enough that Estelle was done with this audience, so Ava figured it was better to get out of here before things got too awkward.

"I'm looking forward to it," Gabriel said, and Ava nodded, not sure what else she was supposed to do.

They followed the Dubois *prima* to the front door, where she again said she was sorry that they'd traveled all this way with nothing to show for their efforts. After that, however, she seemed glad to have them leave, and within a few minutes, they were back out on the sidewalk, the steamy air surrounding them once again.

"What now?" Ava asked, relieved that Estelle was gone so she didn't have to hide the disappointment in her voice.

"I suppose we should go to our hotel and check in, then decide what to do next."

She gazed up at him, trying to read something of his inner state in his expression. Unfortunately, she couldn't see much; he appeared serene enough, despite the bad news. He would have made a good poker player.

And even though she knew she could have dipped into his thoughts and taken a quick peek to see how he was really doing, no way in the world would she betray his trust by using her magical talent like that. "Sure," she said. If Gabriel could roll with this latest punch, then so could she. No one had said this was going to be easy. "I'll get us a cab."

Luckily, the app Ava already had installed on her phone worked as well here in New Orleans as it did in Santa Fe, so she requested a pickup at their current location and then slipped her phone back into her purse. The cab arrived only a minute later, which didn't give her and Gabriel much time to talk.

Just as well. They'd go check into their Airbnb, drop off their few pieces of luggage, and then…

...well, she supposed she'd just have to see. She knew she'd be lying to herself if she didn't admit that she was excited at the prospect of exploring the city with Gabriel, despite the disappointment they'd just experienced.

And who knew? In a place like this, almost anything could happen....

## 8

GABRIEL MADE HIMSELF FOCUS ON THE PLACE that would be their temporary home for the night. It was a well-appointed second-story flat just around the corner from Bourbon Street, with a balcony that overlooked a courtyard filled with containers of brightly colored flowers, and what appeared to be a thoughtful combination of interesting antiques and modern conveniences. Ava had chosen well.

Two bedrooms, and two bathrooms. No need to worry about sleeping arrangements, but of course, he should have expected that. Although he thought he'd noticed a few subtle signals from her —the way her gaze lingered on him longer than it needed to from time to time, the way color would touch her cheeks despite there being no real reason for her to blush—he couldn't definitely say that any of these signs meant she felt some sort of attraction to him. There was certainly no reason for her to have gotten them a flat with only one bedroom.

Too bad. Losing himself in her arms would have been a good way to forget what Estelle had told them. All this way, and for nothing.

All right, maybe not for nothing, he thought as he watched Ava emerge from her room. She'd said she wanted to get freshened up a bit before they headed out to explore, and she did look more relaxed now, as though she'd faced the bad news Estelle had given them and was ready to move on. Her dark hair fell in shining waves over her shoulders, and she had a pale blue sweater draped over one arm, a sweater that went well with the floral knee-length dress she wore.

Still, considering the warm, humid air outside, he wasn't sure a sweater was strictly necessary. Ava must have caught the sideways glance he sent at the garment, because she let out an embarrassed-sounding laugh and said, "I know it's hot. But we might end up someplace that's super air conditioned."

"True," Gabriel allowed. He got up from where he'd been waiting in the living room area of the flat and glanced over at the clock on the wall.

Not quite five o'clock yet. At this time of the year, the daylight would linger for quite some time. "Ready to go?"

She nodded. "Do you know where we're going?"

"Not really. I thought we'd start walking and see what we find."

Apparently, she didn't have a problem with this particular plan—or lack thereof—because she replied, "Sounds good."

They descended the stairs to the ground level and emerged into the muggy heat. Gabriel turned right as they left their building, more because it felt better to go that way than because he had any particular destination in mind. For a few moments, they walked in silence, Ava's bright eyes taking in the shops, the crowded sidewalks and even more crowded streets.

Once they had turned another corner, onto a street that ran parallel to a river—which one, he wasn't quite sure, although he thought it might be the Mississippi—she spoke again. "Do you want to talk about it?"

He really didn't. What was there to say, after all? Another hope dashed, and at this point, he didn't have many left. However, he made himself smile and say, "I'm not sure what there is to talk about. I can't even blame Estelle for what she and her clan did, since I helped burn the de la Paz books for much the same reason."

"True, but...." Voice altering, she went on, "Look, I think we can cut across the street here to the riverwalk. It's less crowded over there."

Gabriel glanced over at the crosswalk, then on toward the path that bordered the river. Plenty of people milled about on that walkway, but she was right—they would be afforded a little more privacy in that location, since at least there weren't any shops with people coming and going. "Yes, that sounds like a good idea."

They waited for an opening, then hurried across the street, past several storefronts, and onto the asphalt path. Next to them, the river flowed, wide and placid, gray-tinged under the partly overcast sky. Here, he could feel something of a breeze, not quite strong enough to be truly refreshing, but better than the thick, heavy heat that had accompanied them on their walk over here.

Once they were in a spot where their nearest companions were a good ten paces or so away, he went on, "It was not as though Toulouse's books were a certainty. They offered possibilities, nothing else."

"I suppose so," Ava said, although the downcast expression she wore seemed to tell him she had been expecting a good deal more than merely possibilities. "I just wish I could think of another alternative. I've been wracking my brains, but I can't come up with anything."

"Well," he replied as a sudden thought struck him, one probably inspired by the odd artifacts in the window of one of the shops they'd just passed, "we are in New Orleans. Isn't this city known for its voodoo practitioners? Perhaps I should explore that avenue."

She stopped on the path, and so he was forced to pause as well. Her arms were crossed, and she turned away from him, pretending to look at the river, at the large boats slowly cutting through the muddy-looking water. "That is really not a good idea," she said, and although she spoke in an undertone, he could still hear the vehemence in her voice.

Somewhat startled by her reaction, he said, "No? Why not?"

Her lips pressed together. "Because…because that kind of magic isn't like ours. Our magic comes from within"—she touched a forefinger to her collarbone, as if indicating the powers that lay deep inside her, and, by extension, within all witch-kind—"but people who practice voodoo are calling on outside powers, outside entities. They don't know what they're playing with. It's dangerous."

"How do you know that for sure?" Gabriel

asked, genuinely curious. "Are there people who practice voodoo in Santa Fe?"

"No, of course not," Ava replied, looking a bit offended by the suggestion. "But I asked my mother about it once, mostly because I had just read a book where people were using voodoo and I wanted to know whether it was real magic—magic like ours, I mean—or whether it was something made up. She said that it might seem as if there are different kinds of magic in the world, but our kind, the kind that's born within us, is the only true magic. The rest of it is civilians playing with powers they don't understand and can't control. Yes, we all know there are beings…entities…whatever you want to call them…that exist outside us—"

"Like your Loc, for instance," he said, and she nodded.

"Right. Loc turned out to be one of the good guys, but a lot of them…aren't. And those are the kinds of entities people are reaching out to when they're practicing voodoo. You don't want to get mixed up in that."

Gabriel had really been half joking when he made the suggestion, but he could tell that Ava was deadly serious. She was worried for him… worried about him. Despite the disappointment he carried within like a lead weight, he had to be somewhat cheered by her concern. It meant she cared, that she wanted to make sure he stayed safe.

"I won't," he said. "It was just a thought."

"I can understand why you might consider doing something like that, but we can figure out something else."

Even though neither of them had any useful suggestions to give at the moment. Possibly, there were other witch clans here in the U.S. who had amassed libraries similar to the one Nicholas Toulouse had collected, but, as Loc himself had pointed out, he'd never found anyone who could help him with his particular situation, so Gabriel saw no reason why he should have any better luck. Besides, he couldn't roam the country indefinitely, looking for an answer to his problem. Sooner or later, he would have to accept his lot, would have to realize there was no going back and he would be without magic for the rest of his life.

If that happened, he doubted Ava would want to have anything to do with him. She was a beautiful witch with a strong talent, and could do far better than a magic-less exile with nothing to offer. He thought no less of her when accepting this probable outcome. They barely knew one another; there was certainly no reason for her to sacrifice her future to be with someone like him.

About all he could do was say, "You're right, of

course," and then begin walking again. He didn't know precisely where he was going, but he spotted some tall buildings off in the distance and figured that one or more of them were probably hotels and presumably had restaurants where he and Ava could get some dinner. Curiously, he realized he was hungry, even though he found it amusing that he had an appetite at all when the bottom had just fallen out of his world.

She didn't ask if he had a destination in mind, but gamely kept up with his long strides as though she knew he needed this time to walk and ponder his situation. Gabriel wondered if some of her obviously empathetic nature had been born from her peculiar talent. It made sense that someone who was able to see into the thoughts of others would be more understanding of people's troubles. Whatever the reason, he was grateful for her concern, for the way she was able to instinctively know how to respond to him.

As they drew closer to the hotels he'd spied from far away, he realized they looked very glossy and modern. They didn't seem to offer the sort of New Orleans experience he had been looking for, so instead, he paused on a street corner and said, "Should we go up this street and see what we find?"

His companion blinked up at the sign above

them. "Natchez Street? Sure…it's not like I know where we're going anyway."

She offered him a rueful smile as she spoke, something about her expression so endearing that he wished he knew her better, knew her well enough that he could lean down and kiss her on the cheek as a way of saying thank-you to her for being so adorable. However, since he had no idea how she would respond to such a gesture, he thought it better to only say, "Neither do I. Not really. But I thought that with any luck, I would see someplace that looked appealing, and we could have an early dinner there."

"That sounds good. I didn't think I would get hungry this early, but I know I could eat something."

Her comment made him feel somewhat relieved. At least he wouldn't be forcing her to eat when she wasn't hungry.

They crossed the road when the light turned green and began to walk again. When they reached the intersection with Magazine Street, he looked in either direction and was gratified to see a green and white striped awning with the name "Bon Ton Café" written on it in an elaborate golden font.

"What about there?" he asked, pointing toward the restaurant in question.

Ava looked at the restaurant's façade and

frowned slightly. "It looks kind of fancy, doesn't it? We don't have reservations or anything."

Possibly, but they would be arriving early enough that reservations shouldn't be much of an issue. As for the relative "fanciness" of the place…. "You're wearing a dress," he pointed out. "And I have on a dress shirt. It should be fine."

She still appeared somewhat dubious, but then her shoulders lifted slightly. "I suppose so. If we don't fit the dress code, I suppose they'll tell us."

Possibly not the most enthusiastic endorsement, but at least she was willing to go along with him and see what happened. And actually, once they entered the building and waited at the hostess stand, Gabriel saw that the interior was homier and more relaxed than he'd anticipated, with red and white checkered tablecloths and exposed bricks on the walls. A pretty young woman around Ava's age approached them and asked if they had a reservation.

"No," Gabriel said. "We saw the restaurant and thought we would like to have an early dinner. But if it's a problem—"

"Not at all," the woman replied. She looked like she was probably of mixed blood, with her soft brown skin and curly black hair, and her smile was bright and friendly. "It's early enough that I can seat you now. This way."

She led him and Ava to a table up against the wall and off to one side. True, the spot wasn't completely secluded, but at least they wouldn't have dinner companions on all sides. And, as the hostess herself had pointed out, it was early enough that the dining room wasn't yet full. He should be able to speak with Ava about important matters as long as the tables around them didn't fill up.

They sat down and took the menus the hostess handed them. Although Ava hadn't said much up to this point, her eyes widened a bit as she looked down at the menu she held. "It's kind of expensive."

"That isn't a problem," he told her, which was only the truth. Even taking into account the money he had spent to get to New Mexico, he still had plenty left over from his modeling days in Mexico City. "You bought me a drink and some food yesterday, so I'll return the favor now."

"I'm not sure it really comes out even—"

"It doesn't have to come out even," he said. "Order what you like."

For a moment, her expression seemed to indicate that she wanted to protest further. But then she gave a shrug, returned her attention to the menu, and said, "Okay. It's probably going to take me a while to figure out what I even want to order. I don't recognize half this stuff."

This observation could have been extended to Gabriel himself, since he, too, couldn't quite decipher many of the items on the menu. Regional cuisine, he supposed, dishes that would be very different from what Ava was used to in New Mexico, or what he himself had consumed in El Salvador and then later on in Mexico City.

But there was an abundance of seafood dishes, and he thought a platter of grilled Gulf fish topped with shrimp sounded good and something that wasn't too foreign. Ava decided on trout —"because at least I know what that tastes like"— and a moment later a waiter came to take their orders. Gabriel asked for a glass of white wine, with Ava following suit.

Then they were left alone again, looking at each other from across the red-checkered tablecloth.

"Well," she said.

"Well," he echoed. It was as good a sentiment as any. They didn't have their wine yet, but he raised his water glass and said, "To making the best of things."

She touched her glass to his. "To making the best of things." A glance around the restaurant, and she sent him a smile that had the faintest hint of guilt to it. "I can't lie—I always wanted to visit New Orleans and never thought I'd ever have the chance. So it's good to be here, even if I wish we had a better reason for coming to the city."

"I can understand that." He set down his water glass. "And I never thought I would have any reason to visit America. At least, not until I realized it was here that I had my greatest chance of finding help."

Her face immediately fell. "I'm sorry."

"Don't be." On impulse, he reached across the table to where her hand rested on the brightly patterned cloth and touched her fingers, giving them a very gentle squeeze. She stared at him in surprise, color once more flaring in her cheeks… but she didn't try to move her hand away. No, she actually twined her fingers with his and held on.

Just that touch was enough to send a wave of warmth, of need, through his body, but he willed himself to remain calm. Their eyes met, and she smiled.

Oh, yes, he knew what that sort of look meant. She might have been trying to hide her feelings before now, but he could tell that she must be experiencing the same sort of attraction to him that he'd been feeling toward her.

This could complicate matters a great deal… and yet, he couldn't quite find it within himself to be overly concerned. Feeling her delicate fingers pressing against his right then was the most important thing in his world.

But then she abruptly pulled her hand away. Not, Gabriel realized with some relief, because she thought she'd made a mistake with even that simple gesture, but because the waiter had returned with their glasses of wine. Gabriel and Ava thanked the man, who said their food would be out in a little while, then both stared at one another now that they'd been left alone again.

"So...." Gabriel said.

"So," Ava responded. She managed to smile, but it looked somewhat lopsided.

"I didn't mean to make things awkward between us."

She reached for her glass of wine and took a sip. "I think maybe they already were. It was just neither of us wanted to acknowledge what was happening."

Her remark only confirmed what he'd thought just a few moments earlier. "I do like you very much, Ava."

Rather than demur or look away, she met his gaze directly. "Why?"

Nonplussed, he stared back at her. "Why do I like you?"

"Yes."

He chuckled. "A variety of reasons."

Her eyebrows lifted, but she remained silent, clearly waiting for him to go on.

Very well, then. "Because you're kind and

intelligent, and you reached out to help a stranger when you had no reason to get involved. You could have shuffled me off to your *prima* and washed your hands of the problem."

"I would never have done that," she protested.

"Exactly," Gabriel said. Then he added, feeling daring, "I have never met anyone like you."

Now she smiled as she lifted her glass of white wine to take another drink. "You must not get out much. I'm pretty ordinary."

"I don't think so." He straightened in his chair, even as he wished they didn't have this large table separating them. This would have been easier if he could have reached over and taken her in his arms. "My life in Pico Negro was somewhat circumscribed, true. But I met a great many women while I was living in Mexico City, and I can say with all confidence that none of them were anything like you."

The color returned to her cheeks. "Okay. I mean, I'm not going to argue with you, mostly because that will just make me sound as though I'm fishing for more compliments, which I absolutely am not. But there really isn't anything that special about me. I've never done anything important, never been anything more than a rank-and-file witch in a clan with lots of powerful witches and warlocks."

"You're doing something important now, I think."

"Maybe," she allowed, then added hastily, as if she didn't want him to think she considered their mission trivial, "I mean, yes, it's important to you, important that you're able to stop your brother from making some kind of big mistake. But if I weren't helping you, someone else would. It's not like I can do anything that someone else couldn't."

For a moment, Gabriel didn't reply. It seemed to him that Ava was going out of her way to deprecate her abilities, and he couldn't really understand why. Her gift was a rare and strong one—even the Escobars didn't have a member of their clan who could read another's thoughts. True, it possibly wasn't as showy a talent as her brother's ability to summon the wind, but wind-summoning was only a subset of the broader gift of being able to control the weather, which Tony Castillo could not do.

However, Gabriel realized he knew very little of Ava's past, of what her childhood had been like, whether her relationships with the others in her immediate family had been troubled. He knew that she had gone to the university in Albuquerque and that she was several years younger than her older brother. The little he had seen of her family home when he had gone to remove the de la Paz grimoires from their hiding place had told him it was a large and beautiful house. Clearly, she hadn't suffered any kind of material wants growing up, but that didn't necessarily mean all that much. For some reason, she seemed to think of herself of lesser...a notion he would happily help her abandon, if she would only let him.

"I'm not so sure of that," he said. "But I don't want to argue with you. Just know that I appreciate you helping me, that I'm glad you came here to New Orleans to offer your assistance, even if it turned out that the Dubois clan couldn't do anything for me after all."

A small smile touched the corners of Ava's mouth, and something about her seemed to relax, even if she didn't respond immediately. Her slender fingers with their tipping of shimmery pink polish played with the stem of her wine glass. Now looking downward, as if mesmerized by the straw-gold contents of the glass, she said, "I want to help you, Gabriel."

In a way, she already had, if only to remind him that the world wasn't full of people like his brother Vicénte, or the dark-hearted man who had fathered both of them. Yes, he knew that there were those in the Escobar clan whose hearts weren't black, who daily showed small acts of kindness to the others in their witch family...but none of them were strong enough to stand up to

Vicénte, or to the elders, who seemed to delight in carrying out their own cruelties. If he was ever granted the grace to become *primus* of that clan, Gabriel knew he would make sure the elders were replaced by those who took no joy in hurting others.

Unfortunately, that day appeared to be farther off than ever. Once again, he'd been thwarted in his quest to restore his powers, and it seemed that he would be forced to return to Santa Fe empty-handed. Ava had already said that her clan would take him in, but he didn't want to be a hanger-on, an object of pity. It was one thing if he could feel as though he might contribute something to the Castillos. As it was, with him no better than a civilian—worse, because he had not been raised a civilian and therefore possessed no useful skills he could even offer to his benefactors in trade—he would only be a burden to them.

To Ava.

She was watching him with some concern, obviously waiting for him to reply. "You are helping me," he said softly. "You may not believe that, but it's the truth."

Her mouth opened, and then she paused. Whatever she'd been about to say, she appeared to have reconsidered, because she said softly, "I believe you, Gabriel."

And he knew he would have to be content

with that. Whatever was happening between them…whatever it might turn out to be…he knew Ava would tell him the truth. Indeed, he guessed that she could do little else, since her talent had taught her there was no refuge in lies.

Right then, he thought she was the only true thing in his world.

## 9

GABRIEL DIDN'T KISS HER WHEN THEY CAME back to the Airbnb. Ava hadn't really been expecting him to, and yet some part of her had secretly hoped that he might reach out once they'd gotten safely inside, might take her in his arms and press his mouth to hers.

Instead, he'd suggested that they watch some TV to relax. They'd walked through the French Quarter after dinner, enjoying the sunset and the slight cooling that the end of the day brought with it, but he hadn't taken her hand, had seemed friendly but remote, as if he wasn't quite sure whether he knew what to do now that things between them had changed, if only a little.

She'd agreed to watch television, since saying no would have just made her seem petty. Luckily, the Airbnb's satellite service had some premium channels, so they watched a harmless action movie, then said good night and went to their respective bedrooms.

Which was why she lay here now, eyes wide open as she watched the reflected light on the plaster ceiling shift subtly when a car went by on the street below. This flat had fairly good sound-proofing in place—and it helped that the weather was so warm, because everything was shut up tight as the central air conditioning labored to keep the interior of their Airbnb cool and dry—but she could still hear the occasional sound as it drifted up from Bourbon Street. Echoes of laughter, faint music, low and smoky, with a saxophone singing its blues into the warm New Orleans night.

She wished she could be down there with all those other people, enjoying herself, having a night on the town. That would be much better than lying here wakeful in bed, her thoughts fixed on the man who slept in the bedroom down the hall.

If he even slept. For all she knew, he was just as wide awake as she was.

Should she have tried to make some kind of move while they walked through the French Quarter, or maybe after they got back to their Airbnb? Ava didn't know. Her experience in these sorts of things was horribly limited, and the couple of times she'd been at all intimate with a guy, he'd been the one to make the first move. What if she'd reached out to Gabriel and had been rebuffed, despite that small bit of hand-holding they'd engaged in at the restaurant? She didn't know if she would have been able to handle that kind of rejection.

*Stop second-guessing everything,* she told herself. *Go back to sleep.*

While that was sensible advice, her brain didn't appear willing to take it. Instead, it kept rattling on in the background, going over everything she and Gabriel had done and said during the evening, trying to find the moment when things could have been different but somehow weren't.

And, as if that wasn't fun enough, the mental playback went even further, to their meeting with Estelle Dubois. All right, Ava knew she hadn't done anything to embarrass herself during the interview, but she also couldn't quite shake the feeling that the Dubois *prima* had been a little impatient with them, was annoyed that they'd come here to intrude on her territory when everything could have been handled with a simple phone call.

Maybe that was only the truth, and yet Ava couldn't help but feel a stir of impatience of her own. She knew if she'd had those spell books in her possession, she might have decided it was best to destroy them in the end, but she damn well would have looked inside first to make sure they didn't contain anything that might be of some use to her clan.

That thought seemed to clang around inside her head.

*I would have looked inside first....*

She sat up in bed, mind working furiously. Estelle hadn't given them any real details on what precisely had happened to the books after they were taken from Nicholas Toulouse's house. Yes, they'd been destroyed, but had someone in the Dubois clan looked at them before setting them ablaze?

Because if they had, that meant the memory would still be located somewhere in their mind. And if that memory existed, it meant Ava would be able to see it.

The realization felt like a zing of electricity had just shot through her. All right, she had to admit she had no idea whether Estelle Dubois would grant permission to take a peek at one of her clan member's thoughts...

...but what if she did?

Ava pushed herself out of bed, pausing to grab the lightweight robe she'd laid across the chair over by the window. Right then, she wasn't too worried whether Gabriel was awake or not. This sort of possibility was the sort of thing that was worth being woken up for.

His door was almost closed, but not completely. She paused at the entrance, took a quick peek inside. Although she couldn't make out much, she could see the outline of his form under the light-colored duvet that covered the bed, thought she could glimpse the darkness of his hair against the white pillow case.

For a moment, she wavered. Maybe she should wait until the next morning to tell him about her idea. It wasn't as though they could call Estelle tonight, not when it was nearly eleven o'clock. On the other hand, if hers and Gabriel's roles were reversed, Ava knew she would be irritated to learn that she'd been allowed to sleep calmly when such an alluring possibility had presented itself.

That seemed to decide things. She pulled in a breath, then knocked on the door frame and said in a tone just a little above a whisper, "Gabriel?"

He sat bolt upright, moving so quickly that she couldn't help but flinch. "What the matter?" he demanded.

"Nothing," she replied. "It's just—I've had an idea."

His fingers must have found the lamp's switch, because a second later, it flared on. Ava blinked. As her eyes adjusted, she saw that Gabriel was shirtless, showing off a torso that definitely looked as though it belonged to a male model.

Damn. She swallowed, then went on hurriedly, "I was thinking…."

"It seems you were," he observed dryly. "Come in."

She entered the room, doing her best not to stare at the muscles in his chest and arms, the smooth brown skin that seemed to accentuate the contours of his physique. The bedclothes covered his stomach, but she guessed it was probably just as impressive. Another swallow, and she said, "I was thinking about our talk with Estelle, and how she was really vague about what they did with the books."

"She said that they burned them," Gabriel remarked, his tone flat. He reached up to rub at his eyes. It was pretty obvious that he'd been dead asleep when Ava knocked.

Well, at least one of them had been getting some rest. Since it felt horribly awkward to be standing there next to his bedside, she pulled out a chair that had been placed against the wall and sat down. "Yes, but she didn't give us any kind of timeline or anything, didn't say how long the books were in her clan's possession. That made me wonder if Estelle or someone else in the Dubois family glanced through the books before they were destroyed. If that's the case, then I think I could look into that person's mind and see the spells the books contained. All I'd have to do is transcribe them—"

"—and then it would be like having a whole new grimoire," Gabriel finished for her, looking both hopeful and somewhat bemused, as though he was a bit astonished by the mental leap she'd just made.

"Exactly. Or at least, that's what I was thinking." Ava stopped herself there, since she knew there were probably a million ways someone could poke holes in her theory.

"It's a good idea," Gabriel said. Now he appeared approving, and a happy little flush went through her. Or at least, she hoped that flush was strictly due to happiness. It could have been from her continued view of his impressive bare chest. "But…do you think Estelle would even let you do something like that?"

About all she could do was shrug. "I have no idea. If she was completely unwilling to help us, then she probably wouldn't have allowed us to come here to New Orleans at all."

"But when she granted us permission, she really didn't know why we wanted to speak to her," Gabriel pointed out.

Well, that was true. Ava pursed her lips and wished she'd gotten herself some water before she came in here. Her throat felt awfully dry.

Or maybe that was just from the effort of trying to seem cool and calm while doing her best not to look at Gabriel's bare chest and exposed arms.

"I know," she said, after a pause that felt awkward but hopefully hadn't been too noticeable. "And I know it's an intrusion to ask for something like this. Even witches and warlocks aren't too open to letting someone walk around in their heads."

"It doesn't feel bad," he told her. "Actually, it doesn't really feel like anything at all."

Ava knew that, because she'd heard pretty much the same thing from those members of the Castillo clan who'd allowed her access to their minds. Still, it wasn't the physical discomfort that was the problem, but the realization that you were opening the most private part of yourself to someone else, even if that person's intentions were pure.

"You wanted me to see your thoughts, though," she said. "You *needed* me to, since that was the best way to convince me you were who you said you were. This is something entirely different. Estelle doesn't need to help us."

Gabriel's expression grew grim. "If she knew what my brother Vicénte was capable of, she might be more interested in helping me."

"Maybe," Ava allowed. "But maybe not. I

mean, I understand that he's a threat, because I've seen inside your mind. I saw what he did to you. For Estelle, it's a lot more abstract, especially since we're talking in hypotheticals here. Your intuition tells you that Vicénte is getting ready to make some kind of move, but you don't know that for sure."

These arguments only made Gabriel frown more deeply. "I know my brother. There is no one to keep him in check. Before, I could talk reason into him…sometimes. And also, although I never openly threatened him, he knew deep inside that I would always be there to act as a constraint on him if necessary. With me powerless and gone…." The words trailed off, and he gave an eloquent lift of his shoulders.

"You've been gone for months," Ava said. "Wouldn't that have been enough time for Vicénte to start, I don't know, flexing his muscles?"

"Possibly," Gabriel replied, his eyes narrowing as he appeared to consider her question. "But possibly not. Even Vicénte would not act too quickly. He would take time to make a plan he thought would work."

"With assistance from your clan's elders, I'm guessing."

He nodded, the dislike on his face obvious even in the soft light from the one bedside lamp. "Yes. They are as cruel as they are powerful—my father made sure of that. No soft-hearted elders for the Escobars, I fear."

"Could you really fight all of them?" Ava asked, fear stirring within her. Even though she'd heard from Tony and Cassandra how powerful Gabriel had once been, there had to be *some* limit to his magical gifts.

"I think so," Gabriel said. There hadn't been any hesitation before he responded, which seemed to indicate he wasn't terribly concerned about facing down so many powerful adversaries. "Or at least, I think I could if my powers were restored to me."

It was good he was so confident, but.... "And what about the null?"

His eyelids dropped and he turned away toward the window, as though responding to a sound he'd heard outside. However, Ava hadn't noticed anything, so she had a feeling this was his way of concealing something of his expression from her. "I would have to kill him, I fear."

A chill worked its way down her back. He'd sounded almost casual as he spoke, and with his face still angled away from her, she couldn't get much of an idea as to what was really going through his head...well, not without taking a surreptitious peek inside, which Ava knew she would never do. She forced herself to speak. "*Could* you?"

Although she'd meant the question in more of a moral way, Gabriel appeared to take her literally. Now turning back toward her, he said, "Unlike my father, who had the powers of a null in addition to all his other gifts, Alessandro is only a null and nothing more. He has no way of defending himself against a magical attack…or a physical one, if it came to that. And with him out of the way, it would be easy enough for me to challenge my brother and the elders."

The cool tone of his voice sent a chill down Ava's back. She had no idea how she was supposed to respond to those remarks. Maybe somewhere in the back of her head, she could coldly acknowledge the necessity of what Gabriel was proposing, and yet it seemed too awful to think of killing a man just because his magical talent could possibly prevent Gabriel from carrying out his mission of stopping Vicénte Escobar.

The words came out before she could stop them. "That sounds awfully bloodthirsty."

"No, it's practical." Gabriel's tone sounded calm, though; if he was irritated with her for making such a comment, he wasn't showing it. "Besides, he has allowed himself to be the elders' lackey ever since his power manifested itself. He is certainly not blameless."

Maybe not. Ava had never been to Pico Negro, had never met any of these people, and so she knew she didn't have the whole truth of the situation. Still, she felt compelled to say, "If he doesn't have any powers besides being a null, maybe this Alessandro person feels as though he can't really stand up to the elders or your brother, no matter what he might think or feel inside."

For a long moment, Gabriel didn't reply, only sat there with his hands folded calmly on top of the duvet. Then, to her surprise, he smiled. "As I told you before, you have a kindly heart. You don't wish to see harm come to anyone, even if they are not deserving of your compassion."

"I think everyone deserves compassion," she replied. "Even people who've done terrible things. Maybe that's naïve. But you have to start somewhere. I don't know this Alessandro, so I won't pretend to understand his motivations. All I can do is tell you how I feel about these things."

Another pause, and then Gabriel nodded. "Very well. I will promise you, Ava, that if my powers are returned to me somehow, and I do go to Pico Negro, then I will do my best to show mercy to Alessandro, since he is only a pawn. And I will give the elders and Vicénte a chance to redeem themselves. But if they are determined to walk the dark path, to think only of the trouble and suffering they can bring to others, then I see no reason to be merciful. To be honest, I will think it a mercy to rid this world of them, because their deaths will guarantee that many others may live."

Ava knew she probably couldn't ask for much more than that. And besides, as she'd stated earlier, they were talking in hypotheticals here. The most likely scenario would be that Estelle would refuse to allow Ava to see inside her mind to access the secrets hidden in the books which had been destroyed—or that she would inform them those books never had included the kind of information which would allow Gabriel to regain his powers. It was a long way down the line from either of those possibilities to his return to El Salvador to seek revenge against the clan members who had wronged him.

Because of all that, she only nodded and said, "Okay, that's fair. I'll call Estelle in the morning and see what she has to say." And because there didn't seem to be anything else left to talk about now, Ava added, "Good night, Gabriel."

He murmured a good-night to her as well, but she'd already gotten up from the chair and hurried out. Maybe it was foolish, but she didn't want him to see the disappointment she knew she wore on her face.

~

Although he had been slumbering peacefully

enough before Ava came in to wake him, Gabriel knew it would probably be quite a while before he felt calm enough to fall asleep again. He sat up in bed, the light on the table next to him still on as he stared at the framed painting of a market stall full of flowers on the wall opposite him and brooded on what she had come to tell him.

He wouldn't have admitted it to Ava...and didn't much like admitting such a thing to himself...but the constant tug of war with his emotions over the past two days had begun to wear on him. A hope offered, a hope taken away, over and over again. While he knew that she was only trying to help, he had to wonder if she understood how tiring this was. Some part of him —a cowardly part—wanted to say enough, that he would simply have to reconcile himself to this new existence. But he knew he wouldn't give up, especially now that his conversation with her had awakened all the plans he'd once dismissed as impossible.

It had hurt to see the disappointment in her eyes when he spoke of what he intended to do to Vicénte and the elders, to Alessandro. Gabriel knew that Ava had begun to have feelings for him —feelings he wholeheartedly reciprocated—but he worried that she was having a hard time recon-ciling his harsh words with the man she thought she cared about. However, better to be honest with her now than to have her feel misled in the future. There was not much room in the Escobar clan for kindness or mercy. Once upon a time, he might have felt sorry for the null, since in a way, his peculiar power made him something of an untouchable, but now he was only another obstacle, something that must be removed in order for Gabriel to defeat his brother.

Well, he would have to hope Ava would come to understand that sometimes hard things must be done in order to achieve a greater good. It gave him no real pleasure to contemplate any of these possible actions, except perhaps a certain satisfaction in knowing that Vicénte would no longer be able to plot against the world's civilian population, and that the cruel reign of the clan's elders might finally be ended.

But he was getting ahead of himself. First, he and Ava would have to meet with Estelle once more, and hope that this discussion might end on a better note than their first one. Otherwise, he truly would have to return to Santa Fe empty-handed…and hope that Ava might still want him.

Even if he was truly no better than a civilian, and apparently had no real hope of being anything else.

## 10

THIS TIME, ESTELLE HERSELF MET THEM AT the door. Even though it was only a little past ten in the morning, she looked just as impeccable as she had the day before, this time in a crisp linen sheath dress in a soft periwinkle shade. A bluish-purple stone that Ava thought might be a tanzanite glittered on the ring finger of her right hand.

"Come in," she said. "Although I'm not sure what else I can do to help you."

Gabriel and Ava stepped inside the foyer. Meeting the *prima's* expectant gaze, Ava said, "I had an idea last night. I'm sorry for being vague on the phone, but—"

"It's all right," Estelle cut in. However, her tone seemed to indicate that it wasn't really all right, that she was beginning to lose patience with them. "What was your idea?"

They were all still standing in the entry hall, and, judging by the way the Dubois *prima* stood there with her arms crossed, she wasn't in any mood to extend the same courtesy of meeting them in the salon and serving them iced tea that she'd shown them the day before. Fair enough; Ava had been purposely vague on the phone, mostly because she'd thought their mission would have a better chance of succeeding if she was able to broach the subject in person.

However, with Estelle Dubois' sharp blue eyes feeling as if they were trying to bore right through her skull, Ava was beginning to question the wisdom of her approach. Unfortunately, the die had been cast, so there wasn't much she could do except brazen her way through this and hope she didn't sound too ridiculous.

"I was thinking about the grimoires you destroyed," she said, glad to see Gabriel give her a very small but encouraging smile. She wouldn't lie to herself and say that she wasn't still somewhat disturbed by their conversation the night before, but despite all that, there seemed to be something intrinsically reassuring about his presence, about just knowing he was there with her. It would have been a lot more difficult to carry out this errand on her own.

"Yes," Estelle said, obviously not overly thrilled about this opening.

"Did you look inside the books?"

That question earned her an even more piercing stare. "Why in the world would it matter whether I looked inside them or not?"

"Because—" Ava hesitated, then glanced over at Gabriel for some additional encouragement. He nodded, and she went on, "Because my talent is reading thoughts…seeing inside someone's mind. I thought that if you'd gone through the books at all, had seen the spells they contained—"

"Then you'd be able to pull the information from my mind?"

"Well, yes," Ava said, glad that she'd been able to get the words out after all. Doing so hadn't been quite as hard as she'd imagined it would be.

However, her relief was short-lived, because Estelle was frowning, well-groomed eyebrows drawn together so tightly, they formed a distinct line in her otherwise smooth skin. "Why on earth would you think it appropriate to ask such a thing of a clan's *prima?*"

Uh-oh. Ava paused again, trying to come up a way to reply that sounded simultaneously respectful but urgent. Luckily, Gabriel stepped in for her.

"We would never ask such a favor if we had any other options," he said. "Believe me, Ava does not make such a request lightly. But those books and what was in them may very well be my only chance to regain my abilities. If you had lost all your magic, wouldn't you do anything in your power, explore every possibility, to get it back?"

For just a moment, the forbidding expression Estelle wore wavered slightly. Ava hardly dared to breathe, hoping that Gabriel's words would somehow get through to her, that she would allow herself to see the situation through his eyes. There was no impertinence in their request...only desperation.

But then a certain stillness settled over the *prima's* features, and she shook her head. "I only looked in one of the books," she said. "That was enough to tell me the knowledge it contained was the sort of thing that's been forbidden for centuries."

"You saw the spells, then," Gabriel returned, his voice somehow flat and insistent at the same time. "If you could only let Ava look—"

"No," Estelle cut in. "I have some sympathy for your situation, Mr. Escobar, but I can't allow someone I barely know to go wandering around in my mind. It's...dangerous."

Because she'd heard these sorts of protests many times before, Ava wasn't upset. Or rather, she allowed herself a flicker of irritation, one she pushed away before she spoke. "I wouldn't 'wander.' I know how to look for a certain set of memories, nothing else."

"It's a risk I can't take," Estelle replied. "I'm sorry. You'll have to think of something else." Tone sharpening, she added, "How long do you plan to stay in New Orleans?"

"Not long," Ava said. She knew exactly what the Dubois *prima* had intended by that question, so she only went on, "In fact, our plane leaves in about three hours. So you don't need to worry about us hanging around here and causing more trouble."

Was that a flicker of contrition on Estelle's face? Maybe, but even if she had begun to feel a little sorry for the way she'd treated them, it was obvious that she had no intention of allowing Ava to look into her mind. "Well, then, you have a little time to see a bit more of the city before you go. I won't keep you."

The dismissal was obvious…and that appeared to be that. Disappointment stabbing through her, Ava wondered if she should make one more attempt to change the *prima's* mind, but the firm set of the older woman's mouth seemed to indicate she wasn't open to hearing any more arguments.

Better to escape with their dignity intact.

"Thank you for seeing us," Ava said, her tone as polite as she could make it. Next to her, Gabriel shifted his weight from one foot to the other, and she worried that he might try to argue, might try to make one more desperate plea, even though it was pretty obvious that Estelle didn't think his plight was worth giving up even a little bit of her privacy for.

But then he let out a breath and said, "We're sorry to have bothered you," then put his hand on the doorknob and turned it. They went outside into the muggy heat and didn't look back, although Ava heard Estelle shut the door behind them.

"Not a very understanding woman, is she?" Gabriel remarked as they began to walk slowly away from the house, back toward the main street that had led them here.

About all Ava could do was offer a helpless lift of her shoulders. "I guess not. I mean, I can understand why a *prima* might not want to open her mind to someone who's practically a stranger, but I was hoping she'd take pity on us."

"She doesn't seem to have much pity in her heart."

No point in arguing with that comment. Possibly Estelle was more gun-shy than another woman might have been in her particular situation, just because the incident with Nicholas Toulouse really wasn't that far back in her past. She was probably just being extra cautious.

Still, even if that caution was warranted, all it had done was effectively torpedo the one decent idea Ava had left. She certainly didn't have the luxury of hanging around here until inspiration struck...especially with their plane leaving in less than three hours. Besides, there was no point in staying in New Orleans, not when it was clear the Dubois clan wouldn't offer any further assistance.

They'd failed.

Before they'd gone farther than a few more steps, however, an unfamiliar female voice called out to them from behind. "Hey!"

Ava paused and looked back to see who had hailed them, while Gabriel turned as well. Standing just behind them was a girl probably around Ava's age, maybe a little bit older. She had long, honey-blonde hair that fell in careful waves down her back, and she was very pretty in a sort of popular-girl, cheerleader sort of way. In fact, she reminded Ava so much of the girls who used to tease her about her weight back in high school that she had to make a conscious effort not to dislike her on sight.

Despite the way her hackles went up, she could tell from the tingle at the back of her neck that this stranger was another witch. Obviously a Dubois; her coloring was similar to Estelle's, although her features weren't quite as much a carbon copy of the *prima* as Martine's, the *prima*-in-waiting, had been.

Gabriel said politely, "Can we help you?"

"More like I can help you." Her gaze went up and down him, frankly appraising, which made Ava tense that much more. No, she didn't have any real claim on Gabriel, but that didn't mean she wanted some strange witch to be looking at him the way a kid might look at an ice cream cone on a hot summer day. "I overheard what you were saying to my mother."

That remark seemed to confirm what Ava had already suspected. Still, she made herself sound faintly skeptical as she said, "Estelle Dubois is your mother?"

"Yes. I'm Celeste." She shot a quick glance over her shoulder. "Is there someplace we can go talk in private?"

"Of course," Gabriel said. In fact, he'd replied so quickly that Ava felt a flicker of unease pass over her. Did he think Celeste was pretty? She knew she shouldn't be feeling jealous, not when they had so many more important things to be worrying about, and yet....

But then he spoke again, and a rush of relief went through her.

"However, our flight is leaving soon, so we don't have a lot of time to spare."

A wry smile quirked Celeste's pink-glossed lips. "You may want to cancel that flight."

~

They sat in the small living room area at the Airbnb, which Ava had had the foresight to keep past the time they'd planned to depart…just in case. Now Gabriel could only be glad for her prudence, since it seemed obvious they wouldn't be leaving New Orleans this afternoon.

"I saw inside all of Nicky's spell books," Celeste said, then drank from the glass of ice water Ava had given her.

"He let you read them?" Ava asked, her tone a mixture of curiosity and disbelief. From the quick sideways glance she sent him, Gabriel guessed she wasn't quite sure what to make of the Dubois witch's latest revelation. For himself, he wasn't quite as surprised; men did strange things when under the influence of a beautiful woman.

A shrug from Celeste, one that sent a shining lock of warm gold hair slipping over her shoulder. Yes, she was very pretty, this witch…and she was also all too aware of her effect on others. It was not too surprising to think that Nicholas Toulouse would have drawn her to him, not the least because a warlock who'd kept himself alive far past the years allotted him would have been glad to have someone so youthful, so vibrant, in his clutches.

However, Celeste Dubois' beauty was not the sort that Gabriel found appealing. It was hard and bright, not gentle and welcoming like Ava's warm brown eyes and beautifully curved mouth. He wished he could tell her that, could let her know she had no reason to feel threatened by the presence of the other witch. Because he could tell she was not happy about Celeste being here in the Airbnb, even if the Dubois witch might possess the knowledge they needed so desperately.

Unfortunately, Gabriel had no way of making such reassurances…not now, anyway. Perhaps later, when he and Ava were once more alone together, he could reach out to her, tell her how much she had come to mean to him in such a short time.

For now, though, they needed to focus on what Celeste was telling them.

"Well, I don't know about 'let,'" she said with a smile, her gaze lingering on Gabriel. He sat calmly in his chair and did not react, and her smile faded slightly. "More like, he probably knew I was peeking, but since he also knew I didn't have the magic to do anything with what I was reading, he figured it was harmless."

"How many books?" Gabriel asked, and Celeste gave a careless shrug.

"I don't know. Probably around forty books, maybe a little more. He kept them all on a special shelf in his library. There was an illusion spell on them to make them look like regular leather-bound classics—you know, *Huckleberry Finn* and *Great Expectations* and that sort of thing—but when you opened them up, you could see that they were filled with all kinds of weird symbols and charts and words in languages I've never even heard of."

"Forty books," Ava said. She bit her lip, her expression dubious. "That's a lot of spells to transcribe." A pause, and she sent the other witch a sharp look. "Why are you helping us?"

The direct question didn't seem to bother Celeste in the slightest. Another lift of her slender shoulders, and a sly smile touched her pink-glossed lips. "Why? Because it would piss my mother off. And besides, just because she turned you down doesn't mean I have to do the same thing. She likes to think she controls me, but I do what I want."

Gabriel was not sure he wanted to get in the middle of a power struggle between the Dubois *prima* and her younger daughter. Clearly, being set free from Nicholas Toulouse's control hadn't done a lot to show Celeste that her wild ways could still get her in a good deal of trouble.

On the other hand, he didn't have much of a

choice. If he wanted any hope of having his powers returned, he needed Ava to look inside Celeste's mind and transcribe what she saw there.

Still smiling, Celeste went on, "Besides, I'm curious what you two are going to do with those spells once you have them written down. If you really had all your powers taken away, Gabriel, then it's not like you can use them. And it's not like those grimoires were hiding someone's secret recipe for bread pudding. That shit is dark, you know? Is your Girl Scout girlfriend over there going to draw the circles, summon the demons you'll need to give you your powers back?"

Ava's mouth opened, as if she wanted to protest being called his girlfriend. And while Gabriel himself certainly wouldn't mind thinking of her in such a way, he had to admit that she was no such thing. A friend, yes, a truer friend than he had expected to find among the Castillos. But....

"We thought we would take this one step at a time," he said calmly. "Of course, we hoped that there would be someone among the Castillos who could help us at that point."

"Like that mega-hot demon lord of yours?"

"If you mean Loc, then possibly," Gabriel admitted. He'd been a bit startled to hear Celeste refer to the demon lord so casually, but he reminded himself that of course the Dubois witch must have been there when Loc came to rescue his lady love, so she would know something of his presence among the Castillos. "The particulars needn't concern you."

This remark seemed to annoy Celeste, but then she made another casual toss of her bright blonde hair. "Whatever."

"And if not among my clan, then maybe the de la Pazes," Ava offered, as if trying to prevent the other witch from getting too irritated with them. "Because Gabriel helped one of them as well, so they owe him a favor. But all of this is academic if we can't access what's inside your head and get it written down."

"Then go ahead and try," Celeste said. "I told my mother I was going shopping and to the movies, so she won't expect me back for a while."

They'd stopped at a stationery store on the way over here, and had purchased several reams of paper and a package of pens. Those items were already waiting on the Airbnb's dining room table.

Ava glanced over there now. "Okay. Let's go sit at the table, and I'll see what I can see."

"Sure," Celeste replied, now sounding almost too casual, as if she didn't want them to know that she might inwardly be a little nervous at allowing another witch to look into her mind. "But I need to pee first."

She got up from the couch and went out of the living room area to the bathroom. After the door shut behind her, Gabriel sent Ava a questioning glance.

"Are you sure you're ready for this?"

Without hesitation, she said, "Yes. It's our only chance. And it's not like I don't have experience going in other people's minds. I'll admit there are probably things in Celeste's head that I really don't want to see, but I suppose that's just an occupational hazard."

About all Gabriel could do was smile, heartened by her acceptance of the situation. Yes, she was the kind of woman he wanted by his side—willing to do the hard things, someone who did not seek the easy path.

If they were successful, would she follow the paths he knew he had to tread?

But then Celeste returned, and he knew the things he wanted to say to Ava would have to wait.

Now was the time to see what secrets the Dubois witch held in the depths of her mind.

Ava asked Celeste to sit quietly with her eyes closed. To her relief, the other witch didn't argue, but obediently shut her eyes and sat in the prim little white-washed chair, hands folded in her lap, mouth shut, as if she didn't quite trust herself not to talk if she didn't keep her lips firmly pressed together.

It was times like this that Ava was really glad her particular talent didn't require her to reach out and physically touch the subjects of her mind-reading forays. She had a feeling that making physical contact with Celeste would have felt beyond awkward.

As it was, she still had to get past a few things she would rather not have seen to access the hidden memories of Nicholas Toulouse's grimoires. Ava knew nothing of the dark warlock except what other people had said about him, and so she had to focus on his name as she dove into Celeste's mind. She saw a man who must have been the warlock himself—tall and thin, with light brown skin and striking pale eyes. Not someone she herself would have thought attractive, and yet she felt something of Celeste's attraction to him, to the power he wielded, to the rich honeyed baritone voice that made her name sound like a caress.

Then, thankfully, she was past those memories, was now watching as Celeste reached up and took one of those leather-bound books from the shelf where it rested, saw as she opened the book and realized this was not *Mansfield Park* but something much, much darker.

And, almost without thinking, Ava reached

out as well, only this time to take up the pen from where it rested on the tabletop, to start scratching away on the blank paper that had been waiting for this moment. It would have been easier to dictate into her phone, but of course these spells couldn't be uttered out loud. Doing so would only awaken the dark magic they contained. Transcription by hand was the safest way to go about the process, laborious as it might be.

On and on she went, pen moving across the sheets of paper, setting them aside once they were full. At some point, the pen she was using ran out of ink. Then she felt Gabriel's warm fingers on hers, taking the spent pen away and putting a fresh one in her grasp.

More writing, faster and faster. Dimly, she was aware of her fingers cramping up, of her back aching as she sat there, bent over her work. All that time, Celeste sat quietly, almost as if she was in a trance of some sort, as though the connection between her mind and Ava's was so strong that she had no desire to do anything except sit there until they were done.

Which happened at last, many hours after they had first seated themselves at the table. Ava set down the pen and leaned against the back of her chair, muscles now aching with exhaustion. Celeste's bright blue eyes flared open, and she looked around in confusion, as if she couldn't quite remember where she was.

"It's all right," Gabriel said, coming over to the table. He held two glasses of water, and set each of them down by the two women who sat there.

"What time is it?" Ava asked. Her voice sounded rough and hoarse, raspy, dry. She lifted the water he'd brought for her and took a large gulp. It was cool and soothing on her throat, welcome as an oasis in the desert.

Next to her, Celeste did much the same, while Gabriel replied, "It's nearly eleven o'clock."

"*Eleven?*" Celeste repeated in a startled squeak. "Oh, shit, my mother has got to be crapping egg rolls."

Probably. The Dubois witch had given her mother something of an alibi, but a movie and some shopping wouldn't have taken the better part of ten hours. Alarm flashed through Ava and she said, "She wouldn't be able to figure out where you went, would she?"

"No," Celeste replied, now looking slightly contemptuous. "Do you think I'm a complete amateur?"

"Well, she is the *prima*—" Gabriel ventured, but Celeste shook her head.

"No, she used to have a couple of warlocks try to follow me, but she gave up on that a few months back after I kept giving them the slip.

Besides, after a while she realized I wasn't going to get into any trouble—any *real* trouble, anyway—and so she gave up."

Well, that was something of a relief. As irritated as Ava was with the Dubois *prima,* she couldn't help but be a little sorry for Estelle. Having a daughter like Celeste had to be exhausting. In the bad old days, Estelle probably would have married her off as quickly as possible in an effort to end her troublemaking adventures, but that sort of thing wasn't really an option anymore.

"Still," the Dubois witch went on, "I need to get going. I can always say I went to a club or something—in fact, I might stop by one on the way home, just to get some vape smoke smell on me—but if I'm out for too much longer, she's going to send out the bloodhounds."

She got up from her seat and looked down at the pile of papers on the tabletop. Although Ava had the vaguest of recollections of transcribing all those spells, she was still astonished to see sheet after sheet covered in her neat, round writing—pretty, girly writing that almost made the strange runes and sigils and diagrams look harmless.

Almost.

"Cool," Celeste said. "I hope there's something in there that can help you."

"Thank you," Gabriel said. He looked tired but relaxed. "Thank you for doing this for us."

"Oh, I didn't do it for you," she returned. "I did it because I know my mother will blow a gasket if she ever finds out. 'Night."

She let herself out, and Gabriel gazed at the door for a moment, expression somewhat bemused, before he shrugged and came over to Ava.

"Are you okay?"

"I think so," she replied. Even though her muscles didn't want to cooperate, she forced herself to get up and out of her chair, to stretch out her arms and lift her shoulders in an attempt to unkink her abused muscles. "I'm just not used to sitting in one place for that long."

"I can imagine." For a moment, he was quiet, and then he went on, "It was fascinating to watch —to see your hand moving as if on its own, your eyes open and fixed on something only you could see."

Privately, Ava thought it sounded more creepy than anything else, but she only smiled. "If you say so. I'd think it would get boring after a while."

Now Gabriel grinned, some of the fatigue leaving his expression. "Well, I'll admit that at one point I turned on the TV—with the sound off and the subtitles on, of course, so as not to disturb you. And I ordered in some food, since I thought you might be hungry once you were done."

As soon as he said the word "hungry," Ava's

stomach woke up and told her that yes, it was really hungry, and what the heck was she thinking, working like that for hours and hours without pausing to take a single bite.

"Starved, actually," she said. "Thanks for that."

"I'll just heat it up."

He went over to the small kitchenette, spooned something out of a plastic take-out container onto one of the plates the Airbnb had provided, and then put it in the microwave. Ava couldn't tell exactly what it was, but it sure smelled good.

A minute later, he set the plate in front of her. "It's something they call jambalaya. I tried to get something that would be easy to reheat."

By that point, she probably could have eaten the proverbial horse, so she wasn't going to be picky. Anyway, as soon as she put a spoonful in her mouth, she knew he'd made a good choice. The jambalaya was spicy without being over the top, hearty and warm and thick with shrimp and chunks of crab.

"It's great," she said after she was done chewing.

Gabriel looked pleased, although his only response was to pour her some more water from the pitcher in the fridge. "Here. You're probably thirsty, too."

Which of course she was. She punctuated

bites of jambalaya with swallows of water, and within a few minutes, she started to feel like her old self again. Or at least, she was fairly certain she'd be herself once she was done with this food…and after she'd gotten a good night's sleep.

As she ate, he started leafing through the sheets of transcribed spells, a frown pulling at his straight, elegant black brows. Ava didn't like to see him looking so troubled, prompting her to ask, "Do you recognize any of it?"

"No," he replied at once. "That is, some of it seems like Latin, and I think some of it may be Greek, but this is not a kind of magic I've ever used."

For some reason, his answer comforted her. She didn't like to think of him playing around with forbidden magic, something she thought might not be quite the taboo in the Escobar clan that it was in so many other witch families. But clearly, he had no real idea what they were looking at, either.

She nodded and ate another mouthful of jambalaya. Still looking troubled, he said, "I don't suppose this is the sort of thing you can decipher, either."

"No," Ava told him. She drank some more water, then looked down and realized she'd eaten all of the jambalaya Gabriel had heated up for her. Telling herself she'd had plenty, she pushed the empty bowl away. "I wrote it all down, but I have no idea what any of it is."

Which made it sound as though they were back to square one. Yes, they had the contents of Nicholas Toulouse's library in their hands, but what were they supposed to do with it now?

Most people would have thought they'd come to an impasse…and yet, Ava knew better. She knew of one person who'd be able to read those spells, no problem. Actually getting her to do such a thing was an entirely different proposition, however.

"There has to be someone out there who can help us with these," Gabriel said, his hand resting on top of the pile of paper. "We just have to figure out who it is."

"Oh, I already know that," Ava returned.

At once, his eyebrows lifted, and a certain glint sparked in his dark eyes. "You do?" he demanded. "Who?"

"You're not going to like it," Ava said, which was only the truth. Actually, she didn't like it much, either, but they didn't have any other options.

Gabriel didn't respond, only stood there with his hand still on top of the transcribed spells, body suddenly tense. "Who is it?"

She let out a sigh. "My mother."

# 11

"HAVE YOU LOST YOUR MIND?" SOPHIA Castillo demanded, and Ava couldn't quite keep herself from wincing at the outrage in her mother's voice. All right, she'd known from the beginning that this interview probably wasn't going to go all that well, but....

Next to her on the couch, Gabriel shifted but didn't say anything. She could only imagine how hard it must have been for him to come here and face the woman he'd struck down magically last November when he came to Santa Fe to steal the grimoires. Well, imagine was exactly what Ava had had to do, since when they'd discussed how to approach her mother, he hadn't tried to get out of this meeting, hadn't tried to tell her that maybe it was better if he didn't participate. He hadn't said anything except that he understood why such a discussion was necessary…and he certainly hadn't revealed anything of how he felt about such a confrontation.

Maybe it wasn't quite as spectacular a show of bravery as sending Tony and Cassandra away so he could face his brother and clan's elders all alone, and yet Ava had to think his being here proved he certainly wasn't lacking in courage.

"No, I haven't lost my mind," she said, doing her best to sound calm. All during the flight back from New Orleans, she'd told herself that she couldn't fall into her old habits, couldn't act like a snotty teenager arguing with her mother over her curfew or why it wasn't her turn to take out the trash. She'd taken on the responsibility of helping Gabriel, and so she had to be strong and cool and rational. Otherwise, they wouldn't have a chance of convincing her mother to give them the help they so desperately needed.

"I know we are asking a good deal of you, Mrs. Castillo," Gabriel said. This was the first time he'd spoken, beyond the brief introduction he'd made when Ava first brought him to the house. He leaned forward slightly, but he, too, seemed to be making an effort to avoid a confrontation. "Believe me, if there were someone else who had your same magical talent, then of course I would have gone to them first. I am truly sorry for what I had to do to you in order to take the grimoires, but I had little choice. My brother threatened the life of my own mother, an innocent civilian who was treated horribly by Joaquin Escobar. I could not allow her to suffer any further harm…and I did what I could to make sure you suffered no lasting hurt, either."

These words seemed to have some effect, because Ava's mother sat up a little straighter. Her mouth, which had begun to open, closed again, as if she'd planned to offer some kind of argument but was thwarted by the obvious sincerity in Gabriel's tone. Her well-manicured fingers played with the heavy gold bracelet she wore on her left wrist—a rare nervous gesture, since Ava knew her mother did what she could to remain rigidly in control at all times.

"No lasting hurt at all," she said, lips lifting in the barest of smiles, one she obviously hadn't planned to offer at all. "But I'm worried that neither of you knows what you're doing here. Whatever is in those spells"—her gaze strayed to the stack of papers Gabriel and Ava had brought with them, now resting incongruously on the travertine and glass coffee table—"has to be very dangerous. I doubt they were in Nicholas Toulouse's library because they promised to bring light and good to the world."

Probably not. There were those who held their noses and dabbled in dark magic because the benefits outweighed the risks, but there were others—the kind whispered about at family gatherings, where the consensus always was that no one in the Castillo clan would ever play with that kind of magic—who seemed to delight in following the left-hand path, who wanted nothing more than to surround themselves with the magic of pain and darkness and power sought for its own delights.

She'd never met him, but Ava had a feeling that Nicholas Toulouse was definitely one of the latter types of warlock.

"True," she admitted. "I'm not going to lie and say that the spells we need to use are anything we'd want to work with under normal circumstances. Right now, though, we don't have a choice. The only precedent we have is that Gabriel's half-sister used some kind of forbidden magic to restore their brother Matías' powers, so we know it can work."

Her mother crossed her arms, mouth compressed. Watching her, Ava felt her heart sink a little. When Sophia Castillo looked like that, it generally meant she'd already made up her mind on a topic and wasn't going to budge.

But she had to budge. She had to help them. Otherwise, she'd be dooming Gabriel to a life without his magic...and possibly allowing the

Escobars to expand their reign of terror into a sphere no one had yet imagined.

When she spoke, Ava's worst fears seemed confirmed. "That kind of magic is forbidden for a reason," her mother said. "I don't know the whole story, but I know Cassandra has said that her paternal grandfather was killed by this half-sister, that her mother's estranged husband was also dead by her hand. What if I do you this favor and read the spells for you, find the one you need to restore Gabriel's powers? What if it turns out the only way it will work is if human sacrifice is involved?"

"Then of course we wouldn't use it," Gabriel said, even though the question had clearly been addressed to Ava and not her companion. "Every day I feel the loss of my magic like the loss of a limb—or rather, all of them—but I would never ask such a thing of Ava or anyone in her clan. Right now, though, we don't know what is in those spells. We don't know if one of them can return my powers to me...without a need for blood to be spilled in the process. And if you won't read the spells that Ava worked so hard to transcribe, then we'll never know. Isn't it better to be certain, one way or another? Only then can we make an informed decision."

It seemed as though he'd made his point, because Ava's mother frowned slightly, faint lines appearing between her brows as she appeared to consider what he'd said. Ava barely dared to breathe; the last thing she wanted was to do or say anything that might interfere with her mother's thought processes. And she knew this had to be difficult for myriad reasons. Sophia Castillo might expect a great deal from her children, but she also had always been there for them, was the kind of mother who always made sure to participate in school fundraisers, to offer her home for meetings or bake cookies for friends' birthday parties or basically do whatever needed to be done. She had to know how much this meant to her daughter. And while Ava had done what she could to avoid any awkward questions about why precisely she was so invested in helping Gabriel, she also realized that her mother was a very smart woman and could probably read between the lines. No, nothing had happened with Gabriel except that one moment of hand-holding at the Bon Ton Café, but Ava sure wanted more to happen…and she had a feeling her mother knew that just as well.

Then again, it didn't take a rocket scientist to figure out that your somewhat socially inept daughter would of course develop a crush on a handsome stranger who just happened to be in dire need of some assistance.

*It's not a crush, though,* Ava told herself. *This is…more. A lot more than that.*

Maybe they'd wasted an opportunity in New Orleans. She'd worked so late on transcribing the spells that of course they'd stayed another night, had caught a flight back to Albuquerque the next morning. But possibly there could have been a moment when she'd tilted her head up at Gabriel at exactly the right angle, one that would have told him she wanted him to bend down and touch his mouth to hers, that she wanted to know he felt the same way about her that she did about him…and also to let him know that while she'd do whatever she could to help him restore his magic, it was also all right if his powers never returned. She cared about *him,* Gabriel the man, not his magical talents.

If that moment had occurred, though, she'd managed to miss it entirely. They'd both gone to bed around midnight, and the next morning they were all business, packing their things and tidying the Airbnb before they went out to catch the cab that would take them back to the airport. The whole time, Ava had been on edge, worried that Estelle Dubois was going to show up and read them the riot act about peering into her daughter's mind to retrieve the information they'd needed so badly, but they'd left New Orleans without incident.

Without anything at all happening between her and Gabriel.

She didn't have a chance to dwell on what might have been, however, because her mother spoke then, still frowning, with a hesitancy to her words that showed how reluctant she was to find herself in agreement with Gabriel's argument about how knowing something was better than remaining in the dark. "Possibly," she said. "Maybe." Her fingers tapped on the knees of her crisp khaki slacks; even in warm weather, she would never allow herself to relax enough to wear jeans. A long pause, and then she added, "You both have to swear to me that you will not use any of these spells if they require you to—to hurt someone to make them work."

Ava wanted to be insulted—did her mother actually think she would be capable of such a thing?—but at the same time, she understood why she needed them to make this pledge. Desperation could make people do terrible things, after all.

"I swear," she said softly. "There's no way we would go any farther with this if it meant hurting another person."

"And I swear as well," Gabriel said at once, his tone firm. "My powers mean a great deal to me, but not that much. I am not my brother…nor my father."

His remark seemed to reassure Ava's mother, because she let out a breath and allowed herself to lean against the back of the chair where she sat. "All right. Let me look through the spells and see what I can find. It's going to take a while, though."

"That's all right," Ava replied. Relief was already singing through her veins, even though she tried to tell herself that she had no idea what her mother would find in those closely written sheets of paper. Even after all this effort, it still might turn out that there really was nothing to help Gabriel. "We'll go outside on the patio so we're out of your hair while you read."

"There's lemonade in the fridge," her mother said. She was reaching for the first piece of paper on the pile as she added, "Make sure you use the acrylic drinkware."

That request was so typically her mother that Ava could only smile. Yes, she was about to read through reams of dark magical spells, but she needed to make sure no breakables were taken out on the patio in the meantime.

"We will," she promised, getting up from the couch. Gabriel rose as well.

"Thank you, Mrs. Castillo," he said.

She slanted a look up at him, the type of glance Ava recalled all too well. It said, *I might be doing a favor for you, but don't think that means I'm going to let you get away with any nonsense.*

Whether Gabriel recognized her mother's

expression for what it was, Ava couldn't be sure. Based on the few things Tony had told her about Gabriel Escobar's past, it didn't sound as if he'd had any kind of mother figure around to raise him. Maybe some of the clan witches had looked after him—she couldn't imagine Joaquin Escobar ever lowering himself to change a diaper—but that wasn't the same thing as having a mother, someone who knew you better than you knew yourself.

He was quiet, though, as Ava led him into the kitchen and poured some lemonade from the fridge into a pair of the acrylic tumblers her mother had requested, then handed one of the drinks to him. "This way," she said. "We can get onto the deck from the family room."

They went out into the sun and warmth of a beautiful late May day. A fresh breeze ruffled the aspens that ringed the backyard, and while the sun was bright, the air itself was mild, not yet truly hot. Ava wanted to drink in that air, so refreshing, so different from the damp heat they'd left behind in New Orleans.

"That went better than I'd hoped," Gabriel commented, then took a sip of his lemonade.

"I was worried, too," Ava said. Of course, she hadn't allowed him to know just how worried she actually had been, how much she'd feared that her mother would flat out refuse to offer them any kind of assistance. But as rigid as Sophia Castillo could be about some things, she was also fair and hated the idea of any kind of bias. Possibly that was what had made her listen to their plea; she wasn't the sort of person who'd want to be accused of allowing her own prejudices to blind her to Gabriel's plight. "But I think we actually have a chance of making this work."

He smiled then, and once again, Ava could feel a warm little thrill move through her. What an amazing smile he had. Actually, every single part of him was amazing. He'd only held her hand that one time, and yet it was as though she could still sense the warmth of his touch, the pressure of his fingers against hers.

But then his expression darkened, and he looked away from her, fine chin lifting as he gazed toward the mountain peaks high above them. "Even if your mother finds something that might work, we'll still need someone to cast the spell," he said.

Maybe he wasn't allowing himself to hope too much, for fear their whole endeavor would still fall apart. Ava supposed that was a real enough worry, but she also didn't want them to get too ahead of themselves. "First things first," she replied, and took a sip from her own glass of lemonade. She'd always liked the way her mother made it, fresh and tart, not sugary at all. "A lot depends on what kinds of spells were contained in Nicholas Toulouse's books. Your half-sister restored Matías' powers with a blood sacrifice, but the books I transcribed could have contained an entirely different type of magic. We just can't know for sure until my mother is done looking through all the spells."

"True." However, he still looked worried, dark brows drawn together, jaw set. "Unfortunately, what I've heard of Toulouse doesn't seem to indicate that he would be the sort to collect the more harmless types of magical books."

Ava wished she had an argument she could give him to explain why he was wrong in making such a statement...but she didn't. Even though she didn't know a whole lot about the dark warlock who'd once lived in New Orleans' Garden District, she'd heard enough to realize he would have been hoarding forbidden spells, just like the ones he'd used to keep himself preternaturally young.

"Maybe," she allowed. "But 'dark magic' is kind of a catch-all for a whole spectrum of spells and potions and other things. Just because something has been forbidden doesn't necessarily mean it involves human sacrifice, you know."

Those words appeared to cheer Gabriel a little, because, although he didn't smile, the frown disappeared and a certain brightness returned to his dark eyes, helping to ease the knot of worry at the back of her neck. "You're right, of course," he said. He lifted his glass of lemonade to his lips and took a sip. "This house has quite a view," he remarked next.

The change of subject was abrupt, and yet Ava thought she understood why he'd made it. They could stand here and hash over possibilities for the next few hours—or however long it would take her mother to skim through the pile of transcribed spells—but in the end, none of that would matter if those spells turned out to be useless to them. Better to talk about something else, if for no other reason than to take their minds off the sad reason for their quest.

"That's why my parents bought the place," she said. "I mean, the house itself is very nice, of course, but being able to come out here in the summer and look across Santa Fe all the way out to the Jemez—that was always something special. The place we lived before this was down in town, so it didn't have much of a view."

"Those are the Jemez?" Gabriel asked then, shielding his eyes as he stared at the mountain range to the west. "Those mountains over there?"

"Yes. I guess there's good skiing there, too, but I've never been."

"And people ski these mountains?" He

pointed up toward the crest of Tesuque Peak, thousands of feet above where they stood.

"Every winter."

He shook his head, something like wonder in his expression. "It is hard to imagine this entire landscape being covered in snow."

"Oh, believe it," Ava replied with a rueful little chuckle. She wondered if she should tell him that they'd had snow as late as Mother's Day weekend this year—only a few weeks before the bright, sunny day they currently were enjoying now—but she guessed he wouldn't believe her. It had been hard enough for her to believe at the time, although everyone agreed that you really weren't safe from snow in Santa Fe until after the second weekend in May. Luckily, the storm hadn't been a heavy one, and the snow had melted quickly enough that it didn't seem to have damaged any of the tender buds and shoots in people's gardens, but still, snow in May felt like a slap in the face.

"Do you ski?"

That question made her want to laugh. She'd never been what anyone could call athletically inclined, had spent most of her school years with her nose in a book—or rather, glued to the screen of a tablet or phone, immersed in the latest electronic tale she'd bought with her chore and babysitting money. A lot of the time, her parents had practically been forced to use a pry bar to get her to go outside. Needless to say, skiing was something she'd avoided at all costs. She'd had a feeling that she would have ended up plowing right into a tree or going ass over teakettle on one of the steeper slopes. Better to keep her feet on solid ground.

"No," she said. "It was never really my thing." Figuring he might as well know the worst, she went on, "I'm not really an outdoorsy person. On a cold, snowy day, I'd rather be inside reading a book."

To her relief, he smiled at that particular confession. "I spent a lot of time reading, too. That was how I taught myself English. Well, and watching some of the satellite shows. Vicénte used to laugh at me, but I wanted to learn."

"Your brother doesn't speak English?" Ava asked. Hopefully, they weren't edging back into dangerous territory by discussing his brother, but since Gabriel had brought up the subject first....

"No, he speaks good English," Gabriel replied. "Not as good as mine, I don't think, but good enough. He had a tutor when he was a little boy. Our father spoke English as well, and he wanted his son to be fluent."

"But you didn't have a tutor?"

A shadow seemed to pass over his face, and he shook his head. "No. If my father had stayed in Pico Negro, I suppose he would have seen to it that I was taught. But he never returned, of course, and Vicénte did not see the need for his half-brother to have the same advantages that he did. I suppose that was why I became so determined to learn the language—I wanted to show him that I did not need him to do me any favors."

Vicénte sounded like a real prize. Depriving his younger half-brother of an English tutor could only have been an act of true pettiness, because magic didn't care which language you spoke. He'd only acted like that to show Gabriel that he didn't have any true power in the Escobar clan except what his older brother was willing to relinquish to him.

Pointing any of that out didn't seem like a very good idea, though. Ava had a feeling that Gabriel knew every single one of Vicénte's character flaws, so there was no need for her to rehash them. Instead, she only commented, "Well, you did a great job of teaching yourself English. So obviously, you really didn't need a tutor after all."

"I'm glad you think so," Gabriel said, but something about his tone was absent, as if his mind had already moved on to other matters. And, judging by the quick glance he sent over his shoulder toward the house, Ava could guess exactly what those concerns might be.

"Why don't we go down into the garden?" she suggested. "There's a bench at the end of the walk

—it's a great place to sit and look down into the city."

"That sounds good," he responded, even though he didn't sound terribly enthusiastic. "Lead on."

Since she'd committed to this course, there wasn't much to do except head down the set of two steps that led into the garden itself, Gabriel a pace or two behind her. As she went, she couldn't help wondering whether she should have worn a skirt rather than the jeans she'd put on earlier in the day. Did her butt look enormous to him? Yes, she'd managed to walk everywhere and semi-starve herself down to a size six those last few months of college, but....

They reached the bench and she sat down gratefully, glad that she was no longer offering him such an up-close view of her rear end. This part of the yard wasn't fenced, only had a low border of local drought-tolerant plants, so there was nothing to obscure their view of Santa Fe, from the tall spire at the Cathedral to the graceful pueblo-style bulk of the art museum on the northwest edge of downtown. All the trees were fully leafed out now, providing fresh green accents against the various stucco buildings in the historic city center.

"It is a beautiful town," Gabriel said. The

breeze was playing with his short-cropped dark hair, sending one lock dipping over his forehead.

Ava had to resist the urge to reach out and brush that piece of hair back away from his face. No way in the world were they intimate enough for her to make such a familiar gesture. As it was, she had to force herself to focus on the view rather than how close they sat now, with barely a foot separating them. Not because she'd planned it that way, but only because the bench wasn't big enough for them to sit much farther apart.

"Yes, it's beautiful," she agreed. However limited she might have felt in her existence, that wasn't really Santa Fe's fault. God knows Tony had been able to keep himself endlessly occupied here. Unfortunately, she'd never possessed her big brother's ability to be comfortable in any social setting, and so she'd always found herself on the fringes, feeling awkward and uncomfortable. It had been a lot easier to live through books than to attempt to do such a thing in the real world.

"But...?" Gabriel prompted, somehow guessing that she had left something out.

"But nothing," Ava said firmly. "It was a good place to grow up. Maybe it would have been nice to see more of the world, but that's just how witch clans operate. We stick to our own territories. I should probably be glad that all of New Mexico is Castillo territory, so I've had my chances to get out and about. There are a lot smaller territories than ours, after all."

For a moment, he was quiet, as if absorbing what she'd just told him. Then, still without speaking, he reached over and put his hand on top of hers. It felt heavy and solid, as if it was the only real thing in the world right then.

Ava hardly dared to breathe. While she'd been wishing he would make some kind of overture, now that it had happened, she wasn't quite sure how to respond.

Luckily, he saved her from having to react by saying, "I'm glad I was able to go to New Orleans with you." He shifted, turning so he faced her rather than the breathtaking vista in front of them. Voice lowering a bit, he went on, "I find myself wishing you would travel even farther than that with me...perhaps all the way to Pico Negro?"

A small thrill moved through her. The hope in his eyes was so obvious, Ava knew she couldn't be mistaking it for anything else. Sure, she might have allowed herself to dream that she would help him follow his quest all the way through to its logical conclusion, but even so, she'd never really believed that he would ask her to come with him on his journey to set the Escobar clan on the right path.

Before she could get her muddled thoughts

together, he shook his head at himself and said, "But I know I am asking a great deal by making such a request. It is too dangerous. I shouldn't have asked such a thing of you."

"Of course I'll go," she blurted out, knowing she had to say something before he got entirely the wrong idea about why she'd taken so long to reply. Somehow, she managed to keep herself from adding, *Don't you know I'd go anywhere with you?*

But the thought lingered in her mind all the same.

A smile as bright as the sun blazing overhead touched his lips, and then he leaned forward.

And then…and then….

Then he was kissing her, mouth strong and sure and tasting of lemonade. Heat that had absolutely nothing to do with the warm day rushed all through Ava's body, along with a sort of singing, delirious joy that Gabriel was kissing her, kissing *her*, Ava Castillo, the girl Danny Trevino had cruelly nicknamed "Ava Cattlecar" back in fifth grade, the girl who was always chosen last for softball teams and soccer teams and just about any other team a person could think of.

When he ended the kiss, he didn't pull very far away, but sat there with his hand still covering hers, eyes somehow hot with desire but terribly earnest at the same time. "Was it all right for me to do that?"

"Very all right," she said. Thank God that had come out sounding mostly normal, not wobbly or high-pitched or something else equally embarrassing.

Something about the set of his shoulders seemed to relax a little, and he reached out with his free hand and pushed a stray strand of hair away from her face. "I've wanted to kiss you for a while, but it didn't seem as though New Orleans was the appropriate place."

*And my mother's backyard is?* Ava thought, but she only nodded. "I get it. Santa Fe seems…safer."

A grin. "I am not sure how safe I am around you, Ava Castillo," he said. "I should be thinking of other things…and yet, you are what occupies my mind."

Happy warmth spread through her at the realization that apparently he'd been obsessing over her just as much as she'd been obsessing over him. This was how it was supposed to be when a witch and a warlock recognized their soul mates, but for some reason, she'd never thought such a thing would happen to her. Too many years of being awkward and chubby and overlooked, she supposed. If no one wanted her on their dodgeball team, why would they want her for a soul mate?

And yet it seemed Gabriel did want her, enough that he was willing to ignore the promptings of caution and ask her to come with him to El Salvador. Of course, they still had a lot of work to do before such a trip was even feasible, but the mere fact that he'd asked was enough for her. Right then, she was pretty sure she'd follow Gabriel to the ends of the earth.

It was a good thing he'd ended the kiss when he had, though, because in that moment, Ava saw her mother coming down the path toward the bench where the two of them sat. From this angle, with the back of the garden bench blocking part of her view, she probably couldn't even see how her daughter and the Escobar warlock were holding hands.

Even so, Ava pulled her hand from underneath Gabriel's and stood. A moment later, he rose as well.

"Come inside," her mother said. "I think I've found something."

## 12

FOR SOMEONE WHO'D JUST FOUND THE proverbial needle in a haystack, Sophia Castillo didn't look all that happy. She brought Gabriel and Ava inside and back to the table where all the transcribed spells had been resting, then asked them to sit down. He could tell that Sophia had gone through a larger portion of the stack than he would have thought possible in the scant hour that he and Ava had been out in the garden, but possibly her magical gift of being able to read any spell, no matter how obscure, had also allowed her to read such spells more quickly than the average witch or warlock.

"There is something," she said, lifting one sheet from the stack so she could set it down on the table for all of them to see. It was written in what Gabriel thought was Latin, although with names and words mixed in that he couldn't recognize, along with diagrams picked out in strange runes and sigils. "This is a very old spell, a restoration spell."

*Restoration.* That was exactly what he needed.

"What does it restore?" Ava inquired. Her cheeks still bore a faint flush, although he wasn't sure whether that was a residual effect from the kiss they'd shared or merely the effect of being out in the sun and wind for the greater part of an hour.

Sophia let out a breath, one not quite heavy enough for a sigh. "Basically, anything. The object of the restoration comes from the spell-caster's intent."

That sounded easy enough. Or rather, he thought a spell so basic was something that Miranda, the Castillo *prima,* should be able to manage. If the spell was a simple one, then it shouldn't matter whether or not Miranda had any training in such things. Her raw talent would be enough.

Ava appeared to have thought much the same thing, because she said, "Then it shouldn't be too hard to find someone in the clan who can cast the spell."

"I'm afraid it's not that simple," Sophia replied, and Gabriel frowned at her.

"What do you mean?"

She pointed a manicured finger at one of the intricate diagrams on the page. "You see this? It's a spell of summoning. It's not the spell-caster who restores whatever it is that he or she needs to have fixed, but the being this spell brings into our world."

"Like a demon?" Ava asked, worry replacing the bright hope that had filled her eyes just a moment earlier. Gabriel recalled her concerns when he'd brought up using voodoo as a way of solving his problem, and wondered if she viewed this as the same thing. But then, this would be a witch or a warlock performing the summoning, not a civilian who couldn't possibly control the being they had called to this world.

"Not exactly a demon," her mother said. "Something other. An intelligence not of this world."

"Like Loc, then?" Gabriel said.

Lips pursing, Sophia gave a reluctant nod. "Something like him. But not him," she added quickly, as if she could tell he was about to suggest that they have Loc cast the spell. "This is a very particular spell to summon a very particular being…entity…whatever you want to call it."

"But if we can summon him, then we can ask him to restore Gabriel's powers," Ava said.

"In theory." Sophia sat back in her chair, as if she wanted to put some distance between herself and the piece of paper before her with all its arcane scribblings. "But this isn't something any of us can do."

"Can't, or won't?" Ava asked then, the challenge clear in her voice. In a way, Gabriel was surprised she would be so bold about confronting her mother. But perhaps she'd decided this was not the time to be meek.

"Can't," Sophia said firmly. "None of us have the type of magical gift required to cast such a spell, to make contact with such a being."

For a few seconds, Ava was quiet, pretty mouth tight with worry. "There's no one in our entire clan who could do this kind of thing?"

Now it was Sophia's turn to be silent. Her arms were crossed, and she looked uncomfortable, very much as if she wished to be someplace far away. At last she said, "No one that I know of."

"Possibly Miranda would know?" Gabriel suggested. In his own clan, the *primus* had always known exactly which specific gifts each member of the Escobar family controlled. It was a way of keeping track of valuable assets. He had to assume that the witch clans here in the United States worked much the same way.

But Sophia only shook her head. "I doubt it. She's only been our *prima* for a year and a half now. I think she's done a lot to learn as much as she can about the Castillo clan and all the people in it, but as bright as she is, that's a lot of people to keep track of."

"Didn't Genoveva have a database or something?" Ava asked, the strain obvious in her voice. Gabriel could tell she was desperately trying to cover every possibility, just in case they'd overlooked something.

"If she did, I never heard anything about it." Sophia's lips—not quite as full as her daughter's, but still pretty—pursed slightly, her expression more rueful than anything else. "You have to remember, Ava, that I wasn't someone Genoveva took into her confidence. Tony was always friends with Rafe, and so that's why Tony was involved with Rafe and Miranda's wedding, but I can't say that my and Genoveva's relationship was anything as close."

"You don't have clan elders who would keep track of such information?" Gabriel realized he'd never heard Ava mention anything about those who fulfilled such a role in the Castillo clan, but possibly that was only because the subject had never arisen before now.

Once again, though, her mother neatly shot down his suggestion. "No, we don't. It's never been a tradition with the Castillos, for whatever reason. Anyway, I've just never heard of anyone in the clan with the ability to summon demons—or otherworldly entities, if you want to be more scientific about it—and I'm pretty sure that even I would have heard something about a Castillo with such an unusual talent."

For some reason, Ava seemed to go still and quiet upon hearing those words, her big brown eyes dreamy, almost glassy, as if she was looking at something very far away. Then she came back to herself as she gave a quick glance over at Gabriel. "Well, that seems to be that," she said. "If there's no one in the Castillo clan who can cast this spell of summoning, then I guess we've hit a dead end."

He stared at her, not sure why she would be so determined to give up this quickly. "Perhaps not a Castillo, but someone from the de la Paz clan, or the McAllisters?"

"I can tell you for sure that it wouldn't be a McAllister," Sophia said. "They've never dabbled in this kind of magic, never seemed to have anyone whose talent was even questionable. And the de la Pazes might, but I'm not sure whether they'd be all that eager to help an Escobar."

Whether she'd meant that remark to sting as much as it did, Gabriel couldn't be sure. In a way, the members of the de la Paz family had even more reason to view his clan with fear and distrust, thanks to Simon stealing their books in the first place…not to mention the havoc Matías had caused back in the day. Knowing he sounded nearly as desperate as Ava had just a moment earlier, he said, "What about the Wilcoxes? I know their reputation isn't exactly as good as the McAllisters'."

"A few decades ago, I would have said you were right," Sophia replied. "But things changed a great deal once Connor Wilcox took over from his brother Damon. I don't think you would get any help from them, either."

"Gabriel, I think we need to let it go for now," Ava put in. She got up from the sofa where she'd been sitting, then let her fingers brush against the sheet of plain white paper that contained the problematic spell. "Do you mind if we take this with us? Maybe if we puzzle over it some more, we'll figure something out."

For a second, Sophia hesitated. Then her shoulders lifted, and she said, "It's fine. I'm not sure what good it will do you, but with no one who can cast the spell, it can't cause much harm, either."

"Thanks, Mom." Ava looked down at Gabriel. "Let me take you back to your hotel. You probably would like to rest for a bit, wouldn't you?"

He wanted to protest that resting was the last thing he felt like doing, but getting into an argument with her in front of her mother was something he would prefer to avoid. Besides, he knew that there truly wasn't much either of them could do right now. They might as well get away to more neutral territory, and then he could sit down with her and attempt to discover why she was suddenly so eager to abandon their quest when only a little while earlier, she'd seemed ready to leave behind everything she knew and come with him to El Salvador.

"Yes, going to the hotel sounds good," he agreed, then also stood up. He extended a hand to Sophia and added, "Thank you very much for all your assistance. I'm sorry I took up so much of your time."

"It's not a problem at all," she replied, clearly ready to be gracious now that it seemed they were in no danger of actually finding a solution to his predicament. "I wish I could have been of more help."

"That was not your fault."

There didn't seem to be much else to say, and so Ava thanked her mother again, and then she and Gabriel left, heading out to the driveway so they could get back in Ava's compact SUV and return downtown. She seemed tense, fingers gripping the steering wheel, even though the car's self-driving mechanism had been activated and there was no reason for her to be guiding the vehicle at all.

Taking note of her mood, he remained quiet in the passenger seat, watching as the streets with their old adobe houses and enormous, ancient trees passed by. And although he didn't pretend to know downtown Santa Fe very well, he could have sworn she didn't turn where she should have to return him to the La Fonda, but kept going on a road that appeared to be heading directly away from the city's heart.

"She was lying," Ava said abruptly, and Gabriel shifted in his seat so he could look directly at her.

"What?"

"My mother. She was lying to me…to us."

With anyone else, he might have asked how she could be so certain. But someone with Ava's particular talent would of course know whether someone was hiding something. "You looked in her mind?"

A brief nod as she pressed her lips together, her expression…even in profile…troubled. "It's not—that's not the kind of thing I usually do. I try really hard not to invade other people's thoughts. But…I could tell she was lying, so I took a peek. I saw what she was hiding. There is someone in the Castillo clan who can read that spell, summon the entity that can restore your powers."

Hope surged through him, but Gabriel willed himself to stay calm. He had been fed false hope far too many times already to get terribly excited now. "You're sure of this?"

"Yes."

"And that's why we're not going to the hotel?"

"Exactly." Now she finally smiled a little and looked over at him, a mischievous glint sparkling in her big brown eyes. "We're going to Las Vegas."

From the way Gabriel stared at her, it was clear he thought she'd lost her mind. "'Las Vegas'?" he repeated, looking confused. "There are Castillos there? I thought your clan only lived in New Mexico."

"We do," Ava told him. "The person we're looking for lives in Las Vegas, New Mexico. It's a little over an hour from here."

That is, assuming what she'd seen in her mother's mind was accurate. Despite the terrible necessity that had driven her, Ava couldn't help but feel horribly guilty about the way she'd intruded into her mother's thoughts. After all, hadn't she spent years trying to convince everyone in her clan that she would never read someone's mind without their express permission? But then again, if she hadn't known in her very bones that her mother was hiding something, she would never have taken that peek in the first place.

Probably she was rationalizing, but did it

matter? She'd seen the information they needed so badly, and that was the important thing.

"Ah," Gabriel said. He now seemed tense as well, fingers of one hand clenched around the shoulder strap of his seatbelt. Well, she couldn't blame him for that. They'd had so many false starts lately, she knew he must be wondering if this was only going to be yet another in a very long series of disappointments.

Somehow, though, she didn't think so. Ava knew her mother had been lying about the person they were going to see because she feared she would be able to cast the summoning spell.

"Her name is Elena Salazar," Ava went on. "Some kind of distant cousin, but we don't have a lot of interactions with the branch of the family in Las Vegas. I mean, they'll come into town for the annual Castillo gatherings we have every summer, just because pretty much everyone comes to those if they're able to. Elena is about a year older than I am, which means I should know her, since the cousins who're around the same age tend to hang out together when the clan gathers. But I know I've never met her."

"Possibly she doesn't like to socialize," Gabriel suggested.

That sounded plausible enough, but Ava knew it wasn't the real explanation. "No, it's more like she's never come to *anything*. I've never heard anyone mention her. And it's not as if I pretend to have every single person in the Castillo clan memorized, but I at least know all the people in my basic age group. From what I could see in my mother's mind, it's like they decided to keep Elena locked away from everyone once they realized what her power was."

"That sounds excessive."

Ava thought so, too. The details weren't all completely clear, since she'd known better than to spend too much time rummaging through her mother's thoughts, but she'd gotten the impression that isolating Elena had been pretty much Genoveva's idea. That sounded like the sort of draconian maneuver the former *prima* would make, although Ava thought she could kind of understand why Genoveva would do such a thing. Most of witch-kind started to exhibit their powers when they were around ten or eleven years old, and having a kid that young with the talent to summon super-powerful beings from another dimension sounded like a recipe for disaster. Even so, one would have thought that Elena would have been able to start mingling again once she was safely past the first couple of years of coming into her power.

They'd finally reached the on-ramp to I-25, which would bring them all the way to Las Vegas. Ava waited until the car had safely merged them into the freeway traffic before she said, "I didn't have time to see all the reasoning behind what happened. At this point, I suppose it doesn't really matter. About all we can do is hope that Elena will help us."

"Or be allowed to help us," Gabriel said darkly. "If her family has controlled her to the point where she can't even mingle with the rest of the clan, then she might not be free to provide any kind of assistance."

He had a point, but Ava hoped that Elena's continuing absence from the greater Castillo clan was more due to habit than anything else. She also had to hope her distant cousin's powers wouldn't be so rusty from disuse that she wouldn't be able to work the spell of summoning.

"Well, we'll just have to see what happens," she said lightly. "This is the only real lead we have, so we need to follow it."

"Oh, I understand that," Gabriel replied. A corner of his mouth quirked as he went on, "After all, it is not as if there was anything useful I could have done with this time. Resting at the hotel didn't sound that appealing."

Ava's own lips twitched a little. She was glad to see he still could maintain some perspective about the situation. "No, I could tell you weren't too interested in that."

They drove in silence for a while after that

exchange, passing through Glorieta and Pecos and on to the wide-open areas beyond those small settlements. As she often did when passing through New Mexico's sparsely populated countryside, Ava found herself wondering why certain areas had been settled while others appeared to be mostly ignored. Was it all about access to water? She had to admit that she'd never really done a lot of research on the topic…and she realized as the miles flickered by that she'd only been to Las Vegas once, all the way back when she was a freshman in high school. There certainly hadn't been any mention of an Elena Salazar during that visit, even though Ava's mother usually tried to get her to meet any cousins who were around her age.

Sooner than Ava had expected, the first exit for Las Vegas approached. She touched the button for the nav and said, "One thirty-one Sixth Street."

"How did you know the address?" Gabriel asked.

"I saw it in my mother's mind," Ava replied. "Or at least, I saw the house and I saw the number on it, and somehow the name of the street came along with the rest of the information."

"How did she know? That is, assuming she also wasn't misrepresenting her relationship with your former *prima*."

Good question. As she'd told Gabriel, Ava hadn't dug too deep when retrieving the information about Elena Salazar from her mother's mind. She supposed Genoveva must have said something at some point. Why she would have done such a thing, Ava had no idea, and at this point, she supposed it really didn't matter one way or another.

"I don't know," she said frankly. "I didn't want to spend too much time rooting around in her thoughts. But I somehow know this is the address we need to go to."

The car turned into a neighborhood of old homes, some of them probably of the same vintage as the Victorian house Tony had bequeathed to Ava. This area looked more working class than the distinctly gentrified area where Hillside Drive was located, though. Her late-model compact SUV felt conspicuous here, even though it was nowhere near as flashy as her brother's shiny black Fiat Spider convertible.

They came to a stop in front of a two-story brick house with a white-painted front porch and a somewhat threadbare lawn out front. Unlike some of the other homes on the street, the entire yard was enclosed with a brick wall. The gate in that wall was closed, and all of the blinds at all the windows were firmly shut, even though it was the sort of fresh, sunny late spring day when you would normally want everything open to let in a breeze.

Looking at the house made an uneasy sensation stir in the pit of her stomach, but Ava knew they'd come too far to turn around now. Hoping she sounded braver than she felt, she said, "I guess this is it. Let's see if anyone's home."

Gabriel nodded, then opened his door and got out. Ava climbed out of the driver's seat and came around to meet him on the sidewalk. She felt a little better once she was standing next to him; there was something reassuring about his height and the breadth of his shoulders, the way his chin lifted as he glanced around him, as if to familiarize himself with his surroundings before they went any further. Yes, he didn't have any magic to command, was in his way even more defenseless than she when it came to that sort of thing, but she was still very glad to have him next to her.

Besides, the little she'd seen of his memories told her that he was no slouch when it came to a good old-fashioned physical brawl, although she sincerely hoped this encounter wouldn't end in anything quite so dramatic.

A thrill went through her as he took her hand in his. Fingers entwined, they approached the gate. It was padlocked on the other side, but since the wall surrounding the house was only a little more than three feet high, Ava could reach over and touch the lock with her free hand, using this simplest of witchy gifts to make it unlock. Even as she did so, however, she had to wonder why they hadn't used a combination lock, something even a witch or warlock would have difficulty getting past.

*Maybe it's more to keep civilians out,* she thought as Gabriel unlatched the gate and they both entered the yard. *Although it sounds as though Elena's family wanted to keep her away from everybody, not just nonmagical people.*

She also realized they were now officially trespassing, but she had to hope the minor infraction would be overlooked once they explained why they'd come here in the first place.

There was a large "No Solicitors" sign prominently mounted next to the front door, which didn't seem to bode well for their errand's success. Still, all they could do was try.

Gabriel gave the sign a jaundiced look, but then shrugged ever so slightly and reached over to push the button for the doorbell. When he did so, he let go of Ava's hand. She wished he hadn't, even though she guessed he thought it might look better if they weren't touching.

A long silence followed the hollow ring of the doorbell. Ava shifted her weight from one foot to the other, then glanced up at Gabriel. Once again, his shoulders lifted, but he didn't say anything.

A minute crawled past. He let out a breath and reached for the doorbell again, pressed the button. The bell sounded even louder this time, even though Ava knew that was only her imagination. The anxious, crawling sensation in the pit of her stomach worsened. Deep down, she knew that they could stand here and ring the doorbell all day, and if whoever was inside this house didn't want to see them, they could just ignore their unwelcome visitors until she and Gabriel finally gave up and went away.

That outcome seemed too ignominious to contemplate, but she knew it was a distinct possibility. But just as Gabriel was raising his hand to touch the doorbell button for a third time, the door finally opened. Standing there was a woman around Ava's age, with long brown hair and slate-blue eyes, startling against her olive skin. In fact, she was much prettier than Ava had been expecting, since in her mind she'd envisioned Elena Salazar to be some kind of pasty recluse, like something out of a Victorian gothic novel. Realistically, she should have realized that Elena probably would look like any other girl in her early twenties…at least, any other girl who could summon demons.

She blinked at the two of them, and then her gaze settled on Ava, obviously startled by the presence of a strange witch on her doorstep. "You're…you're a—"

"I'm Ava Castillo, one of your cousins from Santa Fe," Ava said. "And this is my friend Gabriel." She figured it was probably safer not to mention his last name up front, just in case Elena had heard anything of what Simon Escobar had done eighteen months earlier. This was going to be hard enough without poisoning the well like that. "Can we come in and talk to you for a minute?"

This suggestion made Elena cast a worried glance over one shoulder. "I'm not supposed to let anyone in the house."

"Even a cousin?" Ava asked, with what she hoped was a reassuring smile. "I just want to talk."

Another hesitation, and then Elena seemed to gather her courage, because she said, "Okay. My father's at work, and my grandmother went to the store. We should have a little time."

That sounded promising, although it was strange that she'd been left alone when it sounded as if she'd basically been under house arrest for the past decade or so. Whatever the reason Elena was by herself, Ava sent a silent prayer winging upward that she and Gabriel had managed to arrive when no one else was home. "Thanks."

Elena stepped out of the way so Ava and Gabriel could enter the house. Immediately inside was a small entry hall. A plain table of dark wood stood between the two doorways directly opposite the front entrance, and above that on the wall was an ornate crucifix of wood and silver. Normally, Ava wouldn't think twice about spotting such an artifact in a Castillo house—her clan tended to be pretty conspicuously Catholic—but she had to wonder whether Elena's family had one hanging here as a defense against demons.

"We can go in the family room," Elena said, leading them through the right-hand doorway and down a short hall to what had probably been a parlor back when the house was built but now seemed to serve as a TV room of sorts. A large television was mounted on the wall above the fireplace, which appeared to be nonfunctional, since it held a row of saints' candles and nothing else. "Can I get you anything? Some water?"

Actually, Ava realized she was thirsty…but she also didn't want to lose any of their precious time with Elena by having her go fetch drinks for them. "No, we're fine," she said hastily.

Gabriel seemed to understand, because he also murmured a demurral. Then he said, "I hope you don't mind us intruding like this, but we were hoping you might be able to help us."

"'Help' you?" Elena echoed, looking from one of them to the other with surprise…and a measure of wariness...in her startling eyes. "I don't think I'm in a position to help anyone."

Her tone was more than a little bitter, and Ava couldn't really blame her cousin for feeling that way. She doubted she would be in a very good mood if her family had kept her basically locked up because her magical talent was one that everyone feared.

"You might be surprised," she said gently. From inside her jeans pocket, she pulled out the piece of paper with the transcribed spell of summoning on it, then unfolded the paper and handed it to Elena. "Do you know what this is?"

Now appearing warier than ever, Elena took the piece of paper and glanced down at it. Her expression shifted to one of shock. "Where did you get this?"

"Um...it was transcribed from a grimoire we found," Ava replied. Close enough. They didn't have time for her to launch into a full explanation of the spell's provenance.

"And you know what it's for?"

"Basically," Gabriel said. "But we can't use it. We were hoping you could."

A heartbeat, then another...and another. Elena only stood there, staring down at the spell, her face now almost a blank, as if she was trying her hardest to hide what she was actually thinking. "I'm not supposed to use my magic," she said at last. "It's dangerous."

"I know," Ava said gently. Even as she spoke, she could practically feel time sliding past them, slipping out of their hands. What if Elena's grandmother chose to come home right now? She'd throw out the interlopers without a second thought, most likely…and would probably call Miranda to complain as well. Not that Ava was too worried about how Miranda would react, but any complication might be enough to keep Gabriel from recovering his powers. "Or at least, I guess that's what you've been told. But have you or anyone else ever actually suffered any bad consequences from you using your powers?"

This question made Elena's fingers tighten on the piece of paper she held, crinkling it slightly. "No," she said at last. "But I was always told that's just because I got lucky."

"Or maybe it's because your power protects you and those around you from harm, even when you're calling up these beings," Gabriel suggested.

"Maybe." Elena glanced down at the spell again. "Why do you need me to call him?"

"'Him'?" Ava echoed.

"The one who can restore whatever it is you've lost. Belshegar."

Gabriel's dark eyes glinted with curiosity. "That's his name?"

"It's our version of his name, I suppose." Elena's slender shoulders lifted. "Anyway, it's close enough that it'll work to summon him." A pause, and she tucked a strand of long brown hair behind one ear, exposing a thin silver hoop earring. "But why him particularly?"

Ava pulled in a breath and glanced over at Gabriel, not sure whether she should be the one to explain or whether it was his place to tell his own story. He seemed to think it was the latter, because he said, "My powers were taken from me by the elders of my clan because I dared to help Ava's brother"—he nodded toward her—"and a witch of the de la Paz clan. It was the right thing to do, but I suffered for my decision."

To Ava's surprise, Elena didn't ask how such a thing was possible. Maybe the stories about Miranda's parents and how they'd done the same thing to Matías Escobar had made it all the way out to this branch of the Castillos in Las Vegas, or maybe she'd also realized that they didn't have the luxury of going into in-depth explanations.

"And so you need me to call Belshegar so he can restore your powers."

"Exactly," Gabriel said. "We've exhausted all other options. This is our last chance."

Again, Elena went quiet as Ava held her breath, praying silently that they hadn't come all this way for nothing. Her cousin's eyes scanned the piece of paper she held. When Elena finally looked up, her face seemed full of a steely resolve, as if she'd wrestled with something deep within her and come to a decision.

"Okay," she said at last. "I'll help you."

## 13

GABRIEL WASN'T SURE WHETHER HE SHOULD allow himself to breathe. "You will? You'll really help us?"

"Yes," Elena said. She folded the piece of paper with the spell and slid it into her jeans pocket. Now her gaze slid toward Ava, as if she knew her cousin was the person she needed to appeal to next. "But you need to do something for me in exchange."

"Um, sure," Ava replied quickly, although she looked troubled as she spoke. No doubt, she was worrying whether she was making promises she couldn't keep.

Something about Elena's posture seemed to relax. "I want you to get me out of here."

"That's not a problem," Ava told her. "Your

family shouldn't be keeping you here anyway. I mean, you're an adult, right?"

"I'm almost twenty-three," Elena said. "But you know how it is in witch families."

Yes, they all understood that the dynamics which might apply in the world of civilians weren't exactly the same when it came to those born into magic. However, Gabriel guessed that Miranda would be sympathetic to the young witch's plight and would do what she must to help her.

"Anyway," she went on. "It's not as easy as it sounds. I can't exactly walk out the door." A pause, and then she added by way of clarification, "That is, I can walk out the door, but I can't leave the property. My father has a ward on the wall that makes it give me a shock if I step within a foot of it."

"They did that to you?" Ava demanded, tone full of righteous indignation.

"I guess they figured it was the easiest way to get me to stay put." A shrug, and she added, "They take it down every once in a while, like if I have a dentist appointment or something. But it's definitely in place now. Otherwise, my grandmother would never have left me alone here."

That explained why Elena was by herself. Gabriel had to admit he was somewhat stunned by the measures her family had taken to make sure she was trapped here. However, something occurred to him. "When you say that it gives you a shock when you step near the wall, does that mean you wouldn't get shocked if you weren't actually standing on the ground?"

Elena seemed to consider the question. "You know, I'm not really sure. I never tried pole-vaulting over it, if that's what you mean."

"What are you thinking, Gabriel?" Ava asked. "That you could carry her?"

"It's worth a try."

Ava's eyes began to shine. "Definitely." She glanced over at her cousin, "We've got a car right outside. Are you willing to risk it?"

Her answer was a broad smile. "Hell yes, I am."

"Do you need to bring anything?" he inquired.

"Just a few things. I'll be fast."

Before either Ava or Gabriel could reply, Elena had hurried out of the room. A moment later, he heard her footsteps on the stairs, light and quick.

"I hope we're doing the right thing," Ava said. Nervous fingers played with the hem of her blouse, and she cast a worried glance over one shoulder in the direction of the front door. "I mean, I know we couldn't really leave her here, not when her family's treated her this way, but my mother is going to completely freak when she finds out what I've done."

Probably, but Sophia Castillo's reaction was not what troubled Gabriel now. He wanted to get out of here before the grandmother returned home. Elena's father he wasn't as worried about, since he probably wouldn't come back until he was done with work for the day. Or at least, Gabriel hoped he wouldn't; possibly he dropped in to check on his daughter at unexpected intervals, just to make sure she wasn't getting up to any mischief. Most likely, though, the wards he'd set in place had been keeping her trapped here for so long that he took their efficacy for granted.

He was going to be in for quite a surprise.

Since Ava still looked anxious, he said reasonably, "As far as your mother's reaction goes, you're also an adult and can make your own choices. And I'm sure Miranda will understand once the circumstances have been explained to her."

A bit of the worry seemed to leave Ava's face. "Let's hope so."

Footsteps on the stairs again, and Elena was standing at the door to the family room, a small canvas bag dangling from one hand. "Let's get out of here," she said.

"On our way," he replied.

The three of them began to move toward the front door—only to hear a slam from somewhere toward the rear of the house. Elena startled, her smoky blue eyes wide with fear.

"It's my grandmother," she whispered. "Hurry!"

A woman's voice called out, *"¡Elena! ¿Dónde estás?"*

*"En la sala de televisión,"* she called out in reply. *"Estaré allí en un minuto."*

Hopefully, that minute would be enough for them to get away…and hopefully, Elena's grandmother's ears weren't too sharp. The trio tiptoed down the hall and went out through the front door, with Elena closing it gently behind them.

In unspoken agreement, they began to run as soon as they'd descended the creaky front steps. Not a moment too soon, because even as Gabriel's fingers began to lift the latch on the gate, the front door banged open and a stout woman in her sixties emerged, dark eyes blazing with anger.

*"¡Elena! ¿Quienes son esas personas? ¿A dónde crees que vas?"*

Elena said in a quick undertone, "Her power is throwing fireballs, but she doesn't dare do it in front of the neighbors."

Thank God. It was good to know that her grandmother wouldn't use her formidable power any place it might be witnessed by civilians. Or at least, he hoped she wouldn't be so desperate that she might still risk such a thing. He paused for a moment, gesturing for Elena to climb on his back. She did so without hesitation, arms around his throat, legs wrapped around his waist. There was no intimacy in their closeness, though, only a desire to get out of there as quickly as possible. Ava yanked open the gate, and the two of them hurried through it, Gabriel letting out an internal sigh of relief when it seemed that they were able to get through the ward without it affecting his unlikely burden in any way. The key fob for Ava's SUV was already in her hand so she could unlock while they were still several yards away…and she turned on the motor as well, the low hum of it starting up one of the most welcome sounds he'd heard in recent days.

As soon as she was on the other side of the fence, Elena called out in English, "No more cages for me, *abuela!*"

"You stop now!" her grandmother shouted back in the same language. "You can't do this. Come back inside!"

But Elena only ran to Ava's compact SUV, flung open the passenger-side rear door, and climbed in. Ava ran around to the driver's side, while Gabriel got into the passenger seat. He'd barely shut the door behind him before Ava stomped on the accelerator, sending the vehicle charging forward. In the rearview mirror, he could see Elena's grandmother come surging out through the gate, gesticulating wildly and mouth still moving, although he couldn't hear her over the whine of the overstressed motor.

He guessed that Ava had taken manual control of the vehicle because the auto-drive function would never have allowed her to accelerate so quickly in a residential neighborhood. Luckily, the map from their trip here was still on the dashboard display, so all she needed to do was glance at it to refamiliarize herself with the route in order to retrace their steps. In only a few minutes, they were back on the interstate and heading toward Santa Fe.

"You okay back there?" she asked, glancing quickly over her shoulder toward her cousin in the back seat before she returned her attention to the road.

"I'm fine," Elena said. Her eyes were shining; apparently, she wasn't too concerned about anything her grandmother might do now. "Thank you."

"Not a problem," Ava responded. Her fingers were still wrapped tightly around the steering wheel, but a little smile played around her mouth, as though she, too, was pleased with how things had turned out. "I've always wanted to make a quick getaway like you see in the movies."

Elena chuckled then and settled herself back against the seat. "I don't think my *abuela* could believe what she was seeing." Her expression sobered, and she added, "I'm sure she's on the phone to my father as we speak."

"Will he come after us?" Gabriel asked, worry flaring along his nerve endings. Yes, they had done the right thing, but he also didn't want to get bogged down in trying to fend off an angry and overprotective Castillo warlock.

"Maybe." Elena glanced out the rear window, almost as if she expected to spot some sort of pursuit, even though of course it was far too soon for anyone to have started chasing them. "But then, while I suppose he'll probably guess that we were headed to Santa Fe, it's not as if my grandmother would even know who you are. She hasn't been to visit family there for at least ten years. I assume you looked a little different ten years ago, Ava."

Elena chuckled, but Ava's expression wasn't particularly amused. In fact, she appeared almost grim, as if thinking back to ten years earlier didn't give her any joy. Was there something about her childhood that had been difficult? Gabriel realized there was still so much that they didn't know about each other, so much they still had to learn.

With any luck…if all went well…they would have plenty of time for that later.

"Just a little," Ava remarked. "You don't have

any magical trackers in your branch of the family, do you?"

"No. So I think we're safe."

"Good." She glanced over at Gabriel. "I assume we should work the spell at the house."

"It seems the safest place," he said, glad that she was ready to move on to the next order of business. Despite the disappointments he'd suffered so far, he couldn't quite prevent a thrill of anticipation from working its way down his back. In the next few hours, he might very well have his powers restored.

And that was when the real work would begin.

They arrived at her house without incident, although the entire drive there from Las Vegas, Ava kept expecting her phone to start ringing at any second. Surely that hour and some change was plenty of time for Elena's father to have gotten in contact with Miranda to let the *prima* know what had happened.

Only…maybe luck had been with them, and Elena's grandmother hadn't gotten a good look at either her or Gabriel, hadn't been able to note much about their car except that it was a small silver SUV. Maybe all she'd really seen was a man and a woman, dark-haired, in their twenties and driving a compact silver sport-utility vehicle. Even in the Castillo clan, such a description could have fit a large number of people, and maybe Elena's father hadn't wanted to reach out to Miranda until he had something a little more concrete to go on.

Ava had to hope that was the case. Sooner or later, they'd have to come clean about what they'd done, just because it was pretty obvious that Elena had no intention of returning to Las Vegas, and so they'd have to make some kind of accommodation for her here in Santa Fe.

In the meantime, they had work to do.

The three of them drank some water and fortified themselves with a snack of some fruit and cheese—no crackers, because Ava knew better than to keep any spare carbs around the house. While maybe it wasn't the most satisfying meal in the world, at least it staved off their hunger for the moment, which was all they needed.

After looking at the rooms on the ground floor of the house, Elena decided the living room would be best for the summoning.

"There's the least amount of furniture to move out of the way," she said, a remark that made Ava wonder whether Victoria, the home's resident ghost, would drop in to scold them about rearranging things. She was so horribly particular about what the residents of the house did with the furniture.

*She's probably not going to like us summoning a demon, either,* Ava thought as she helped Gabriel lift the heavy antique-style sofa off the Persian rug so they could place it up against one wall. *But oh, well.*

With the space cleared, they were ready to begin.

"You can stand over there," Elena said to Gabriel, pointing toward the wall where they'd just set down the sofa. "I have to do the summoning by myself, so it's better if you're out of the way but still close enough to come over when Belshegar is ready to restore your powers."

Ava noticed how she said "when" and not "if." Was Elena really that sure of herself, or just trying to make them all feel more relaxed about what was going to happen next?

Probably better not to ask.

"Is there anything else I need to do?" Gabriel asked.

"No. You just need to wait."

"And you're sure he's going to be okay with you summoning him like this?" Ava said, her anxiety getting the better of her, even though she knew it probably would have been wiser to keep her mouth shut and allow Elena to work.

Her cousin smiled. "I'm not sure if 'okay' is

exactly the right word, but it's going to be fine. None of them have ever minded when I had them come talk to me."

"'None of them'?" Ava repeated, not sure she'd heard Elena correctly. "How many times have you done this?"

A small, secretive smile, one that would have been worthy of the Mona Lisa herself. "More than my father or my grandmother realize. I wanted someone to talk to, and they wouldn't let me socialize with anyone, so…."

"…so you summoned some demons for a chat."

"Basically. Although they really don't like to be called demons. It's not what they actually are. They're just…different from us."

Of course. Ava glanced up at Gabriel, and he gave a very small shrug. Probably he also didn't quite know what to make of a girl who called demons to her because she was feeling lonely and needed a sympathetic ear.

"I think they're lonely, too," Elena went on. "At least, they never seemed to mind hanging out for a while. I couldn't let them stay too long, though, because I couldn't let my grandmother or my father know what was going on."

No, it probably wouldn't have gone over too well if either of Elena's immediate relatives had discovered she was having slumber parties with demons in her room. The whole thing sounded crazy, although Ava tried to reassure herself that at least it seemed her cousin had enough experience interacting with these "beings" to make sure the current situation didn't go sideways.

"Well, take as much time as you need with this one," was all she said, and Elena's eyes crinkled a little, as if she was amused by her cousin's remark.

"I will," she responded.

Then her expression grew more serious, and she pulled the piece of paper with the spell out of her pocket, looking it over one more time.

"I don't need to create the summoning sigils," she said. "Those are for magic-workers who don't have my talent. I'll go ahead and read the spell, though, just because it'll get Belshegar's attention faster than if I used my power on its own."

Thank God there was no need for Elena to draw the spell circles. Victoria would probably have popped right out of her corset in indignation if Ava's cousin had started marking up the burnished oak floors.

"Sounds good," Ava managed.

Then the room went quiet as Elena stood in the center of the open space they'd created by moving the furniture out of the way. She closed her eyes for a moment. Still with her eyes shut, she began to recite the words of the spell. They were heavy, ponderous, seeming to reverberate somewhere in Ava's midsection like the low, low notes of a bassoon, as though they came from a throat that wasn't quite human.

Gabriel's fingers found hers, warm and reassuring. Or maybe he'd reached out for reassurance because he didn't like the sound of the spell any more than she did. Maybe this was as casual an act for Elena as calling to order a pizza, but Ava could feel the hairs on the back of her neck lifting, an odd ache somewhere near her ear making her want to cringe.

A strange, blurry darkness began to form in the center of the room, only a foot or so away from where Elena stood. The piece of paper with the spell written on it had disappeared back into her pocket, as if she really didn't need it to work this magic, had already committed all the words of the charm to memory. She looked up to the dark shape hanging in the air in front of her, a smile back on her full mouth, eyes shining as though she was about to meet a friend she hadn't seen for a long time.

Actually, maybe that was exactly what was about to happen.

The darkness grew solid, grew tall and broad. Now it had a nearly human shape, although it was much taller than any human being could possibly be, its head coming dangerously close to the crystal chandelier that dangled from the twelve-foot ceilings. No wings, though; Ava had heard from Tony that Loc's original form had wings, but apparently this demon…entity…wasn't the same kind of being.

And then it was standing there, its skin a gleaming copper shade, a mane of black hair falling down its back. *His* back, Ava corrected herself with a shiver. That thing wasn't human, but as she looked at the bulging muscles of its back and arms, the heavy thighs covered in some sort of strange, glinting metallic fabric, she knew that Belshegar was definitely male. Thank God she had Gabriel standing next to her, or she would have been tempted to flee the room.

"Elena," the strange being said, his voice a deep rumble that seemed to shake the floor beneath their feet.

"Hi, Belshegar," she replied, clearly not at all discomfited by the apparition who stood so close to her. "How are you?"

"I am well." His gaze flickered over to where Ava and Gabriel stood next to the wall. As she stared at him, Ava realized his eyes were entirely black, with no distinguishable pupil or iris. "Who are your friends?"

"This is my cousin Ava and her friend Gabriel. They need your help."

Belshegar bowed slightly. "How can I be of service?"

Maybe demons had been getting a bad rap all these years. Despite his frightening appearance, he seemed surprisingly civilized.

Elena said, "The elders in Gabriel's clan stripped him of his powers because he went against their wishes in order to save the life of Tony, Ava's brother. We need you to restore them."

"Ah." Belshegar moved closer to Gabriel, whose fingers tightened on Ava's. "May I see for myself?"

"'See'?" Gabriel repeated, obviously not quite sure what this strange being was asking of him.

"See into your memories."

Before Gabriel could reply, Belshegar laid one huge hand on the crown of Gabriel's head. Startled, he let go of Ava's hand but then stood stock still, as though worried that doing anything else might prompt an unwelcome reaction. As for Ava, about all she could do was remain where she was and try not to look frightened out of her wits. True, the demon hadn't done anything remotely threatening, but he was just so huge and, well... hot. Not hot as in attractive, but actually physically hot, as if his entire oversized body was radiating an enormous amount of heat. A strange sulfur smell seemed to drift from his hair, which was heavy and black as a horse's mane, and Ava felt her nose twitch.

"Ah," Belshegar said after a moment. "Your powers were quite prodigious, for a human. I can see why they were such a loss."

Elena came over to stand next to her other-worldly friend. "Can you help him?"

"Of course," the demon replied. "This is a simple enough matter. I am glad I can assist."

A warm, golden glow surrounded the hand that still rested on top of Gabriel's head. His eyes shut, then flared open, full of wonder and rapidly developing joy.

Surely that could mean only one thing....

"Did it work?" Ava whispered.

"Yes," Gabriel replied, voice as full of wonder as his expression. "My powers are back." He stared up into Belshegar's sharply planed, inhuman features. "Thank you."

"It was a worthy cause," the demon said. "You should not have been punished for doing the correct thing. It is your elders who deserve to have their powers stripped. They are not very good people, I fear."

Did Ava want to reflect on the irony of this otherworldly being—this demon—passing judgment on the Escobars?

Probably not.

"Still, thank you," Gabriel said. He wore a

dazed expression, as if he hadn't quite absorbed what had just happened to him.

"Yes, thank you," Elena chimed in. To Ava's surprise, her cousin took one of Belshegar's oversized hands in both of hers and gave it a squeeze. He looked down at her, expression strangely gentle.

"And you—you will also be doing better now, I think."

"I think you're right," she replied with a smile. "At least, it seems as if things are looking up."

"Curious expression." He removed his hand from hers, but only so the two of them could exchange what suspiciously looked like a fist bump. "Don't be a stranger."

And then he was gone, disappearing with an odd whistling noise that might have been the air collapsing where he'd stood just a second earlier.

Ava could only stare at her cousin. She wasn't sure what to say first, so she blurted out the first thing that popped into her mind. "You know Belshegar? You've summoned him before? Why didn't you tell us?"

"Well," Elena said reasonably, her expression all innocence, "you never asked."

## 14

HAD HIS MAGIC ALWAYS HUMMED IN HIS VEINS like this, always made him feel such a sense of well-being, as though someone had bottled the most perfect day possible and he had just drunk that sublime beverage?

Gabriel didn't think so, but he couldn't remember for sure. Once upon a time, he might have taken this feeling for granted. Now he knew he would never be so careless again.

Elena's familiarity with the being who had restored him to himself didn't bother him all that much, although he could tell Ava was still somewhat flummoxed by how friendly the two of them had been with each other. In a way, he could understand why Elena would have reached out to these entities, had been friendly with them.

Thanks to her strange gift, she had nothing to fear from any of those beings, and since her family had been so determined to make sure she had no friends in this world, she had gotten them the only place she knew she could.

And he knew he would be eternally grateful to both of them—to Elena, for rebelling against her family in order to help him, and to Belshegar, who'd restored his powers without argument, without expecting anything in return. Was he always so selfless, or had he only been helpful in this instance because Elena had asked him nicely?

In the end, Gabriel supposed it didn't matter one way or another. The important thing was that he had become himself again, and that meant he could move forward with his plans.

Ava's cousin still wore a slight smile, as though cheered that it had been so easy to grant the favor he'd requested. She reached over and picked up a square of pale yellow cheese from the plate that still sat on one of the living room's side tables, then shot Ava a speculative glance. "So...what now?" she asked. "Are we just waiting to see how long it takes my father and grandmother to figure out where I am?"

"To be honest, I don't think I thought that far ahead." Ava sent a rueful glance over at Gabriel. "Did you?"

Actually, he had…up to a point. At least, he guessed that it probably was not a good idea for Elena to linger here, just in case Miranda came sniffing around. Suspicion would probably fall on him and Ava at some point, simply because they'd been fairly open about his troubles, about his need for help. And Sophia Castillo knew they'd taken the summoning spell with them. It wouldn't require too much deduction to realize they'd gone to Elena Salazar for help.

"It's probably better if you don't stay here," Gabriel said. "I'm sure this house is one of the first places Miranda will look, once your father and grandmother reach out to their *prima* for help. But I have a room at a hotel downtown. I was thinking you could have that room, and I could come stay here." His gaze moved to Ava, whose cheeks flushed as he looked at her. "Would that be all right with you, Ava?"

"Um, sure," she replied as she grew even pinker—no easy feat, considering the warm olive tones of her skin. "I'll just have to put some fresh sheets on the guest room bed. Also," she went on, speaking more quickly, as if in an attempt to cover up her awkwardness, "the La Fonda is owned by civilians and the Castillos don't tend to hang out there, so it would be a good place to lie low for a while."

For some reason, Elena didn't look overly thrilled by this solution. "So I'm going from being locked up in my house to being locked up in a hotel?"

"It's only temporary," Ava said hastily. "Just until we can figure out something more permanent. And I wouldn't exactly call it locked up—the hotel has a great restaurant and a nice bar, and there are a lot of shops on the ground level that are safe to visit, since they're also owned by civilians."

Her description appeared to hearten the other witch, because she nodded. "That doesn't sound so bad."

"It's not," Gabriel put in. "It's a very nice hotel."

A thought seemed to occur to Ava, and she said, "And I'll print out a map of downtown and put stars on the stores and restaurants that are owned by Castillos, so you'll know which ones to avoid. To be honest, we don't hang out downtown all that much since there are always so many tourists around. But with a few precautions, you should be able to see a lot more of Santa Fe than you might have thought."

These arguments appeared to convince Elena. While she didn't exactly smile, she did seem more relaxed. "And what will you do while I'm luxuriating at the La Fonda Hotel?"

There were a great many things Gabriel would like to do now, although he doubted whether Ava would appreciate him describing them in any detail. The mere thought of being alone with her in this house was enough to set his blood racing. He told himself there would be plenty of time later, that he needed to focus on his return to El Salvador and what he would do once he was there, and yet all he could think of was telling Ava there was no real need to make up the bed in the guest room…was there?

Luckily, Ava came to his rescue, saying, "Now that Gabriel's powers are back, we're going to work on getting him home to El Salvador. After that…we'll see what happens."

"You're not planning to stay here in Castillo territory?" Elena asked, her expression openly curious. It seemed obvious to him that she couldn't understand why he wouldn't want to remain in Santa Fe, especially since it was probably clear enough to anyone who possessed a pair of eyes that he and Ava had formed some sort of connection.

"I have unfinished business back home," he said, and hoped that would be enough. While he was grateful to Elena, she didn't need to know all the details. In a way, it was probably better if she didn't. If Miranda discovered her eventually, Elena wouldn't be able to give away much information.

Because he'd realized that whatever he and Ava decided to do, they would have to do it secretly. If her family discovered their plans, they would do whatever they could to prevent her from taking the dangerous trip to El Salvador. It didn't matter that she was an adult and could make her own decisions. Even an adult could be stopped by a *prima's* orders, if that *prima* decided the business at hand was far too risky. After all, a clan leader's first obligation was to make sure her people remained safe.

At least, such concerns were supposed to be their first obligation. He feared that such noble intentions had fallen by the wayside in the Escobar clan long ago…if they had ever existed in the first place.

For one fragile second, he wondered if it would be better to stay here, to become part of the Castillo clan and forget that he had been born an Escobar. He certainly owed his family nothing; they had actively worked to hurt him, to destroy the very essence of what he was. And yet…

…and yet he knew he couldn't abandon them. With Vicénte in control, there was far too great a risk that they would be led down a path which could lead to their destruction…and possibly the destruction of other witch families as well. The elders must be removed, true, and those who had been their willing toadies somehow dealt with. But there were many in the Escobar clan who had committed no crimes, who were guilty of nothing more than trying to live their lives as best they could. Surely they did not deserve to meet a dark fate.

Elena's slate-blue eyes narrowed slightly, but she didn't probe any further. As someone who'd spent the past ten years or so carrying her own secrets, she probably knew not to ask questions that were better off left unanswered.

"We might as well get you settled," Ava said. "We'll all need to go, since I have to drive, and Gabriel has to be the one to transfer the room to you."

"No problem," Elena replied. "It's not as if I'm not already packed."

True enough; the bag she'd brought with her still sat in a corner of the room where she'd dropped it earlier. Now she went to retrieve her single piece of luggage, slinging it over her shoulder. When she straightened, she looked almost cheerful as she glanced over at her cousin.

"Hey...does the La Fonda offer spa treatments?"

~

It had been a little more complicated to transfer Gabriel's room than Ava had expected, but after they'd spent the better part of a half hour getting Elena set up at the hotel, everything seemed to be squared away. At least her cousin actually had a state-issued I.D., if not a driver's license. It was in her own name, but that was a risk they'd have to take. Ava supposed that Elena's father and grandmother might try calling hotels in their search to locate their runaway. However, that sort of search could take them a very long time, considering how many hotels and motels and Airbnbs New Mexico's capital city contained. And also, how would they even know she'd come to Santa Fe? She could have gone anywhere in New Mexico, since it was all Castillo territory.

"Just call me if you need anything," she told her cousin. "I wrote my number on the back of the downtown map I gave you."

"I will," Elena replied. She didn't look too worried about being left to her own devices, but that was probably because she'd already inspected the brochure that described all the hotel's spa services. Luckily, Ava had stopped in at one of the places that catered to tourists and made a serious dent in her checking account by loading up a prepaid Visa with three thousand dollars, just so her cousin would have plenty of money on hand to get her through her stay at the hotel. Of course, if she spent hundreds on spa treatments every day, it might not last that long, but she had to hope that Elena would ease up a little once the novelty began to wear off.

To Ava's surprise, Gabriel went over to her cousin, took one of her hands in his, and gave it a brief squeeze. "Thank you again. I know there's nothing I can do to repay you for what you and Belshegar restored to me, but—"

"It's okay," she said hastily, looking horribly embarrassed. "I'm glad I could help. Belshegar, too. He said once to me that he was kind of bummed about not being called to help people as much as he used to. So I know he was happy that this was something he could do for you."

An altruistic demon. Who knew? All the same.... Ava hesitated for a moment, then said, "But you're not, um…going to invite him over to say thanks, are you?"

"Here?" Elena grinned and shook her head. "Being stuck in my house for ten years might have made me a little *loco,* but I'm not that crazy."

About all Ava could do was smile back. Would she have been able to retain her sense of humor if she'd gone through everything Elena had? She honestly didn't know. But at least it seemed as if they didn't have to worry about her cousin getting into any trouble here. The biggest risk was her running into a couple of Castillos, and even then, such an encounter didn't have to be a big deal. All Elena had to do was say she was visiting from Las Vegas and leave it at that. Everything about her had been such a secret that Ava doubted most people in the clan even knew she existed. And since Castillo cousins came to Santa Fe all the time, whether just to sightsee or to visit relatives they hadn't seen in years, there shouldn't be anything about her presence to raise an eyebrow.

Well, unless Miranda put out the witchy version of an APB on her.

"I'll give you a call in the morning, see how you're doing," Ava promised, and went over and gave Elena a quick hug. She wasn't sure how such a gesture would be received, but she thought she should do it anyway, just because a part of her felt guilty about leaving her cousin here. Elena would be perfectly safe, of course, but....

To Ava's relief, Elena hugged her back without hesitation. "I'll be fine," she said. "Now, you two go and do...whatever it is you need to do."

Blood rushed to her face, but she managed to reply, "We will. Have fun at the spa."

"And call if you need us," Gabriel added.

"Not necessary, but sure." Elena made a shooing motion with her hands. "Go on, get out of here. I want to see if they have any openings for a mani/pedi this afternoon."

About all Ava could do was chuckle and shake

her head as she and Gabriel exited the suite, but she felt considerably less guilty than she had a few minutes earlier. The hotel was fairly crowded, and so neither of them said much of anything until they were back in the parking garage and safely inside her car.

"It seems as if your cousin is handling all this very well," he remarked as Ava touched the nav and the preset that would send them straight back to her house.

"It does. But I guess she's just happy to be away and someplace where she can be pampered a bit." Not that Elena needed a lot of glossing up, she reflected. Her cousin was just sort of naturally gorgeous. Probably the biggest danger was her attracting all sorts of male attention. Ava doubted the other witch was used to that sort of thing. How could she be? She'd been basically locked up like Rapunzel in the tower ever since she was eleven years old. All right, she'd had some demons to keep her company, but it didn't seem as if those demons were interested in her the way Loc was interested in Cat. Belshegar had been friendly, true, but his relationship with Elena had felt more like a brother with his favorite little sister than anything romantic.

*Thank God,* she thought with an inward shudder. She couldn't quite imagine kissing something that looked like Belshegar.

On the other hand, she could definitely imagine kissing Gabriel…except she really didn't have to, since they'd kissed once already and it had been sublime. Would it feel different now that he had his powers back?

Only one way to find out….

"I'm glad I could give her my room," he said. He shifted a little in his seat, dark eyes fixed on her. There was something about his gaze that made a shiver tickle its way down her back, and she swallowed. "You don't mind, do you?"

"'Mind'?" she echoed. "Mind what?"

"That I invited myself to stay with you."

"No," she replied at once, not sure why he would think she might have a problem with the arrangement. "I mean, it was the logical thing to do. We needed someplace to put Elena, and we needed a place that people wouldn't immediately think to look. My house has lots of space, so it makes sense that you would come stay in the guest bedroom instead of continuing to spend money on a hotel."

One of his eyebrows lifted, the movement echoed in the way one corner of his mouth quirked slightly. "Am I going to be staying in the guest bedroom, though?"

Damn. Ava swallowed, then wished she was driving instead of letting the Honda do everything for her. At least that way, she'd have something to occupy herself instead of being basically forced to meet his gaze. "I…probably not."

There went the blood flooding to her cheeks again. She felt it, but since she couldn't do anything to stop it, she only pulled in a breath and waited to see what he would say next.

He paused. When he spoke, his voice was low, gentle. "I don't want you to think I am putting any pressure on you."

"You're not," she said. "I mean, when you kissed me earlier…I knew right then where all this was going to end up." Did that sound horrible? She wasn't sure. And really, the actual truth was that almost from the moment she'd met Gabriel, she'd guessed where all this was heading. Or at least, where she hoped things might go. She'd never been so attracted to anyone in her life. That had been a purely physical reaction, but after spending time with him, getting to know more of who he was, she knew that attraction had become something much deeper.

His hand moved, went to touch hers. Just a brush of fingertips against the back of her hand, but that was enough to send heat flooding through her, to make her heart speed up and the world seem to spin a little. Good thing the car was driving with no need of her admittedly shaky input.

"I thought so, too," he said, his tone quiet,

intense. Then he smiled slightly. "I suppose the inside of your vehicle is possibly not the best place for this sort of discussion."

"Maybe," she admitted. "But it's okay."

He lifted his hand from hers, settled back in his seat. "I'm glad it's okay."

By that point, they were almost at the house, since the hotel was barely five minutes away from her place. Ava touched the button to open the garage door and let the SUV park itself inside. Neither of them said anything as they went through the garage's back door and on through the garden. It was beautiful, the hollyhocks waving in the breeze, the roses so vibrant, it almost looked as if they were glowing from within.

Or maybe everything looked so resplendent because of the way she was feeling inside.

She barely had a chance to drop her purse on the kitchen counter before Gabriel pulled her into his arms. His mouth touched hers, hungry, and her lips parted so she could taste him, so he could taste her. Their bodies pressed together, and his hands were sliding down her cheeks, fingertips drifting against her neck, moving lower so they brushed against one of her breasts.

A gasp escaped her lips, but at the same time, she could feel herself flinch. No one had ever touched her like that before...mostly because she could never quite get up the nerve to go from kissing to, well, anything else. It wasn't that she didn't want this, but....

At once, Gabriel moved away slightly, his hands falling to his sides. "I'm sorry," he said. "I am going too fast for you."

Damn it. Ava shook her head. "No, that's not it. I—" The problem was, she didn't know what she needed to say to him. She wanted this; she hadn't lied about that. But wanting and doing were two entirely different things.

In frustration, she went to the fridge and got out the pitcher of iced tea, then fetched a couple of glasses. Without even bothering to ask Gabriel whether he wanted some, she poured drinks for both of them. She lifted one of the glasses and took a large swallow. After a pause, he took the second glass and drank some tea as well, his expression growing increasingly puzzled.

"Let's go in the family room," she said.

Still looking confused, he followed her into the space, which always felt a little more homey and prosaic to her because of the TV. It wasn't like the living room, which always looked like something from the set of a living history museum to her.

She sat on the couch, and after a brief hesitation, he seated himself next to her. Not too close, but near enough that she could reach out to him if she wanted to.

That was the real trick, wasn't it? Part of her wanted to…and part of her was scared shitless.

Another bracing swallow of iced tea, and then she said, "You don't know that much about me, Gabriel."

His brows drew together. "Is that what's bothering you? That we are so new to one another? I can wait as long as you need me to."

Of course he would. Because she could tell he genuinely cared about her. That wasn't the problem. The problem was…her.

"I've never been with anyone," she blurted, but he only smiled, apparently not put off by that revelation.

"That isn't so strange for a witch your age, is it?" he responded. "This sort of thing is different for witches and warlocks than it is for civilians."

Damn him for being so understanding, or at least attempting to be understanding. The problem was, he'd completely missed the point, mostly because he could have no way of knowing what the point actually was.

Despite her frustration, she couldn't prevent herself from raising an eyebrow. "Was it different for you?"

He didn't pretend to misunderstand. "No. But I have only been with civilian women. There was no one in Pico Negro who called to my heart, and I did not want to lead anyone on. In San Salvador, it was easy enough to meet those who only wanted to share a night of pleasure and wished for nothing else. I had much the same experience in Mexico City."

Of course he had. Gabriel was so drop-dead gorgeous that Ava was sure he'd never had a problem finding partners. It made her even more uncomfortable to realize that his remark sounded a little too close to the way her brother had managed his own love life, or at least how he'd handled things until he met Cassandra Sandoval. Ava had never told her brother that she knew all about his various conquests, mostly because she'd seen no reason to bring it up. He hadn't wanted to settle down but had wanted to get laid, so pretty tourists seemed like the obvious—and easiest—solution.

"Thank you for being honest," she said.

Gabriel shrugged, although the intensity of his expression seemed at odds with the casual gesture. "You know I would never lie to you, Ava. I always took precautions. But I have experience, yes."

She supposed she should be glad of that. At least one of them would know what they were doing…assuming they got to that point.

"Anyway," he went on, "I hope you don't

think that I wouldn't still want this simply because you've never been with anyone before."

"No, it's...." The words trailed off, and she wanted to kick herself for leading them down this path. Why couldn't she have just let him kiss her and caress her like a normal person?

"It's what, Ava?"

His voice was so gentle, so kind. How could he be so patient with her when she was acting like such an idiot? Worse, he'd just had his powers restored. He should have been able to freely celebrate that particular miracle, instead of having to hold her hand while she worked through her neuroses.

"I used to be fat," she blurted out, and he stared at her, expression both puzzled and startled.

"You're not fat now," he said, pointing out the obvious.

"No," she replied. "But I wanted you to know."

Another frown touched his brow. "Why do you think I would care?"

"Because...because...." She flailed for a moment, then said desperately, "Because what happens if I get fat again? You told me you thought I was beautiful, but I don't *feel* beautiful. I feel like chubby old Ava Castillo, the girl no guys wanted to date."

"Ava."

His tone was still quiet, but something about it made her go silent. He reached over and clasped her fingers in his, then moved his free hand to touch her cheek.

"You *are* beautiful," he said. "Here"—his fingertips traced over her cheekbone—"and here." He paused to touch her temple. "Beautiful, inside and out. If you want to eat *dulce de leche* cake three times a day and get as chubby as my cousin Annabella, I will still think you beautiful."

No way could anyone be this perfect. She stared at him, the impulse to look inside his mind and see whether he was telling her the truth almost overwhelming. But no, she'd already broken that rule once today. That had been in a good cause. This would be only to satisfy her own doubts and her own insecurity. Gabriel deserved better than that.

"Really?" she asked, hating how her voice quavered.

"Really," he said. "I don't know who told you that you weren't worthy, simply because of a few pounds. But you should not allow people like that to have any power over you. I think you are perfect, Ava. You are perfect now, and you will always be perfect, no matter what happens."

She wasn't sure which one of them moved first. Not that it really mattered; their lips met again, and they were kissing one another, Gabriel shifting so he pushed her down against the sofa cushions, his weight on her now, his body strong and hard and so unbelievably amazing. Once again, his hand moved to her breast, only this time she didn't stop him, let his fingertips glide over her, let him push up the cotton blouse she wore so he touched the bare flesh of her stomach.

Such heat in such a gentle caress. She pulled in a breath and hardly dared to let it out, because now he'd pushed her blouse all the way up so the plain white bra she wore was exposed. And damn, if she'd known the day was going to end up like this, she would have worn something prettier, would have gotten out the new dark pink satin bra and matching panties she'd bought last month to celebrate the loss of those last five stubborn pounds. At the time, she hadn't expected anyone to see her in them, but now....

His lips touched the sensitive skin at the side of her neck and she gasped, wondering how that could possibly feel so good. The only boyfriend she'd ever gotten semi-serious with, a guy she'd met at the university her junior year, had kissed her there, but those kisses hadn't felt anything like this.

Then Gabriel paused, his murmur almost a purr in her ear. "Where is your bedroom?"

"Upstairs," she replied, realizing that it probably would be better to do this somewhere other than the family room couch. "The door at the end of the hall."

Those words had barely left her mouth before the room around them vanished, including the couch they were lying on. They fell —or were dropped—onto the bed from a height of about six inches, and again she gasped, although for an entirely different reason this time.

"Sorry," Gabriel said. "I misjudged the height of the bed."

Of course he did. She recalled how he'd managed to teleport Tony and Cassandra right out from under his brother's nose, sending them all the way back here to Santa Fe, to this very house. Compared to that, a short hop from the living room downstairs to the master bedroom must have seemed like nothing, although Ava knew it was going to take her a while to get used to Gabriel having all his powers again.

"It's all right," she replied, sounding a bit breathless. A pause as she kicked off the flats she wore before she added, "I don't mind."

"Good," he responded.

Then he was tugging at her blouse again, this time pulling it over her head. She didn't mind seeing it go, because now he bent to leave a line of kisses across her chest, moving down to one breast, tugging at her bra so it was enough out of the way for him to flick his tongue across her nipple.

*Oh, my God.*

She moaned and, obviously encouraged, he reached back to unhook her bra, then tossed it off to one side. Now his hands closed on both her breasts, caressing them, and she moaned again, feeling her body seem to come alive at his touch, heat building in her core. There had been times in the past when she'd found herself vaguely aroused by something she read or something she saw on TV, but none of that had prepared her for the ravening need he seemed to awaken in her, a throbbing, hungry desire so strong that it felt almost like a separate entity, like something that wasn't completely a part of her at all.

A beast that needed to be fed.

Her fingers pulled at his T-shirt, and he obligingly slid it up and over his head. Now she could see so much more of his body than she had back in their Airbnb in New Orleans; the body he revealed was just as flawless as his face, chest and abs heavily muscled and defined, biceps bulging as he balled up the shirt and flung it onto the floor to lie next to her abandoned bra.

If he saw any flaws in her own body, he didn't seem to notice them. He lowered his mouth to her breast again, suckling, even as his fingers went down to the button of her jeans and unfastened it, then slid down the zipper. Another Ava might have protested, might have said this was all going too fast, but she knew she wouldn't do a thing to stop him, wanted him to ease down her jeans and the panties underneath so they, too, ended up on the floor with the rest of their discarded clothing.

Since her jeans and underwear were now gone, it only made sense to get rid of his as well. She undid his belt, then had to wait while he bent down to loosen the laces on the shoes he wore. Not for too long, though; soon enough, they were gone, along with his socks. At last she could pull down his jeans and the dark gray briefs he wore.

Maybe this should have been an awkward moment, but all she could think of was how amazing he looked, how much she wanted him… all of him. And he must have been thinking pretty much the same thing, because his finger slipped into her, stroking, and she moaned again, louder this time. That was so good…so unbelievably good.

He apparently wasn't content to stop there, though, because a moment later, he bent and touched her with his tongue, tasting her. Dear God. She'd tried to imagine what this might feel like, but those fantasies didn't come close to the sensation of Gabriel making love to her with his mouth as her fingers tangled in his thick black hair and he pushed her closer, ever closer….

The orgasm swept over her, and she knew she was lost, that all she could do was ride the wave of ecstasy flooding through her body until she was finally able to return to herself. Which she did at last, only to see him looking up at her, a smile on his lips.

"You are the sweetest thing I've ever tasted," he said.

A shudder moved through her body. "That was the most incredible thing I've ever felt," she breathed.

His dark eyes glinted. "Oh, I'm not done yet."

He shifted, and now she felt him pressing up against her, felt the heat and the hardness of his shaft. A tremor moved through her body, although she wasn't sure whether that was from anticipation or possibly just the tiniest bit of fear at what was going to come next. Yes, she'd been on the pill for two years, mostly to regulate her periods than because she actually needed it for its true purpose, but....

Somehow seeming to note her hesitation, he paused, still touching her but not attempting to move any further. "Do you want to stop here? I thought...."

"No, I don't want to stop," she said. "I want you, Gabriel."

A relieved smile broke over his face, and he pushed in a little farther. He was big, but it didn't hurt, just felt as though he was filling an empty space she hadn't known existed until this moment. Her legs wrapped around him, pulling him in all the way, and then he began to find his rhythm, moving in and out, while she clung to him and let herself experience all these strange and wonderful new sensations.

Another wave seemed to be building in her, one even deeper and stronger than the first. Her fingers dug into the heavy muscles of his shoulders, and she found herself moaning again and again, gulping for air, as his movements grew quicker and his own breaths became short as well.

He climaxed, spilling his heat into her, but that was all right, because only a few seconds later she came as well, a strangled little cry forcing its way from her throat. This orgasm felt different from the last, not as quick and intense, but welcome nonetheless. For a long minute...or maybe three or four...they both lay there, gasping, bodies still joined as though neither of them wanted to end this moment.

At last, though, Gabriel shifted, pulling out of her even as he bent to kiss her gently on the cheek. "I didn't hurt you, did I?"

"No," she said. "It was perfect. Just like you are."

A brilliant flash of a smile, and then she was in his arms again, being held close so she could hear the strong, heavy beating of his heart, maybe a little faster than normal because of their previous exertions. Ava was glad to stay there, glad to have the man she loved holding her as though she was the most precious thing in his world.

She knew that no matter what happened next, nothing would ever be the same again.

## 15

Eventually, they rose from the bed and put their clothes back on; it was still not even five o'clock yet, and Gabriel supposed it probably wasn't a good idea to lounge in bed naked until they decided what they were going to do for their evening meal...although the thought crossed his mind. However, better to be dressed just in case Miranda put two and two together more quickly than they'd expected, and showed up on the doorstep to demand an explanation for Elena Salazar's disappearance.

When he and Ava made their way downstairs, he thought he caught sight of a pretty woman in an old-fashioned gown standing in the hallway, arms crossed and an expression of severe disapproval on her face. He blinked, wondering whether he was seeing things.

"Is there someone else in the house?" he asked, and Ava startled.

"What?"

"I just saw someone in a long dress standing over there." He pointed toward an antique side table with a burnished gilt-edged mirror hanging above it.

"Oh, that was just Victoria," Ava said. She looked especially delicious right then, hair tousled, her full mouth even fuller from the kisses he'd bestowed upon it. "She's the ghost who lives here."

"'Ghost'?" he repeated.

A grin. "The house is haunted. Victoria is mostly harmless, but she hates it if you try to rearrange the furniture or make changes to the place. I have a feeling she isn't too happy about what we just did in the bedroom."

That would explain the scowl the strange young woman had been wearing. "Well," he remarked, "if she doesn't approve of those sorts of activities, she is always welcome to move on to the next world instead of lingering here."

"I wish it were that easy." Ava headed into the kitchen, where she poured water for both of them and then pulled some of the uneaten cheese from their previous snack out of the refrigerator. "Cat's talent is talking to ghosts. She tried to get Victoria to transcend or whatever you want to call it, but Victoria wouldn't budge. I get the feeling she's going to stay in this house until someone tears it down."

"I'm surprised no one in your clan has done that already," Gabriel said, reflecting that getting rid of the ghost's abode might be the simplest way of dealing with the property's haunting problem.

A pucker of Ava's delicious mouth, and she replied, "We're too big on tradition to destroy a historic home like this. Besides, it seems kind of mean to try to drive her out. She's not really that much of a bother."

"You have a kind heart, my love," he said, and she stared up at him, expression wondering as she seemed to take in the term of endearment he'd just used. Because she looked so surprised, he thought he should make it very clear where matters stood between them. "Yes, *love*," he repeated, emphasizing the word. "For I do love you, Ava. You are a miracle I wasn't expecting, and are that much more precious because of it."

She set down her glass of water and came over to him, then snuggled against his chest. "I love you, Gabriel," she said. "More than...well, more than I ever thought I'd love someone. Of course, I've cared about people, but this...this is different."

Yes, it was. He'd never really expected to give his heart to anyone in such an open, unreserved way. For a long time, he'd suspected he wasn't capable of pure, selfless love, the sort of thing one might read about in books. That wouldn't have been so terribly strange, considering who his father was, the way he'd been raised.

But Ava had shone a light into his darkness, had shown him he was a very different person from the one he'd thought he was. She was so perfect, so pure, so unlike anyone he'd ever met before. Her sheer goodness made him hesitate, made him wonder if he should abandon his plans for revenge. Perhaps it would be better to stay here, to allow himself to become a part of the Castillo clan. At least that way, Ava would be safe…and now, with his powers restored, he actually had something he could offer her and her family, wouldn't be a helpless beggar with nothing of any value.

"Are you okay?" she asked, eyes wide and dark as they caught his gaze and held.

He could have drowned in those eyes, but he made himself reply, "Yes, I'm fine. Possibly, I'm trying to rethink my priorities."

"About going back to El Salvador?"

Amazing how she could go straight to the heart of what troubled him. Another person might have said she'd looked into his mind to discover the source of his current disquiet, but he knew Ava wouldn't do such a thing. She'd taken such a peek with her mother only because she'd known Sophia was hiding the truth from them. Otherwise, Ava exercised an impressive amount of self-control when it came to her unique talent.

"Yes," he said. "But let's go sit down. No need to hover here in the kitchen."

They took their glasses of water but left the plate of cheese behind. Once they were settled in the family room, Ava faced him where they sat on the couch, one leg tucked under the other so she could see him squarely.

"You were so adamant about going to El Salvador," she said. "What's changed your mind?"

*You,* he thought. *You have changed everything.*

However, he only replied, "Several things. For one, my guess as to what Vicénte will do next is only that—a guess. He may very well be satisfied with the situation as it is now, may have decided to marry again and have the family he's always wanted."

"He could be," Ava allowed, although her tone sounded dubious. "But from the things Tony said about him, and the things you've told me, it doesn't seem as if that's too likely."

"I don't know," Gabriel said. Yes, Vicénte's history seemed to indicate that he wouldn't be content to live a simple life, would always want more. And yet, he couldn't know that for sure. People could change. Gabriel knew he had. He let out a breath and added, "I don't want to take you down there on something that may very well be a fool's errand."

This remark was met by a considering silence. Ava wrapped a strand of wavy dark hair around one finger, playing with it as she appeared to ponder his words. "If this is all about protecting me," she said at last, "then you can stop right there. You can't let worry about me keep you from doing the right thing."

Which was exactly what he'd been doing. Gabriel hesitated, trying to think of a way to explain himself without making it sound as though he was ready to abandon the brighter future he'd envisioned for the Escobars, just for Ava's sake. And yet, he knew that was exactly what he'd been contemplating. It seemed far simpler to stay here in this charming—if haunted—house and let the Escobars take care of themselves. They'd survived hundreds of years of *primuses*, some worse than others. Surely they could survive his brother Vicénte.

"Is it the right thing, though?" he asked.

Another pause. Then she shrugged. "I don't know for sure. I've never met your brother. I only have Tony's account to go on, and the few things I saw in your mind when you let me in that one time. But what I saw didn't exactly give me a good impression of him."

No, probably not. Vicénte could be charming when he wanted to, but that surface charm was used only as a tool to mask his underlying ruthlessness. Even his desire for a wife and a son was not so he would have a woman to share his life, or a child he could love without reservation, but because he wanted to make sure the Escobar line continued.

"Would you like to see more of him?" Gabriel said.

She blinked. "You mean, you want me to look into your mind again?"

"Yes. I think it might help if you could see what I've experienced. Then we can decide together."

"I'm not sure—"

"Please, Ava," he said. He put his hand on hers, adding, "It would mean a great deal to me."

A long pause, during which she reached out with her other hand and lifted the glass of water to her lips so she could take a sip. That sip was followed by another. Eventually, though, she set down the glass and gazed back at him, her expression very solemn. "All right. If you think it will help."

"I hope it will. We need to be very clear about the path we take next."

She nodded, then said, "You don't need to do anything. Just sit quietly while I take a look."

Basically the same instructions she'd given him before, only this time they felt even more significant. As he sat there, Gabriel hoped he wasn't making a very great mistake.

After all, she would look into his mind and see everything Vicénte had done…but she would also be able to see what he had done as well.

Usually, when Ava was allowed into someone's thoughts, it was to pick out a single detail, to find a helpful memory that had been buried for too long. This time, though, Gabriel wanted her to see as much of his life as she could so she would have an accurate idea of his brother's character. Or at least, as accurate an impression as this sort of thing could provide. She would be able to see what had happened to Gabriel over the years, but all those events would still be colored by his thoughts and emotions. In the end, she'd need to separate the pure facts from the beliefs.

As she went into his mind, she found herself surrounded by a kaleidoscope of images, a blur of memories and scenes that she had to fight to make any sense out of. This was the problem of not having a single target, one central goal to provide focus.

*Okay,* she told herself, *try to do this chronologically. Go back to the beginning.*

Or at least as far back as Gabriel remembered. She saw a man with a hard, yet strangely handsome face bending over him, and realized the man must be the infamous Joaquin Escobar himself. He was gone quickly, though, and didn't return. Well, that made sense. Joaquin came to the U.S. and never returned to El Salvador. Actually, she was kind of surprised Gabriel had retained even that one memory, since she knew he'd been only a toddler when his father left Pico Negro.

A blur of different people then—several women who seemed to have acted as Gabriel's caretakers, a squat little man who appeared to be one of the Escobar clan's elders, more people who had to have been other members of the Escobar family, a few that Ava thought possibly were civilians from the neighboring village of San Matías.

And she saw Vicénte, a tall, swaggering boy of around thirteen or so, someone who walked around Pico Negro as if he already owned it. In a way, she supposed he did, since it seemed obvious enough that Joaquin had made it clear the boy was in charge, even if it was the elders who actually kept things quietly running in the background.

She saw, too, how Vicénte found subtle ways to torture his little brother, whether it was to hide his favorite toy, or to tear a page from a book he was reading, or to tell the elders about any minor transgressions, such as sneaking a ride on one of the goats when Gabriel thought no one was looking. Possibly none of these things were much worse than some of the ways siblings had been tormenting one another for millennia, but all added up, they showed a pattern of pure meanness, of making sure that his younger brother would never forget his lesser status in the clan. And once Gabriel got older and his truly amazing powers began to develop, Vicénte did what he could to treat his brother as little better than a servant, commanding him to carry out his orders rather than get his own hands dirty, although his reason was always that these things needed to be done for the greater good of the Escobar clan.

Gabriel's memories also showed how Vicénte abused pretty much everyone around him. Even the woman he'd taken for his wife hadn't escaped his harsh tongue and heavy hand. When she died in childbirth, it was called a tragedy, and yet Gabriel overheard the whispers of the healer and the woman who had assisted in the birth, how they'd said that Yolanda would not have perished if Vicénte had not struck her several days earlier, causing her to suffer a bad fall, one that started bleeding neither one of them could stop.

This last was more than Ava could bear, and

she pulled herself out of Gabriel's mind with a gasp, as though she'd been underwater for too long and needed to catch her breath. Their eyes met, and he stared at her soberly, expression calm and somehow resigned.

"So...?" he said at last.

Voice flat, she replied, "Your brother is a monster," then got up from the couch and pushed her hands through her hair. For some reason, she felt dirty, as if some of the evil of Vicénte's actions had managed to rub off on her.

Gabriel released a breath, his hands still lying limp on his knees as if he wasn't sure what to do with them. "Yes."

Faced with such a calm acknowledgment, Ava didn't quite know how she should respond. She crossed her arms and stared down at him. "What should we do?"

"What do you think we should do?"

There was really only one answer to that question. Maybe Gabriel had entertained a fantasy of living a peaceful life here in Santa Fe, but she didn't see how that would be possible with Vicénte still out there in the world. He might have been biding his time, letting himself recover from the loss of the grimoires, but that state of affairs couldn't last indefinitely. Sooner or later, he'd begin to chafe at his circumscribed existence and would start to look again for whatever spell or artifact might give him an edge over all the other witch clans.

He had to be stopped before that happened.

"We have to go to El Salvador," she said. "You have to take the Escobar clan away from him."

No real response, except a slight slumping of Gabriel's broad shoulders. He'd probably known exactly what she was going to say, just as he'd known deep in his heart that there was no running away from his responsibilities in El Salvador. Vicénte's maneuvering—and the clan elders' actions in stripping Gabriel of his powers —might have postponed the day of reckoning, but it couldn't be avoided altogether.

"It will be dangerous," he said.

"You've already told me that," Ava replied, hoping she sounded a lot less rattled than she felt. That was probably the deepest she'd ever gone into someone's mind, and her own thoughts were blurry and unfocused, as if they'd been overlaid by all of Gabriel's memories and emotions. "It's okay. What we need is a plan."

Now he smiled, and patted the seat cushion next to him. "Then come and sit down, and let's talk about it."

She did as he asked, settling herself beside him. It did feel better to be this close to him, to have him drop an arm around her so he could pull her even closer. Ava had to remind herself that they'd made love only a half hour earlier, that they'd been as intimate as two people could be. A good deal of the afterglow from their encounter had been effectively erased by what she'd seen in his thoughts, and she desperately wanted it back.

"We'll drive into Mexico, then take a train down to Guatemala. There, we'll rent a vehicle and drive to San Matías."

Ava lifted an eyebrow at him, wondering why in the world he'd want to take such a circuitous route when they could simply fly and get there in a few hours. "That'll take days," she pointed out. "It's a lot easier to fly."

"True," he said, so quickly that she could tell he'd been waiting for her to make that argument. "But we will set off alarms if we fly into El Salvador, because the elders have warded the entire territory. If we come in by vehicle, I'll be able to mask our natures in a way I couldn't if we were flying."

This explanation didn't seem to make any sense. "But Tony and Cassandra flew there—"

"Yes," Gabriel cut in, so quickly that Ava guessed he'd been ready for that particular argument. "And we knew they were coming. Why do you think I was able to intercept them so quickly, even before the residents of San Matías could reach out and let me know there were strangers in the village? Of course, Vicénte tasked me with discovering what your brother and Cassandra Sandoval wanted, not knowing that I'd already planned to lure them to El Salvador in order to ask for their assistance in getting the grimoires out of my brother's hands."

"All right, that makes sense," she said, then realized they'd been overlooking the obvious. Possibly her brain hadn't yet caught up with the realities of Gabriel being once more in possession of all his powers. "I don't understand why we can't teleport in, though. I mean, you can send the two of us that far, can't you?"

"Yes. But in this case, the element of surprise is one of the few things we'll have going for us. If I use that much magic that close to Pico Negro, Vicénte will surely feel it. My brother thinks I am still safely stripped of my powers, no one who could possibly be a threat. We need him to keep thinking that way."

Ava nodded. She'd have to remember that just because Gabriel was more powerful than his half-brother, it didn't mean Vicénte didn't have a few tricks in his own arsenal.

"Okay, I understand." She still didn't like the plan too much, but at least she realized that their best chance of success lay in flying under the radar and getting to Pico Negro without anyone in the Escobar clan realizing they were in El Salvador at all. "And after that?"

Gabriel's expression grew grimmer. "I have to hope there are those in my clan who have also suffered at Vicénte's hands, who will realize that their lives would be much better if he were no longer their *primus*. Only a few might be enough to turn the tide, since my powers are so much stronger than those of anyone else in the clan."

"Might" being the operative word. That seemed an awfully big condition to be hanging their chances of success on, but Ava knew they didn't have much of a choice. Besides, while she certainly hadn't seen all of Gabriel's life—luckily, she'd managed to avoid his encounters with civilian women, probably because none of those episodes would have involved Vicénte and there-fore weren't anything she needed to witness—she'd seen enough to tell her that the current *primus* was far from universally loved. She'd noticed the way the members of the Escobar clan rarely smiled around him unless he was gazing at them directly, how they seemed to mutter things to themselves when he wasn't looking.

Whereas they'd seemed much friendlier with Gabriel in one-on-one situations, and he appeared to have always reciprocated, had laughed and joked and generally appeared to enjoy their company. Surely if they were given a choice, they'd pick him as their future *primus,* rather than be stuck with the heavy-handed, authoritarian Vicénte.

But first they had to be given that choice.

"Okay," she said. "Any ideas of who you're going to approach first?"

"Paz, our healer. She has no love for my brother…not after what he did to his wife."

"And?" Ava prompted. "I mean, healers are super-important, but they're not generally who you need watching your back in a fight." *And neither am I,* she thought then. Her gift for reading minds came in handy sometimes, but she didn't think it would be of much use in the sort of expedition they were planning.

That observation made Gabriel smile slightly. "Possibly not, but healers are very good people to have around after such a fight."

"You have a point. Still…."

Obviously wanting to reassure her, he named a few other people in the clan, ones who seemed to have the kinds of offensive powers that would be useful for confronting Vicénte and the elders. That all sounded better, but one important detail continued to trouble her.

"What about the null?" she asked softly. "If your brother still has him in his back pocket, then none of the rest of this is going to do us much good."

Gabriel's expression darkened. "Alessandro is

a problem, I know. He's really the person we should approach first, but I'm not sure if that would help at all. Right now, he has a position of some importance simply because Vicénte uses him as a way of keeping the others in the clan in line."

"But does he follow your brother willingly, or is he being coerced like all the rest?"

"I'm not sure." Gabriel rubbed the dark stubble on his chin, eyes narrowed in thought. "He has suffered the wrong side of Vicénte's tongue on more than one occasion, just like the rest of us. But I think lately he has been trying to keep on my brother's good side for an entirely different reason."

"What's that?"

A small, bitter smile touched Gabriel's lips. "You know how I have said that Vicénte has begun to think of taking another wife?"

"Yes," Ava replied, not sure what that had to do with the null.

"Alessandro has a younger sister, Lara. She has grown into a beautiful woman in the past few years, and Vicénte has started to pay her particular attention. I think Alessandro fears what might happen to his sister if my brother should make her his wife."

Considering what had happened to Vicénte's first wife, Ava thought that was a valid concern.

And…. "You said she's grown into a beautiful woman recently. How old is she?"

"Twenty," Gabriel responded. The look on his face grew even more bleak, if that was possible. "Yes, Vicénte is sixteen years older than she. What is worse, Lara and Alessandro's father is dead, and their mother is certainly not in a position to stand up to my brother. I believe that Alessandro does what he can to keep his sister away from Vicénte, but I have no idea what has occurred between them in all the months that I've been away."

"Could you check?" Ava asked. Even though she'd never met this Lara, she couldn't help but fear what might have happened during the time Gabriel was exiled from his clan. She was two years older than the young woman in question, and still the thought of having someone so much older and more powerful pursuing her was frightening, to put it mildly. "I mean," she went on as Gabriel sent her a puzzled glance, clearly not understanding what she'd asked, "You have your powers back now. Can't you, I don't know, take a quick peek to get the lay of the land? It wouldn't take as much magic as the two of us going there, would it?"

"I wish it were that easy," he said. "Vicénte can't precisely track my comings and goings, but he is able to sense when I'm around, especially if I'm expending a great deal of magical energy. I fear that is part of the reason why he was able to corner me and Tony and Cassandra when we went to his house to steal back the grimoires. When the village was my home, this was not as much of an issue, because of course my brother would expect me to be there. But now, if I were to attempt to drop in and do any kind of reconnaissance—even alone—then I would risk him discovering that I was back...and with my powers intact. And although I have many talents to draw on, I am not a seer, or one who can look upon the doings of others from far away. This is why it is so important to get in and work quickly before Vicénte realizes I am there."

Damn. Ava supposed she should have known it wouldn't be that easy, but just once she'd like the universe to cut them a break. Then again, maybe the universe thought it had already done them enough favors, considering that Gabriel now had his powers back, thanks to a friendly, helpful not-demon.

"All right," she said after a long pause, one she hoped he didn't think was a condemnation for him not being all-knowing or all-powerful. He was certainly stronger than any other warlock she'd ever known, but he wasn't a god...even if he might look like one. "Then I guess we need to do this as quickly as possible, I suppose."

He nodded, then reached over to take her

hand, his fingers wrapping around hers so he could give them a reassuring squeeze. "It will be fine. I promise."

She hoped he was right. Because otherwise...

...otherwise he might not have a lot of time left to enjoy the powers he'd so recently had restored.

## 16

Since he knew where they were going and which trains and so on to take, Ava let Gabriel handle that part of the preparations. At least, unlike her brother Tony, she actually had a passport. Not that she'd ever used it...or even really thought she'd ever have a reason or the courage to use it...but more because she'd wanted to have it on hand, her own private insurance in case she ever felt the need to run away, to leave the world that had been suffocating her behind.

Well, she was definitely going to use it now. Of course, Gabriel already had a Mexican passport under his assumed name of Ramón Hernandez, so —on the surface, at least—the travel involved shouldn't be that big a deal. In a way, she could think of a train trip as being sort of romantic and exotic, especially since there was now high-speed rail between Chihuahua and Mexico City that would allow the nearly eight-hundred-mile trip to be completed in less than three hours. Ava vaguely remembered reading about the construction of that particular train route a few years earlier, but she hadn't paid much attention because she'd never thought she'd ever be traveling on such a train.

Except she would be…tomorrow, actually. They'd have to take a bus from Albuquerque to Chihuahua, since there wasn't a train between those two cities, but after that, they'd be able to cover an enormous part of their journey in just a few hours. The train that would take them from Mexico City and all the way into Guatemala would be much slower, and they would have to spend one night on it, since that portion of the trip would take nearly eighteen hours. From Guatemala City, as Gabriel had explained, they'd have to drive. Even so, the two of them should be in El Salvador in less than three days.

That thought made a little shiver go through her. She really didn't want to think about what would happen once they got to Pico Negro. Gabriel sounded optimistic, but optimism would only get them so far. About all she could do was hope he'd been right about the sentiments of the others in the Escobar clan, that they would want to be free of Vicénte's rule.

And that Alessandro Escobar cared more about protecting his little sister than saving his own hide....

All these were pretty big "ifs." However, Ava did her best to push them to the back of her mind, to make herself focus on what needed to be handled here and now. She'd already packed most of what she was taking with her—and had chosen her most lightweight and comfortable clothing, hoping it would fare all right in El Salvador's steamy climate—but now there were a couple of loose ends she needed to tie up. The outcome of this foray into Escobar territory was still very much up in the air. Maybe Gabriel would emerge victorious, in which case he would remain there in Pico Negro to take over the role of *primus* of the Escobars. If that happened, she knew he would want her there with him. They hadn't spoken any words of commitment to each other, not yet, but he wouldn't have asked her to come with him if he didn't expect to have her stay. The prospect both thrilled and worried her. Could she change her life so drastically?

Yes, she realized. Absolutely, if it meant being with Gabriel for the rest of her life.

In which case, she knew that disappearing

under cover of darkness without letting anyone know what she was up to would be far too cruel. On the other hand, she feared if she talked to her parents and told them she was about to head down to El Salvador with Gabriel, they'd absolutely freak out…and probably go straight to Miranda and demand that she prevent their daughter from going.

Ava honestly didn't know whether Miranda would try to stop her. On the other hand, it was probably better not to put that particular hypothesis to the test.

Which was why Ava sat on her bed now, cell phone in hand, as she listened to water run in the bathroom. Gabriel was showering tonight rather than the next morning, since they'd need to be out the door no later than seven o'clock in order to make all their connections. This was the perfect time to make her phone calls, even though something seemed to be preventing her from touching the one entry in her contacts list she'd selected.

At last she pulled in a breath, then put her forefinger on the screen.

The phone rang a couple of times. Was it going to go to voicemail? Maybe that would be easier. But no, she couldn't leave a message about something like this. She needed to be able to deliver this information personally.

But after the third ring, it picked up, and her brother said, "Ava?"

He sounded a little puzzled, as if he couldn't quite figure out why she'd be calling him at nearly nine o'clock at night. Well, that wasn't so strange; they talked, but not regularly, and she generally tried to call in the afternoon at a time when she thought she wouldn't be interrupting anything too terribly important. "Hey, Tony."

His tone sharpened a little. "What's up?"

"I—" The syllable seemed to strangle in her throat, and she wished she'd thought to bring a glass of water up here to the master bedroom. "Gabriel got his powers back."

"He did? That's awesome."

"Yes, it is."

A pause, and then Tony said, "You don't sound very happy about it."

"No, I am," she said quickly. "It's just…now that his powers are restored, he's going back to El Salvador to confront his brother."

"Can't say as I blame him," her brother remarked. "I mean, Vicénte definitely deserves an ass kicking, and if there's anyone in the world who can do that, it's Gabriel."

True enough, and yet Ava sort of doubted Tony would be quite so in agreement with her next statement. "I'm going with him," she blurted out, eliciting a long, shocked pause at the other end of the line.

Then, "You're *what?*"

"I told you. I'm going with him."

"Why?"

*Because I love him,* she thought. Yes, she'd told Gabriel that very thing, but now those words seemed to resonate even more deeply, had popped into her head so easily that she knew they were nothing more than the most basic truth in her world. When you loved somebody, you were there for them, no matter how difficult it might be, no matter what kind of dangers you might face.

Unfortunately, she had a feeling that her big brother might not want to hear that his sister had fallen for an Escobar warlock, even one who had offered some very valuable assistance when it came to the stolen de la Paz grimoires. Then again, Tony wasn't stupid; he'd probably be able to read between the lines and realize that Ava wasn't going along with Gabriel simply out of an over-whelming desire to see Central America.

"Because I told him I would," she said. "I want to help."

These altruistic motivations didn't seem to do much to convince her brother. "Help with what, exactly?" he demanded. "You have a pretty cool skill, Ava, but it's not the sort of thing that's going to help much in a fight between a couple of high-powered warlocks."

Since she'd thought pretty much the same thing herself, she wasn't quite sure how best to counter his argument. Still, she figured she'd better try. "Moral support, if nothing else. It's not as if anyone else in our clan would help him with this."

"Because it's not our fight."

"Well, it should be," she shot back. "I mean, it was an Escobar who killed Genoveva, wasn't it?"

Of course, Tony had an immediate answer to that question. "An Escobar warlock who was born in California and had nothing to do with the rest of his clan back in El Salvador. I'm pretty sure he didn't even know he had a couple of half-brothers down there. Everything that happened here in Santa Fe was a Simon thing, not an Escobar thing." A pause, and then Tony went on, his tone a little gentler, "I'm not stupid, Ava. I don't know exactly what's going on, but I've met Gabriel. Even I can tell he's charming and good-looking… and you're not exactly the most experienced person in the world when it comes to dealing with the opposite sex."

She winced. All right, her brother was only telling the truth, but she still felt as though she shouldn't take that kind of comment lying down.

"Gee, thanks."

"That wasn't a slam. It was just an observation."

"All right, maybe I do care about him," she said, knowing how desperate she sounded. "Isn't that all the more reason to make sure he doesn't go down there alone?"

A long pause. In fact, it was so long that Ava pulled the phone away from her ear and looked down at the screen, wondering if maybe the call had gotten disconnected or something. But no, Tony still seemed to be on the line.

When he spoke, he sounded more tired than anything else. "I can't stop you, Ava. And no, in case you were wondering, I'm not going to rat you out to Mom and Dad. They'd only try to stop you, and it's really none of their business."

"Um…thanks," she said. Although she'd hoped Tony would be cool enough to stay out of things, she hadn't known for sure. Sometimes, he had an overprotective streak that showed up at the weirdest times. Clearly, though, he'd decided she should be making her own decisions. If that meant marching into certain danger in the depths of the Salvadoran rainforest, then so be it.

"You can thank me when this is all over," he replied. There was a hint of grim humor to his voice, as if he was seeing the lighter side of the situation now that he'd made the decision to let her go her own way. "I'm sure Mom and Dad will want to kill me once they find out I knew what you were up to, but I guess the optimist in me is hoping it will all be fine and that they won't have anything too horrible to be angry with me about."

Ava hoped so, too. Her mind wanted to stray to the worst possible outcome—Gabriel hopelessly outmatched, the two of them dead at Vicénte's hands—but she pushed those terrible thoughts away as best she could. If she started this adventure thinking something awful was going to happen, then she was dooming them to failure before they even got stated. She needed to stay positive.

"It will all be okay," she said, so firmly that she almost believed it herself.

A chuckle. "I thought you were a psychic, not a seer."

"I'm not. I mean, I am. Anyway, this is just a feeling, nothing more." She hesitated, wondering whether she should say anything else. But she realized she needed to tell her brother something about her misty plans for the future, even if she and Gabriel hadn't made anything close to formal yet. Not that she was going to confess that she and the Escobar warlock had just made things physical. That would be too embarrassing. Still…. "And Tony?"

"Yes?"

A breath for courage, and she said, "If everything goes well, then…I might not be coming home."

"You're going to stay down in El Salvador."

It wasn't a question. "I will, if Gabriel wants me to. It's just…." She floundered for a few seconds, then went on, "No one really needs me here. But if he's successful, if he gets rid of Vicénte and is going to be the new head of the Escobar clan, then he's going to need all the support he can get."

This explanation only made Tony go quiet again. Ava made herself wait, knowing she needed to allow her brother to say what was on his mind, even if it might be difficult to hear.

Then he said, "I'm going to leave the Vicénte thing aside for now. I don't know Gabriel well enough to guess whether he's capable of killing his own brother or not. But when you talk about 'support' or 'help'—what kind of form do you think that help is going to take, considering your talent? Are you okay with looking into the minds of the Escobars to make sure they're all in line with the change in management, so to speak? I mean, I know you've always been careful about that sort of thing in the past. Would you be willing to spy for Gabriel?"

Sometimes Tony could be too damn perceptive. Ava held the phone to her ear, wondering how in the world she was supposed to answer that question. Of course, she hated the idea of being a spy, of stealing the truth from people's thoughts without them even realizing she'd done such a thing. On the other hand, she could understand why Gabriel might need that kind of intel, might need to know whether there was anyone in the clan planning to stir up trouble.

"I think we'd have a long talk about it before I did anything," she answered at last. "I mean, I can understand how my talent might get abused, and I obviously don't want that to happen. But…the Escobars have caused a lot of trouble in the world. Wouldn't it be nice to know they were no longer any kind of threat, that they finally had someone as their *primus* who wasn't out looking to crush other witch clans and possibly expose us to the rest of the world?"

Tony made a sound that might have been a sigh. "Yeah, I suppose. I guess I just want to make sure you're thinking of all the possibilities. I don't want you to get trapped in a situation you can't get out of."

"I won't be trapped," she said firmly. "Gabriel would never do that to me."

"You know him better than I do. Just…be careful, okay?"

That was a promise she'd have no trouble making. "I will. I'll be extra-super careful."

A bit of a chuckle, and then he said, "All right.

I guess…call me when you can. And call Mom and Dad once you know everything is okay."

"I will."

They made their goodbyes then, and Tony ended the call. Ava sat on the bed, staring at the phone in her hand. She wouldn't lie to herself and say she wasn't troubled by some of the concerns he'd raised, but at least he wasn't going to tell their parents about anything she was up to. They'd be angry to be left out of the loop, and yet she knew she couldn't afford to argue with them right now, or risk them dragging Miranda into all this. Much better to slip quietly away in the morning and present them all with a *fait accompli* once this was done.

There was another call she needed to make, though. She'd already made arrangements with the La Fonda, but she needed to talk to Elena, too, let her know what was going on.

Luckily, she picked up right away. "Hi, Ava."

Of course, her cousin had known who was calling, simply because no one else knew anything about Elena staying at the hotel downtown. "Hey, Elena. Everything still going okay?"

"Great. I went to the spa earlier and got my nails and toes done, and then afterward I had a drink in the bar and met a really cute guy."

Apparently, Elena was trying to make up for lost time. "Civilian, I hope."

"Obviously. He's in town for a conference about hospitality management. He runs a restaurant in San Antonio."

Well, that was a piece of good news. At least her cousin hadn't met anyone local, which might have complicated things a bit. "Sounds like you're having fun."

"I am. I feel like I've been let out of prison." A pause, and then Elena went on, "But you're probably not calling to talk to me about my social life."

"Um, not exactly. That is, Gabriel and I are going away tomorrow morning, but I wanted to let you know that I've paid for your room for ten days, so you're taken care of. I figure by then we'll have handled everything in El Salvador, and I should be back in town to wrap things up here."

"'Should'?" Elena echoed. "What if you're not back, or it takes longer than you think?"

"That's when you'll need to go talk to Miranda. Her house is at 116 Gonzales Street. She'll make sure you're taken care of."

"Yeah, like sending me right back to Las Vegas."

Ava supposed her cousin had a reason to have a jaundiced view of what might happen next, but she knew she had nothing to worry about. "No, Miranda would never do that. If she'd known what your family was doing to you, she would have put a stop to it. What I mean is that she'll find a permanent place for you to live, will make sure you're set up here in Santa Fe and that you're safe."

"You're sure?"

"Positive," Ava replied, hoping she wasn't making false promises. But no, she didn't pretend to be best friends with Miranda or anything, but she knew the *prima* wouldn't send Elena back to her family, would do her damnedest to make sure she was given a fighting chance to have a normal life despite her rocky beginnings. "And I'm sure she'll get you your money, too."

"'Money'?" her cousin repeated, sounding mystified. "What money?"

Oh, damn. Elena's father and grandmother really had done a number on her, had obviously hidden some of the most basic facts about being a Castillo from her. "Everyone in the Castillo family gets a stipend from the clan fund. It's a decent chunk—it's not like any of us have to have real jobs, but we do so we look like normal civilians, contributing to society. You should have started getting yours when you turned eighteen."

For a few seconds, Elena didn't say anything. Maybe she'd been shocked speechless. "You mean I've had money piling up for almost five years and no one told me anything about it?"

"I guess so," Ava replied. "Anyway, Miranda will be able to straighten it all out. Just know that you'll be taken care of, one way or another, even if…." She let the words trail off, wondering whether it would be terribly bad luck to say such a thing out loud.

"Even if what?" Elena asked.

Hoping that she wasn't putting some seriously bad juju out into the universe, Ava replied, "Even if I never make it back from El Salvador."

## 17

GABRIEL HAD HALFWAY BEEN EXPECTING TO get stopped by a group of Castillo witches and warlocks the next morning when he and Ava quietly left the house before seven o'clock, but no one was around to see them climb into the automated cab that would take them to the Railrunner station. Neither did anyone seem to take any particular notice of the two of them as they seated themselves on one of the train cars, their few pieces of luggage held close so they wouldn't get in the way of their fellow travelers, most of whom were only taking day trips to Albuquerque and therefore didn't have anything bulkier with them than a laptop case or a backpack.

So far, so good. He'd wished to make love to Ava again last night, but he knew they needed to be asleep early, needed to save their strength. Instead, he'd held her close as they slept in the big bed in the master bedroom, breathing in the sweet scent of her hair and praying that he wasn't leading her astray, wasn't making the wrong choice in having her come with him. There were so many things that could go wrong, so many chances for his plan to turn deadly. However, he didn't quite have the strength to send her away. He'd been on his own for so long that it was a blessed relief to have her by his side, to know she was taking this enormous risk purely out of love for him.

It was an odd sensation, to know that she loved him. To be honest, he wasn't sure whether anyone had loved him before her. Certainly not his brother, nor his long-dead father. From time to time, Gabriel had wondered if his mother ever thought of him with affection, the child she'd never known, but he didn't see how. She had probably spent the past twenty-five years trying to pretend she'd never lost those months out of her life, to forget that she'd born a child and yet knew nothing of him.

Because the train was crowded with civilians, he and Ava remained quiet for the most part. He already knew that she'd talked to her brother, had called Elena and let her know what to do if seven days should pass without any word. It sounded as though Ava had done whatever she could to make sure all the contingencies were planned for, and so at this point they had little to do except look ahead.

In his mind, Gabriel ran down the list of those he thought would be allies—Paz the healer, and her husband Luis, whose talent was seeing through solid objects, which could come in useful. And Antonio, the village carpenter, who could make a tree grow from a sapling to a towering giant in the span of just a minute, and Stephan, whose gift of causing the earth to shake might also be very handy.

Then there was Alessandro. To Gabriel, the null was the greatest element of uncertainty in his plans, simply because he'd always had a very difficult time guessing what was even going through the other man's mind. They were approximately the same age, Alessandro being not much more than a year older, and they had been friends when they were boys, as often happened in a clan amongst children close in age to one another. However, all that had changed when Alessandro's strange talent began to manifest. Even though Joaquin had possessed the null gift in addition to his other magical powers, the people in the village were wary of Alessandro, wary of the formidable talent that allowed him to blank out anyone else's magic. Luckily, his gift wasn't limitless; a person had to be within three or four meters of the man for his null powers to work. Still, he made people uncomfortable, and Gabriel was told to keep away from him.

That hadn't been terribly difficult to do, since there were plenty of other children in the village for him to play with. However, he had the distinct impression that Alessandro resented him ever since that time, perhaps especially so because of all the various magical powers that began to grow within the boy who had once been his friend.

But that was the past. Now, Gabriel could only hope that the null would be able to put those boyhood resentments behind him, especially if his younger sister was still in danger from Vicénte. Some might say that "danger" was a harsh word to use when it came to a man setting his sights on a woman so she might become his wife, and yet in this case, it was nothing more than the truth. His first wife had died because of his heavy hand, even if there were some who would rather say Yolanda's death had been the will of God and nothing else, and Gabriel feared that Lara might suffer the same fate if his brother took her as his bride.

No woman should have to fear for her life just because a man wanted her.

He glanced over at Ava, who sat next to him,

brown eyes lively with interest as she looked out the train window. There really wasn't all that much to see, but he supposed she was trying to make the best of the situation, attempting to look on all this as an adventure and not as a journey toward danger and an extremely uncertain outcome. His heart swelled with love for her, and he wished he could lean over and take her in his arms, tell her how much it meant to him that she would come with him to El Salvador, even when it meant leaving behind everything and everyone she had ever known.

Whatever else happened, he knew he must do his very best to prove he was worthy of her.

They reached Albuquerque and got off the Railrunner, then walked the block or so to the bus station. It was quite crowded, as was the bus they would be taking to Chihuahua; seeing all the seats filled with various passengers, he was glad that they'd been able to procure tickets at all.

Once they were seated, and once everyone else had climbed aboard, an attendant came by to inspect all their passports. Even though he'd used his false passport on multiple occasions and had never had anyone call out anything suspicious about it, Gabriel couldn't help but release a small breath of relief after it was handed back to him and the man checking the passengers' documents had moved down the cramped center aisle of the bus.

Ava also looked relieved, although she refrained from comment and only put her passport back in her purse. "How long is this going to take?" she murmured.

"Altogether, about nine hours," he replied. "We'll stop in El Paso for an hour break around noon, and so we'll get into Chihuahua at a little after five. There we'll stay until we take the high-speed train the next morning. We'll stay a night in Guatemala City as well, since we'll be getting in quite late. And from there, we'll drive into El Salvador."

He'd gone over this with her before, but he could tell she needed to hear their itinerary again now that they were actually on the road. It was fine, because repeating the details helped him to focus on their goal.

Two days from now, they would be in Pico Negro.

She nodded and offered him a smile, albeit one with a trace of worry around the edges. Gabriel couldn't fault her for that; he was sure that this had all become much more real to her, especially since the bus began to move in that moment, beginning its long journey into Mexico.

He reached over and laid his hand on top of hers, smiling back at her. There was little he could say, since there were far too many listening ears all around them, but he wanted her to know he was there, that he understood everything she was risking to come with him, that he loved her and wouldn't have wanted anyone else sitting beside him now.

Of course, she could have looked into his mind and seen all that—and much more besides —but he knew she didn't need to. Her fingers twined with his, and she glanced up at him through her thick eyelashes, her gaze warm and steady. That glance told him she knew very well what was in his heart.

After holding hands like that for a minute, however, she let go and retrieved her phone from her purse, then navigated to a reading app. It opened to a page that was clearly midway through whichever book she'd been reading when he appeared on the scene. He wondered what it was about, but he wouldn't try to peek; he'd hated it when he was a boy and engrossed in a book, only to have Vicénte come along and pluck it out of his hands so he could see what it was. If he were lucky, his brother would give it back at some point; other times, Vicénte had liked to amuse himself by discarding those books in the rainforest, where they were usually ruined by the damp before Gabriel could manage to locate them.

And because they couldn't talk safely here on

the bus, reading seemed like the best way to pass the time. Gabriel plucked his own phone out of his pocket, then opened the reading app and prepared to dive back into *Like Water for Chocolate*. He wondered if Ava had ever read the novel. If she had, then it would be fun to talk with her about it.

She looked over, saw that he planned to read as well, and smiled. This felt cozy, even though they were surrounded by strangers.

He hoped they would be able to have an entire lifetime to read together.

They only had to survive the next few days.

The hotel in Chihuahua was small but very clean, the sort of place that seemed to cater to local businesspeople and possibly a few adventurous Americans who didn't want to stay in something that felt like every other hotel on their own side of the border. Ava and Gabriel didn't have much luggage, and very little needed to be unpacked, so in less than fifteen minutes, the two of them were already back outside, wandering the streets and taking in the sights. Actually, for some reason, she hadn't expected Chihuahua to be such a big city, bigger than Albuquerque, with gorgeous baroque churches and tall mountains on the east side of town. She found herself wishing that they would be able to stay here longer than just the one night, even though she knew this was no simple pleasure trip, no jaunt into Mexico to see the sights.

Even so, it was fun to walk hand in hand with Gabriel and know they didn't need to worry about any local witches and warlocks detecting their presence, since he'd used his powers to hide their magical natures, just as Simon had done when he came to Santa Fe. Of course, their reason for being in Chihuahua was much more benign, but it was still a weight off her shoulders to know they wouldn't attract any witchy attention. They could pretend to be a couple of civilians and nothing more, could peek into the shops, could find a restaurant that had the most enticing aromas drifting from it, a place with a large outdoor dining area right there on the street, so they could get a table and watch the world—or at least this corner of it—go by.

A lot of the women they'd passed had cast admiring glances in Gabriel's direction, something Ava realized she'd have to get used to. She couldn't even really feel jealous, not when she knew he cared only about her and no one else. That was a strange feeling, to have someone so amazing in love with her. Maybe at some point she'd get used to it, but she wasn't so sure about that. After all, how could she possibly become jaded about being the object of Gabriel's affections?

There were men who stared at her as well, which in a way was even more uncomfortable. She wasn't used to being admired. In high school, she'd been chubby and awkward, and she'd been that way for most of college as well. A few boyfriends, but even they hadn't seemed all that impressed by her, had paid her a few off-hand compliments but never told her she was beautiful, had never gazed at her as though she was the most infinitely precious thing in the world the way Gabriel had.

He ordered a bottle of wine, a Malbec from Argentina. Ava wasn't going to argue; they were only a few blocks from their hotel, and their train didn't leave until nine-twenty the next morning. That gave them plenty of time to recover from any debauchery they might get up to this evening… and she hoped there might be some, at least just a little. The night before, they'd slept in each other's arms but hadn't done anything else, mostly because they'd had to be out of the house so early. Or at least, she hoped their seven o'clock departure was the reason why he hadn't made any overtures.

She couldn't make much sense of the restaurant's menu; she'd taken French in high school, not Spanish. As Gabriel offered to order for her and she gratefully accepted, she realized she would be at a disadvantage down in Pico Negro. He spoke such good English, she'd sort of failed to realize that not all of the Escobars were probably that fluent.

*Then you'll learn,* she told herself, even as she had to acknowledge the irony of someone named Castillo not being able to speak Spanish. True, the family had been in New Mexico for centuries, and many of her family members had never bothered to learn the language of their ancestors, but now Ava wished she'd taken the time. *At least you took French, and they're both romance languages. A lot of the roots are the same. No biggie.*

Still, it couldn't hurt to get a feel for the sort of obstacles she might be facing. "Do a lot of the people where you come from speak English?" she asked, hoping she sounded somewhat casual. And of course she'd been careful not to give the exact name of his village; they might still be hundreds and hundreds of miles away from Pico Negro, but it never hurt to be safe.

"Some," he replied, then took a sip of his Malbec. "Not everyone, of course. Paz speaks a little, and Alessandro and his sister are quite good at it."

"Really?" Ava responded, a little surprised that the null would have taken the time to learn a language he probably didn't need to use all that much.

"Yes. His father also had satellite television, so they learned from that, just as I did. I think Alessandro was fascinated by all the places he saw on the TV, places very far away from everything we all knew."

"You make it sound as if you know him pretty well," she remarked.

"We were friends as children. Later...not as much."

Gabriel didn't seem inclined to elaborate on that statement, and Ava decided it was probably better not to push him, especially here in a crowded restaurant. She wondered, though, what it was that had driven the two of them apart. The simple drifting away that often happened as people grew up and their interests changed, or something else, some kind of actual dispute?

Whatever it was, she hoped it wouldn't prevent Alessandro from helping them defeat Vicénte. Because honestly, she couldn't quite see how all this was going to work if Alessandro remained loyal to his *primus*.

But since she didn't want to ruin this warm, rosy-hued evening with any thoughts of possible defeat, she only said, "I'm sorry to hear that," and reached for her glass of wine.

Gabriel gave the slightest of shrugs. If he was

concerned, his worry didn't show in his expression or his posture. Like her, he lifted the glass before him and took a sip. "It is how these things often go. But enough of that. You like Chihuahua?"

"Yes," she replied. "It's beautiful. Did you come through here on your way to Albuquerque?"

He nodded. "I did, although I only stayed the one night, just as we are doing. I wish we had the leisure to stay longer, but…."

The words drifted off; clearly, he didn't intend to say anything else. And really, what else could he say on the topic? Although Ava had the impression that the Mexican people tended to eat dinner late, even at a little past six-thirty, this outdoor dining area was fairly crowded, certainly not the sort of place where they could discuss any of the real particulars of their reason for being here in the first place.

"Maybe we can visit again someday," she said lightly.

Again, he only lifted his shoulders. Probably he was thinking that if he was successful and became the Escobars' new *primus,* he wouldn't have much time for leisure or travel. Maybe not, although his ability to mask their magical natures took away their biggest impediment to venturing beyond the borders of Escobar territory. It was a lot easier to move around when the *primas* of other witch clans couldn't tell when you crossed into their lands.

Of course, it sounded as though this particular gift wouldn't help much when it came to shielding them from Vicénte. He'd be able to know they were in Pico Negro; Gabriel's masking abilities only went so far. A little shiver worked its way down Ava's spine, and she sipped some more of her wine.

"Don't be worried," Gabriel said. "I know what I'm doing, how I need to handle this."

"I know," she replied. "That is, I can tell you're ready. It's just…your brother scares me."

His expression softened, and he set down his glass of wine so he could reach across the table and gently stroke her fingers. His own hand was warm and strong, and intensely reassuring. Almost at once, she felt herself begin to relax. "I can't blame you for that," he said. "Especially since you've been able to see him through my own eyes. I have no doubt that he seemed like the boogeyman to my younger self."

"Something like that," Ava said, managing a bit of a chuckle. How Gabriel had known almost exactly what she was thinking, she wasn't sure. He didn't have her talent, so it wasn't as though he'd read her mind.

*But he's coming to know you,* she thought then. *Know your reactions, know how you look at things. He doesn't have to be a mind reader to do that...just someone who's very perceptive.*

"With any luck, you will not have very much contact with him," Gabriel said then. "At least, I will do my best to make sure that is how things will work out. This is between him and me, and I certainly don't want you to be a part of that fight."

Those words should have reassured her, but Ava didn't want him to think that she was content to stand on the sidelines and meekly wait to see who emerged the victor in this particular conflict. True, her talent didn't exactly lend itself to a full-on magical battle, and yet she hoped there might be something she could do to help.

"We'll see," she said, her tone noncommittal.

That response seemed to be enough to tell him that she really didn't want to discuss it anymore, because Gabriel abruptly changed the subject, going on to talk about other places he'd visited in Mexico, making it sound as if they were merely normal tourists who were trying to explore more of this part of the world. Of course, Ava knew exactly what he was doing, but she was glad. Their conversation about Vicénte had been couched in the most vague and casual of terms, which should have been safe enough, but they'd begun to tread on ground that could be dangerous even so.

The food was marvelous, and as the evening wore on, she found herself relaxing more, although she guessed the reduction in tension might have been due to the wine she drank. Afterward, they walked the streets some more, paused in a picturesque square where a man not much older than Ava herself played flamenco guitar and a girl who looked as though she must still be in high school danced along. She was slim and graceful and elegant, all the things Ava knew she'd never been when she was that age. Gabriel placed several large bills in the man's guitar case before they moved on, heading back to the hotel.

"I wish we could stay here," she said as they approached the building, and he glanced down at her, expression somehow not all that surprised.

"It is a beautiful place," he agreed. "But Pico Negro is beautiful as well, only in a different way."

She was a little surprised that he'd risked saying the name of the village, although, to be fair, there was no one else around to overhear them. "I suppose it is," she said. "But it's not like this, is it?"

"No." He paused for a moment, then bent to kiss her gently on the cheek. "It is quite different. But there are people in my village who are talented musicians, though, those who play when we gather for feast days and festivals. You mustn't think it is all tragedy, all dark times. We laugh and play and love, just like anyone else."

His hands crept into hers and he pulled her

close, this time touching his lips to hers. A thrill went through her, and she tasted him, savoring the sweetness of wine and the heat of the spices they'd eaten at dinner. "But you're not like anyone else I've ever met, Gabriel," she whispered. "You're amazing."

"As are you, my love." He kissed her again, his fingers tightening against her skin. "But I think we should go upstairs."

Oh, yes. She knew they wouldn't have to worry about sleeping chastely next to each other tonight, not with the way he was looking at her. Hands still clasped together, they made their way into the hotel and then up the graceful curved staircase to the second floor where their room was located. Once they were inside with the door safely closed behind them, they kissed once more, then set about tearing off each other's clothing. On to the bed, where Gabriel pushed her down against the covers, kissing her from the base of her throat, all the way down…down….

She moaned loudly, not even caring whether the people in the room next to theirs could hear. Maybe not; these adobe walls seemed very thick.

That was the first orgasm of the night, but definitely not the last. They made love to each other, touching and tasting, fingers stroking against warm bare skin, until Ava finally lost count of all the times he brought her to climax, until she at last collapsed in her lover's arms, letting him hold her, letting sweet oblivion wash away all her worries, all her doubts.

Perhaps a reckoning was coming very soon. But for now, she was content.

## 18

THIS TRAIN WAS NOWHERE NEAR AS luxurious as the high-speed one that had taken them from Chihuahua to Mexico City, but Gabriel was glad of it nonetheless, glad that this journey would be coming to an end soon enough. In a way, it was a journey that had started more than six months earlier in that anonymous hotel room in Guatemala, the one where Vicénte and the Escobar elders had dumped him so unceremoniously. He hadn't known it yet—hadn't even remembered who he was—but it was on that day that the long, laborious process of coming back to himself had truly begun.

Ava sat next to the window, staring out at the lush, tropical landscape that passed by at a leisurely hundred kilometers per hour. They had sleeping accommodations in one of the cars farther back on the train, but for this early portion of the trip, it was more comfortable to be out here in one of the cars with reclining seats and access to snacks and drinks.

If she was nervous, he could see no sign of it. Possibly their activities of the night before had been enough to relax her. For himself, Gabriel could feel nothing but an overwhelming sense of well-being. Making love to Ava was more satisfying than he had ever imagined such a thing could be. There had been other women, but none of them had answered the need in his soul, the emptiness that lived in the heart of a warlock and which eternally sought the one who would be his true match, the one person who would be at his side for the rest of his life.

In Ava, he had found that person. She was more precious to him than anything else in the world.

Which, he supposed, begged the question as to why he was leading her into such peril. He would not fool himself into believing that they did not face ever-increasing danger the closer they got to Pico Negro. But Ava had insisted on coming along, and he did not possess the courage to dissuade her from this path. This would be easier, knowing she was there.

After a few minutes, she once more lost herself in reading, which made him glad. She should be able to escape for this time, to do her best to forget about what faced them up ahead in El Salvador. However, Gabriel knew he would not do the same, because he needed to think.

Most of the traffic in and out of San Matías, the civilian village closest to Pico Negro, came from the south and west, from San Salvador and some of the other towns and cities in that part of the country. However, he and Ava would travel to Pico Negro from the north, across the border from Honduras. That was rough terrain to traverse, although there were several roads—little more than tracks through the rainforest—that would get them close enough. At the point where the road failed, they would have to cover the last several miles on foot.

He hoped she would be up to the journey. She had already told him she was not overly athletic, and he knew she had no experience of the intense heat and humidity of the equatorial region that was his home. Still, it made the most sense to come in that way, simply because Vicénte wouldn't be expecting anyone to enter Pico Negro from that side. After all, the village was not on any map. You had to know it was there to even bother to travel in that direction.

Also, the house where Alessandro lived with his mother and sister was on the north side of the hidden settlement, a little bit beyond the actual borders of Pico Negro itself. Gabriel hoped that he and Ava would be able to approach the family and make their case before anyone else in the village—including Vicénte—even knew they were there. With Alessandro on their side, their chances of success were much, much greater.

Of course, that outcome was very much a question mark. Although Gabriel knew that the null had no love for the *primus,* it was difficult to say whether his resentment would be great enough to make him embark on such a dangerous course. For all he knew, Vicénte had already taken Lara as his wife, whether or not she was willing. If that had happened, then Alessandro most certainly would not lift a hand against his brother-in-law, no matter how much he might secretly despise him for what he had done to his sister.

"Everything okay?" Ava asked, and Gabriel glanced over to see her watching him closely, her phone lying neglected on her lap.

"Of course it is," he said, doing his best to smile. "Why wouldn't it be?"

"Because you were frowning…scowling, really."

Had he been? He almost wanted to reach up to touch his forehead, just to see whether his worries had engraved a line between his brows, but he resisted the urge. "I suppose I was thinking of what lies ahead for us. Making plans."

This explanation didn't seem to reassure her all that much. "So you are worried."

"No," he responded at once. He didn't want Ava to think he was troubled about what waited for them at journey's end. Of course he was, but hoped she would believe he had everything under control and that there was no reason to worry. "Just thinking of contingencies. That's all. I didn't mean to frown."

Her left hand touched his right where it rested on his thigh. "Okay." She released a breath and looked over at the window again, although there wasn't much to see except mile after mile of trees in various shapes and sizes, everything brilliantly green except the few small villages that broke up the landscape from time to time. Although she didn't say anything else, only squeezed his hand gently, he thought he could guess what was going through her mind—that this all would have been so much easier if he could have simply teleported the two of them right into Vicénte's house and bypassed all this weary traveling.

Well, he couldn't argue with that. On the other hand, he would not have wished to give up the night they had shared in Chihuahua—there had been something magical about the way their bodies joined, about the pleasure they gave and took in one long, languorous, passionate dance. In fact, he could feel himself stir now, just remembering the sweet taste of her flesh, and he did what he could to push the arousal away. There was certainly nothing they could do about it here on the train, and once they reached Guatemala City, they would have more important matters to occupy themselves.

But no, that wasn't quite right. He couldn't think of many things that were more important than making love to Ava. However, this situation with Vicénte was far more pressing. Once his brother was handled—one way or another, although Gabriel's mind shied away from what he guessed could be the only real outcome of their confrontation—then he and Ava would have the rest of their lives to love one another, to continue to strengthen the bond they shared.

Which was why he knew his mind would continue to work away at the problem, to do its best to see whether he could come up with a plan that was truly foolproof.

Unfortunately, he suspected that such a thing didn't actually exist.

Ava wished she could have looked forward to the final leg of their journey with a proper spirit of adventure—after all, she'd never thought she'd have an opportunity to go four-wheeling in the

Salvadoran rainforest—but the hard bed in their sleeper car had given her a crick in the neck, and she felt sticky and not quite herself after not being able to take her usual morning shower.

*Some world adventurer you are,* she scolded herself. *Don't you have bigger things to worry about besides not getting a shower?*

Probably. She had a feeling that she was focusing on her physical discomforts because that seemed a lot safer than thinking about what waited for them in Pico Negro. The Jeep they'd rented in Guatemala City had great air conditioning, thank God...but the Jeep would only get them so far. After that, they'd have to go on foot. And since the few blocks they'd walked from the train station to the car rental agency told her that it was insanely hot and humid here, even worse than New Orleans had been, she guessed that the walk through the rainforest wasn't going to be much fun.

At least she'd brought sturdy hiking boots and her one and only pair of shorts, ones she'd bought on a whim when she saw them on sale. Maybe she looked a little too much like the stereotypical American adventurer in her green cargo shorts and tan tank top and brown boots, but these were the only clothes she had that seemed remotely suitable for the climate.

*Look on the bright side,* she told herself. *You*

*could've been really stupid and brought a pith helmet.*

No, she hadn't been that clueless, although she did have a floppy canvas hat in approximately the same sage green color as her shorts. She figured it would help shield her eyes from the sun, and maybe keep some sweat from dripping into her eyes.

In the driver's seat, Gabriel looked effortlessly cool and comfortable in a white T-shirt and tan cargo pants. And since the T-shirt allowed her to watch his biceps bulge as he maneuvered the Jeep down the rutted highway they were currently following, she wasn't about to complain too much about the bumpiness of the ride.

"I thought Pico Negro was out in some sort of trackless wilderness," she remarked. "This looks like a normal enough highway to me."

"It is," he replied. "And we'll take it as far as we can. If we continued to follow the road, it would lead us into San Matías, the closest village to Pico Negro. But of course we don't want to go to San Matías, for it's far too likely that someone there would spot us and recognize me. In about five more miles, we'll cut off on a forest track and take it to where it dead-ends. From there, it's about three miles to Pico Negro. Not far at all."

No, she supposed a three-mile hike wasn't that big a deal when you were a perfect physical specimen like Gabriel. Ava tried to reassure herself by remembering that she'd spent the last year walking pretty much everywhere she could, but she knew that walking on city sidewalks wasn't exactly the same thing as hiking through the rainforest in ninety-five-degree heat with ninety-five-percent humidity.

*You can do it,* she thought. *You can, because you have to.*

Hopefully, there wouldn't be horrible bugs. She could handle crazy birds and chattering monkeys and even snakes, but enormous tropical insects would be enough to send her screaming into the night. Maybe she was brave about some things; bugs weren't one of them. In fact, she'd almost worn jeans, just because she thought it might be better to have her legs covered. However, dying of heat stroke seemed a more likely prospect than being attacked by hordes of blood-sucking insects, so she'd compromised and worn her cargo shorts, which were nearly knee-length anyway.

Gabriel wore a small smile, as if he'd hazarded a guess as to what might be going through her mind. "I have many tricks in my arsenal," he remarked, even as he slowed to turn off onto a poorly marked track that cut away from the narrow highway. "One of them is repelling any insects within a twenty-yard radius."

Was he teasing her? "Seriously?"

"Seriously." The smile stretched into a grin, and he reached over and patted her on the leg before placing his hand back on the steering wheel again. "I learned how to do it one year when the mosquitos were particularly bad. Ever since then, my meals have been blessedly untroubled by flies."

Ava chuckled, amused despite herself. "Well, that's good to know. And handy. Guess I'll keep you around."

The glance he sent her then was warm, admiring, reminding her of the intimate moments they'd shared...and clearly looking forward to more. "Good. I would like you to keep me around."

After that exchange, though, he had to return his attention to the road...track...barely marked trail, actually. She clung to the handle bolted to the ceiling of their vehicle and was glad of the meager breakfast she'd eaten. Normally, she wouldn't say she was prone to motion sickness, but this muddy, overgrown path through the rainforest had the Jeep bouncing around like a dinghy in a hurricane. Possibly, a few sips of water would have helped her stomach. Unfortunately, she didn't dare let go of the "Jesus handle" she clung to, and even if she had managed to pick up the bottle in the cupholder next to her and get the cap off, she probably would have gotten water up her nose just by trying to take a drink right as the vehicle hit another rut or rock.

Eventually, though, Gabriel began to slow down, crawling along at barely four or five miles an hour, the Jeep's oversized tires grinding their way through the thick, gluey mud. At last, they stopped where the trail ended and an unending thicket of tall trees blocked the way.

"Here we are," he said. "Have some water now. We should drink some before we start walking."

That sounded like a good idea, even though all the bouncing around had made Ava realize she needed to pee. No way would she go out here, though—she'd hold it for as long as she needed to.

They both drank until their water bottles were nearly empty, and then he grabbed them some more out of the pallet he'd stowed on the back seat. He'd also put together a backpack of their most vital items—toothbrushes, toothpaste, a change of clothes, their phones and passports. Of course, there had been no way they would be able to carry their luggage with them on this hike, so they'd pared down to the absolute essentials.

A wall of damp heat seemed to hit Ava the second she stepped out of the Jeep. She took a deep gulp of air, trying to acclimate, but that only seemed to make matters worse, as if she'd swallowed a mouthful of the same black mud that was stuck to their tires.

"It's all right," Gabriel said. He touched her arm, expression concerned but also encouraging. "You'll get used to it."

*Sure I will,* she thought, but she only nodded. No way was she going to hold him back by being a wimp. It was only a little heat and humidity, after all. She gave him a thumbs-up and said, "I'm good."

A quick kiss on her cheek. "Then let's get going."

He began to walk, and she had no choice but to follow. As they went, she realized there actually was a path through the trees and the thick under-growth, although one she doubted she would have ever noticed on her own. Presumably, the residents of Pico Negro must come this way from time to time, even if she guessed that most of the local foot traffic went the other way, down into San Matías.

Birds with brilliant plumage fluttered over-head, squawking at the interlopers. Off in the distance, Ava thought she heard the shrill cackling of monkeys, although they seemed to be keeping their distance. Were they simply wary of humans, or was this more of Gabriel's magic, keeping anything that might be a threat at a safe distance?

In the end, it probably didn't matter. What

mattered was that they were able to keep moving forward without interference, his stride strong but not too swift so she'd be able to keep up with him. And even though she'd doubted his reassurances at the time, it seemed that he'd been right about getting used to the moist, hot air. It was still extremely uncomfortable, but at least she felt as if she was breathing more or less normally, didn't feel as though she was about to pass out at any minute.

She didn't have a watch, which was probably just as well. Otherwise, she would have been far too tempted to keep glancing down at it, trying to see how much time had passed, doing her best to gauge how much ground had been covered in each fifteen minutes, or twenty, or a half hour.

From time to time, Gabriel would pause long enough to glance back at her and make sure she was still soldiering along. Each time, she'd give him an encouraging smile, even though her breathing was getting more and more labored and her tank top felt as if someone had dumped a bucket of hot water on her. Right then, she would have killed for an air-conditioned room and an iced tea. No, scratch that—a mango margarita, one she could sip slowly while cabana boys cooled her down with waving palm fronds.

Too bad that the Salvadoran rainforest seemed notably bereft of cabana boys. Besides, she didn't really need anyone other than Gabriel. Although maybe if she could get him to stand over her with a palm frond, margarita at the ready....

Suddenly, he came to a halt, so abruptly that she almost collided with him. He put one hand on her wrist and another to his lips, indicating that she needed to remain quiet. Puzzled, she stared up at him.

He pointed somewhere ahead of them, then inched forward a step or two, taking obvious care not to step on anything that might make noise. Her heart, which was already beating quickly, thanks to the way she'd been exerting herself, seemed to speed up a little. Was there some kind of wild animal ahead, something that would surely attack them if they made the slightest sound?

Still mystified, she followed him, stepping where he'd stepped so she wouldn't risk treading on a twig that might snap or some rocks that could knock against one another. As she watched, he reached out with one hand to gently move aside the oversized leaves of a plant that looked a little like the fiddle-leaf fig her mother was so proud of and which had a prominent place in her living room. Again, he pointed, and Ava realized what it was that had caught his attention.

Just beyond the section of path where they stood, there was a small clearing, one with several fallen trees that almost but didn't quite block the way. Sitting on one of those trees was a woman— a girl, really, probably a few years younger than Ava herself, and extremely pretty, with long, wavy black hair, big dark eyes, and delicate, graceful features. Even from more than ten yards away, she could tell the girl was crying, slender shoulders shaking as she sat there, something utterly hopeless about her posture.

A few feet away from the girl stood a man, someone who looked to be around Gabriel's age, maybe a little older. He was talking to her in rapid-fire Spanish, gesticulating to punctuate whatever point he was obviously trying to get across. Some vague similarity in their appearance made Ava wonder if they were related, although the man's looks were much more rugged, more sharply etched. Heavy black tribal-style tattoos decorated his forearms, and he looked like the sort of person she probably wouldn't want to get in a confrontation with.

However, the girl didn't seem put off by him. She said something in Spanish, hands spread wide in a gesture of hopelessness, and the man came over to sit down next to her on the fallen tree. He took one of her hands in his, patting it as if to comfort her, and she blinked teary eyes and attempted a very tremulous smile.

More than anything, Ava wanted to ask who

these people were, but she couldn't risk being overheard. True, the couple—brother and sister? —seemed pretty preoccupied. Even so, she doubted Gabriel would be too happy with her if she gave away their position.

No, it seemed as though the only option the two of them had was to wait here and hope the strangers would end their conversation sooner rather than later. Probably they were Escobars, because who else would be out here? They were just far enough away that she couldn't sense whether they were witch-kind or not, but she doubted Gabriel would be hanging back the way he currently was if it had been just a couple of ordinary civilians blocking their path.

Something about his posture changed subtly; his shoulders squared a bit, and his chin went up. From what Ava could tell, it seemed as if he'd reached a decision of some kind or another, although she couldn't guess what that might be. He glanced back at her, then mouthed rather than said, *Follow my lead. Don't be afraid.*

*Don't be afraid?* What the—?

Before she could make any kind of protest, whether spoken or not, he'd pushed aside the large plant that had shielded them and stepped forward, advancing into the clearing. Ava followed him, praying he knew what he was doing.

The young woman who had been sitting on

the fallen tree sprang to her feet, eyes widening, one hand gripping a fold of the brightly colored tiered skirt she wore. She looked like she'd just seen a ghost. Her companion startled, but then his dark eyes narrowed, and his hands clenched into fists.

"Hello, Lara, Alessandro," Gabriel said, as calmly as though they'd just bumped into each other in the local Starbucks. "I've returned."

## 19

UNTIL HE STEPPED INTO THE CLEARING, Gabriel honestly hadn't been sure what he intended to do. Some part of him—the more cautious, measured part—had advised him to wait, telling him that the null and his sister couldn't stay here forever. Once they were gone, he and Ava would have been free to continue on their route.

On the other hand, it seemed as though fate —or God, or Providence—had dropped the very person he needed to talk to directly into his lap, so to speak. Wouldn't it be better to have such a conversation here in this very private place, a location where they were unlikely to be disturbed?

Still, confronting them so openly was a calculated risk. Alessandro couldn't hurt him, precisely, but he could immediately block Gabriel's and Ava's powers, making the encounter much more complicated.

To his surprise, Lara was actually the first to speak. She reached up to wipe the tears away from her eyes, then brushed her damp fingers on her skirt. "G-Gabriel? But we thought—that is, the elders—"

"Yes, the elders took my powers away," he cut in, using English so Ava would be able to understand what they were saying. He realized it was much easier to utter those words now that they were no longer the truth of his existence. "But, thanks to Ava here—and her Castillo clan—I now have them back."

Alessandro slowly unclenched his fists. Otherwise, he didn't move, only remained where he stood, cold dark gaze moving to Ava for a moment before returning to Gabriel. She flinched slightly, as if she'd expected him to use his null powers then and there, but she stood her ground as well. "I can tell this is true," he said quietly, also speaking in English. Out of respect for Gabriel's companion, or merely because he wanted to prove that conducting this discussion in something other than his native tongue was no great hardship? Difficult to say for sure, and Gabriel supposed it didn't really matter one way or another. "Because when the elders took you away from here, there was no trace of your power left, no way to tell that you had once been a warlock. Now I can sense your powers again, strong as they ever were." He looked over at Ava. "How is this possible?"

"Let's just say that the people in the Castillo clan have some very interesting magical gifts," she replied, both her expression and tone almost too neutral. Clearly, she had no intention of telling the null exactly how they'd been able to return Gabriel's powers to him.

"It would seem so," Alessandro said. He crossed his arms, clearly showing off the heavy tattoos he'd gotten in San Salvador when he'd turned nineteen, tattoos that had horrified his mother to no end. As a rule, witches and wizards didn't indulge in any kind of body modifications, mostly because they attracted attention, and it was better to be as inconspicuous as possible. Now addressing Gabriel, he went on, "I'm surprised you would come back here, though. It would have been smarter to stay away."

"Possibly," he admitted. "And yet, I realized I couldn't abandon my clan in such a way."

This statement made Alessandro lift an ironic eyebrow. "I would not call it 'abandonment,' not when the elders forcibly removed you."

He had a point. Gabriel shrugged and said, "All right, let's say it is more that I worried about the future of this clan and the people in it." He shifted slightly so he could meet Lara's anxious, half-fearful gaze. "What is troubling you?" Because while he had been able to tell that brother and sister were sharing some kind of heated exchange, it had been conducted in lowered voices, as if they feared being overheard even all the way out here. He hadn't been able to hear exactly what they were saying…although he thought he could guess at the topic of their discussion.

Lara's gaze shifted toward the vines that crept across the clearing, blurring the path. "I think you probably know, Gabriel."

"Was it Vicénte?"

"Of course it was," Alessandro said. His jaw tightened, and once again his hands wanted to clench themselves into fists, although he shoved them into his pockets once he realized what he was doing. "We have been doing our best to keep him at bay, to tell him that Lara should not be married before her twenty-first birthday, but—"

"But my birthday is next week," she finished for him. The tears were gone now and had left little trace behind. Truly, she was a lovely woman, although too delicate for his taste. He preferred Ava's lush mouth and warm dark eyes, was not particularly interested in the type of female who looked as though she would break if he should kiss her too fiercely.

A little chill went through him as he thought that his brother would like precisely that sort of woman, someone it would be easy for him to dominate.

"And so Vicénte has been putting pressure on you," Gabriel said, and Lara nodded. Next to him, Ava pressed her lips together, obviously troubled, but she remained silent.

"Yes," Alessandro said. "Lara had a crazy notion to run away, but I told her that Vicénte would only pursue her, and treat her that much worse once he found her."

"So, what were you going to do?" It seemed they did not have many options, unfortunately, making Gabriel think that perhaps Alessandro and his sister might be more inclined to listen to his suggestion now that they were truly desperate.

"I was trying to tell her that it would be better to marry Vicénte, that I would do what I could to protect her."

This sounded very noble, but Gabriel knew that the null wouldn't be able to do any such a thing. Not really. Yes, technically speaking, Alessandro could block Vicénte's powers just as easily as he could block those of anyone else, and yet such an act would only prove that he wasn't loyal to his *primus*. Also, just like any other warlock, Alessandro had his limits. He could use his gift to take away Vicénte's magic…and possibly that of the elders as well…but he couldn't block the magic of every single witch and warlock in the Escobar clan.

"There is no protection from Vicénte, I fear," Gabriel said then, and Lara's pretty features grew even more taut with worry, while Alessandro's posture became stiff and wary. "He will do what he wants, without regard for the good of this clan or the safety of the people in it."

It seemed telling that neither brother nor sister bothered to argue with this statement, to say that no, Vicénte was not like that. They knew better, even if Alessandro probably would never admit such a thing out loud.

Lara glanced from her brother over to Gabriel. When she spoke, she sounded frustrated but also plaintive, almost desperate. "Then what are we supposed to do? Did you travel all this way only to tell us it's hopeless?"

"No," he said. "Not at all. I came here because I want to be *primus* of this clan. With your help, Alessandro, I can make that happen."

A stunned silence followed this announcement. Ava shot him a worried look, as though trying to decide whether or not it had been a good thing for him to make such a bold declaration of his intentions.

Then Alessandro laughed, a laugh with no real humor in it. "Oh, is that all? I am beginning to wonder whether losing your powers made you a little bit *loco*."

"I'm not crazy," Gabriel said calmly. "It's common knowledge that my magic is stronger than my brother's. All I need is some assistance to make sure the elders don't interfere."

"Oh, is that all?" Now a trace of amusement found its way into Alessandro's expression, although he still seemed more stunned by Gabriel's announcement than anything else. "And why would I help you? I am already a valuable ally to your brother. I don't need your help to gain more status in this clan."

Because he'd been expecting a question something like this, Gabriel didn't even blink. "You should help me because I will make sure that your sister isn't forced into a marriage she doesn't want. You should help me because I want only for this clan to thrive and prosper, not to be dragged into a mad quest for power that will only bring the wrath of both the witching and the nonmagical world down upon us."

Alessandro was quiet for a moment, brow furrowed. It seemed that he'd guessed at some of

Vicénte's motivations; the null was many things, but stupid wasn't one of them. No doubt, he'd suspected the grimoires had been brought here for a greater purpose than merely expanding the *primus's* personal library. He looked at his younger sister, who was biting her lip in worry, then pulled in a breath.

"I wish I could tell you that you're wrong," he said, his tone heavy. "But he was driven almost mad with anger when the grimoires burned. Ever since then, he's been sending members of our clan out into the world, having them look for books and other items that might help him get back the chance at power he'd lost...thanks to you."

Although Gabriel had suspected such a thing, having those suspicions confirmed only made a cold dread awaken inside him. A shiver walked its way down his spine, despite the stifling heat of the rainforest around them. "Has he found anything?"

"Not yet...but not for lack of trying."

One piece of good news at least. Voice growing more urgent, he said, "Then this is the perfect time to step in, before he does something that can't be undone. You know what's at risk. Like any other witch clan, our safety has come from secrecy. If Vicénte destroys that secrecy, the world will not deal kindly with us."

Again, Alessandro went quiet. Both Lara and Ava were silent as well, as if they knew that all this hinged on the null's cooperation. With him, there would be a fighting chance to remove Vicénte as *primus*. Otherwise....

When the silence went on for too long, though, Gabriel found himself compelled to speak once again. "You know that the tradition is to have the clan run by its strongest warlock. My father allowed Vicénte to be in charge because I was far too young when he left. If he'd known I would be the most powerful of his sons, then he would have wanted me to assume the role of *primus*. The Escobar clan deserves to have a leader who will be strong."

Alessandro shook his head. "And? Vicénte prides himself on his strength. We need more than mere strength. We need wisdom as well. Can you truly say you can offer us such a thing? Because I am not sure it was entirely wise for you to come here, Gabriel. You should have stayed in Castillo territory—clearly, they were willing to offer you help, which means you probably would have been accepted there."

"Does this mean you are saying no?" Gabriel forced himself to speak those words, difficult as they might be. Better to know the worst and plan from there, rather than keep stringing this along.

"I am not saying anything," Alessandro replied. "There are many reasons why I would prefer to have someone else as *primus*, rather than

Vicénte…but you haven't said yet exactly what it is you plan to do."

Should he state the bald truth and hope for the best? It almost seemed as if the null was doing his best to draw him out, to make Gabriel admit that his greatest chance of success hinged on Alessandro's assistance.

"That depends on a great many things," he said. "One of which is your help. If I have it, then this will not be as difficult to accomplish as I feared."

"And if I don't help you?"

"Well, then"—Gabriel shrugged, hoping he still looked calm and assured, and utterly untroubled by the other warlock's insinuation—"I suppose I will have to find another way."

Alessandro smiled. "What if there is no other way?"

And then he felt it—a horrible emptiness inside, the spark of his magic gone as if it had never been. Since his powers had been so recently restored to him, he experienced their loss that much more, like a sudden punch to his gut.

Beside him, Ava gasped, and Gabriel realized the null must have used his terrible talent to take away her magic as well. Face white, she stared at Alessandro.

"Why…?" she said, voice hardly above a whisper. Gabriel reached over and took her hand, felt how cold her fingers were, even though her tank top was soaked with sweat.

"Because I want you to know," the null replied. "I want you to understand what this feels like, to know what it is to have your magic taken away. This is the gift I command, the one that your lover seeks to use in his revenge against his brother."

"'Sandro, stop it," Lara commanded, hands wrapping around her brother's arm as though her pleading touch would be enough to make him see reason. "They haven't done anything to you."

He stared down at her, expression hard. "No, but they are putting me at risk by asking such a thing...putting you at risk as well. You've already seen what Vicénte does to traitors."

"And what will he do to me when I am his wife?" she countered. "We all know what happened to Yolanda. I don't want that to be me, Alessandro, but it will be. You can't stop Vicénte alone...but you and Gabriel working together could."

The null let out a breath, gaze fixed on his sister's pleading face. Gabriel knew better than to speak; all he could do was wait to see if Lara's argument had gotten through to him at all, or whether he would continue to allow himself to be ruled by his fear of the *primus*.

At last, Alessandro turned, dark eyes narrowed

in thought, tension clear in every line of his body. He did not appreciate being forced to this pass, no, not at all. Tone flat, he said, "You will have to kill him, you know."

That particular eventuality had already passed through Gabriel's mind more than once. He did not much like having to consider such a thing, but he had acknowledged the possibility and moved past it, resolve as strong as ever.

"I hope it does not come to that," he said, voice calm. There was no need for the null to know anything of his own private fears or worries. "I still hope that Vicénte will see reason."

"You and I both know that Vicénte is not a reasonable person," Alessandro responded. There was no particular rancor in his tone, only an acknowledgment of established fact. "The only reason he did not kill you before was that the elders persuaded him it was better to leave you alive, and harmless. If you confront him once again, he will do his best to make sure you are dead."

Gabriel couldn't quite allow himself to shrug, although he did tilt his head to one side, as if carefully considering the null's words. "In which case, one could say that any actions I take against him would be purely in self-defense. And that is a very different matter from outright murder."

Now Alessandro let out a reluctant chuckle. "I

suppose you can twist the situation any way you like in order to make it more appealing to you. Whatever works, as they say." He paused, and then Gabriel could feel his magic return, feel the strong, warm tide of it flowing throughout his body. Obviously, the same thing was happening to Ava, because she startled and then shut her eyes for a second or two as she drew in a deep breath, as if accustoming herself to the sensation all over again.

"That's better," she murmured.

Yes, it was. Having suffered the loss of his magic for months, Gabriel certainly had no desire to go through that again, not even for a few scant minutes. He stared at the null. "Does this mean you'll help us?"

"It means I haven't yet said no," he replied. "Come, let us go to my house. My mother will be happy to see you alive and well—she mourned in private when Vicénte sent you away." A glint from his dark eyes, and Alessandro added, "I always had a feeling you were her favorite."

Since Gabriel had harbored much the same suspicion back when he was a boy, he didn't argue, only shrugged. Going closer to the village had its own set of problems, but that had been his original plan anyway—to go to Alessandro's house first and do what he could to enlist the null's aid. That the planned discussion had taken place here in the wilderness rather than in the cozy interior of the cottage which had been home to Alessandro and Lara's family since before he had even been born only meant the timeline had been accelerated somewhat, and nothing else. And in a way, that was a good thing. It was also good that Alessandro hadn't yet given an answer. That could only mean he was still weighing his options, still trying to determine what would be best for him and his family.

"Come," the null said briefly, then turned away from them so he could begin walking down the faint trail that led from the clearing southward, back toward Pico Negro. Lara began to follow at once, although she paused for a second to incline her head, as if reiterating that Gabriel and Ava needed to do the same.

Which of course they did.

He held out his hand to Ava, and she took it with an expression of obvious gratitude in her eyes. Everything about her posture indicated that she was uneasy, unsure as to what might come next. Well, that made two of them. He supposed he should be relieved that Alessandro had not yet given a definite answer to his proposition, but if he truly believed Gabriel had a fighting chance, he probably would have agreed right away to be part of the plan.

Or not. Alessandro had always been wary,

always guarded, even as a boy whose powers hadn't yet manifested themselves. Why he should be that way, Gabriel wasn't sure; certainly, the null's mother had always been loving and kind to her son. Yes, their father had died not long after Lara was born, of a sudden and completely unexpected heart attack. No healer could bring someone back from the dead, and so Teresa had long been a widow. Possibly the suddenness of his father's death had been enough to convince Alessandro that he couldn't take anything for granted in this world, that every decision had to be weighed and considered from all angles.

The path on this side of the clearing was in slightly better shape than the first leg had been. Even so, Ava gripped Gabriel's hand tightly as she trudged along next to him. He could see how the wavy tendrils around her face were stuck to her skin, how more perspiration created trails down the light-colored tank top she wore. Looking at her, he experienced a pang of guilt at bringing her to a place she was clearly ill-suited for. True, she'd insisted on coming, probably would have done her best to follow him if he'd attempted to leave her behind, but....

*In the end, it will be worth it,* he told himself. *You will free the clan from Vicénte's rule, and...*

*...and then....*

He realized this was something he and Ava

hadn't spoken of, not really. She'd sworn to help him, to come here and do whatever she could, but had her thoughts traced this plan to its logical conclusion, namely, that Gabriel would stay here in Pico Negro to lead the Escobars? Had she told herself that she could stay in El Salvador as well, giving up her own clan, her home, everything and everyone she had ever known?

Although he didn't doubt the strength of her feelings for him, he had to wonder if she was quite ready to make that kind of sacrifice. Santa Fe was a beautiful city, with art and culture and many things to distract her, galleries and museums, libraries and movie theaters and shops and restaurants. She would not have those sorts of diversions in Pico Negro, or in San Matías, the closest civilian village. A good deal more could be found in San Salvador, although no one in the clan traveled there on a regular basis, and only went when they needed to procure items or services not readily available in their remote little town.

But he also realized that if he asked Ava outright about any of this, she would probably state that of course she was ready to give up Santa Fe, that she wouldn't have traveled here in the first place if she wasn't ready to make that kind of change in her life. Well, he would have to wait and see what happened. Despite his confident words to Alessandro, Gabriel knew that the outcome of his confrontation with Vicénte was by no means guaranteed.

The quartet walked for another ten minutes or so, and then they came to another clearing, a bigger one this time, with a neat whitewashed house sitting at the far side and a pen with goats directly behind it. Flowers bloomed from pots on the windowsills and on the set of three low steps that led up to the blue-painted front door; Teresa had always loved her flowers, had them growing in various places around the house and made sure to display vases filled with them inside her home.

She was outside, watering one of the flower-pots from a rather battered tin can. Apparently, she'd heard their approach, because she straightened, smiling as she looked at her son and daughter…a smile that turned to a shocked "O" as she raised one hand to her mouth.

The watering can fell to the ground.

"*¡Madre de dío!*" she exclaimed in Spanish. "Are you a ghost, Gabriel?"

"No," he replied, then let go of Ava's hand and moved past Alessandro and Lara so he might reach out his arms to their mother. She immediately clasped him to her, and he was able to smell the rosewater she wore, could feel how frail and thin she felt, even in the loose blouse and bulky skirt she wore. Had she always been this small? As a boy, she'd always loomed tall to him, seeming bigger than she was because of her boundless energy, her refusal to let the world beat her down just because she'd lost her husband while he was still in his prime. "I am no ghost, Teresa. I have returned to Pico Negro because I did not want to think of what might have been happening here in my absence."

That comment made her let go so she could peer up into his face, as if trying to read something of his thoughts in his expression. Her brows —still dark and arched, just like her daughter's— pulled together, and she shook her head. "I am sure you know it is nothing good, Gabriel." Then she glanced past him, clearly noticing Ava for the first time. "And who is this you've brought with you?"

Teresa's gaze strayed down to his left hand, as though she expected to see a band on his ring finger. Smiling, Gabriel said in English, "Teresa, this is Ava Castillo. She and her clan took me in, helped me find a way to have my powers restored to me."

Prompted by this obvious cue, Ava stepped forward and extended a hand. "It's very nice to meet you, Mrs. Escobar."

As Gabriel had expected, this formality didn't sit very well with the older woman. She made a dismissive gesture and said, "Please, I am Teresa to everyone here in Pico Negro. I must thank you and your clan for what you've done for Gabriel."

Ava began to stammer some sort of demurral, but even as she spoke, Alessandro interceded. With a wary gaze in the direction of the village, he said, "I think it's better if we go inside. We have much to discuss."

The look his mother gave him was none too pleased; obviously, she thought her son was being far too abrupt. But she didn't protest, only said, "Of course. I have some fresh tamarind juice and ice, perfect for a hot day like this. Come in."

Teresa led them into the house, which was just as Gabriel remembered it—scrupulously clean, with vases of flowers everywhere there was an available surface. The same carved wood crucifix occupied the place of honor above the hearth, and baubles of colored glass hung in the windows. One new addition was the ductless air conditioning unit that had been installed on the far wall of the main room. Vicénte had had a system put in some five years earlier, and it seemed that others in the clan had decided to follow his lead.

Ava's eyes shut briefly, blissfully, as she obviously felt the cool air wash over her. One hand strayed to the back of her neck, as though she wanted to lift her heavy hair away so she might cool down that much faster. However, she seemed to think better of it, and instead pushed a loose strand away from her face, clearly hoping everyone would believe that was what she'd intended all along.

As Lara murmured for everyone to take a seat on one of the chairs or benches in the large space that served as a combination living/dining room, Teresa stepped through an arched doorway, disappearing into the kitchen. A moment later, she returned carrying a tray with a pitcher filled with the familiar rusty orange tamarind drink, along with five glasses.

Her daughter got up to help pour and pass the drinks around to everyone. Gabriel took his glass and sipped, the sour/sweet flavor of the tamarind juice reminding him of many afternoons spent exploring the rainforest with Alessandro, back in the days before their respective talents drove them apart. He sent a quick glance at the null, wondering whether the taste had evoked the same memories for him. Difficult to say, because he sat on his hard-backed chair and showed very little in the way of expression, although he had offered a brief smile to his sister as she handed him the drink.

"This is very cozy," Alessandro said, after allowing himself a second sip of the juice, irony heavy in his tone. "But this is not exactly a social call, is it, Gabriel?"

"No," he replied. There was no reason to delay

or attempt to misrepresent his reason for being here. Alessandro and Lara already knew the truth, and Teresa…well, she had never had much use for Vicénte, could see past his superficial charm to the cold heart that beat beneath the slick exterior. He turned toward the older woman and went on, "You see, I have returned here because I want something better for our clan, something more than Vicénte can give any of you. I want to be *primus*."

She didn't blink, although the sudden flicker in her eyes told him she was startled…and anxious. Did she inwardly fear that he was not strong enough to confront Vicénte, that he had returned here only to seek his own death? Gabriel could see why she might fear such an outcome, but now the only way was forward.

For a few seconds, Teresa didn't respond. But then she said, "I think there are many in the clan who would be glad to hear such a thing, although of course none of them are brave enough to speak their opinions aloud. There was a great deal of murmuring after you were sent away. Of course, your brother and the elders did their best to paint you as a traitor, and that they were being merciful and kind in only exiling you rather than giving you a traitor's death. But we all knew what had happened…or at least, we could guess. I knew there was something terribly wrong about those books Vicénte brought back here to Pico Negro. I could smell the death and evil on them."

This declaration made Gabriel stare at her, surprised. Yes, they'd felt wrong to him as well, but he'd known what he was stealing from the Castillo clan's hiding place. He had no idea that the books gave off their own peculiar stink.

Teresa shrugged, then took her first sip of the tamarind juice. "My true gift is growing things"— she made a casual wave with one hand toward the riot of color in the flowerpots on the windowsill —"but I can also sense the wrongness in some magic, even if I can't say exactly why it is wrong. Your father...he also carried that wrongness about him."

It was the first time Gabriel had ever heard her say such a thing. Had she kept quiet up until now because she was unsure as to how he might receive such a piece of information? To tell the truth, he wasn't all that surprised to hear her say such a thing about Joaquin; he had very few memories of the man, and no doubt his father had always shown his best face to his son, but history had shown that Joaquin Escobar's heart was a black and shriveled thing.

"And she sees that same wrongness in Vicénte," Lara put in unexpectedly, perhaps emboldened by her mother's own declaration.

Teresa didn't argue, only shook her head. "Yes,

I fear he wishes to walk the same dark path. The only thing that has saved us so far is that he does not have your father's strength. You, Gabriel—you have that strength, only with none of the darkness Joaquin carried within him."

"So you approve of his plan?" Alessandro asked then. His lip didn't precisely curl, but it was obvious that he did not much appreciate hearing his mother praise another.

"I haven't heard it, so I can't say whether I approve of it or not," she replied. Her gaze moved from her son back to Gabriel. "Perhaps you should tell me more."

For a second or two, he paused, trying to think of the best way to state his case. He'd imagined this scenario already, had come up with some very eloquent arguments as to why he should be *primus* of the Escobar clan. Faced by Teresa's bright, dark eyes, however, he realized those arguments probably weren't quite as convincing as he'd thought.

"Vicénte thinks only of power," he said at last. "His own power, nothing more. Those books would not have helped this clan—if anything, they would have aided in its destruction. One of Joaquin's sons should be *primus,* since that is how these things are done in this clan, but there is no reason that man should be Vicénte. Indeed, if he remains in control here, there is a very good chance he will lead you to ruin. And of course, there are other reasons why it is better if he did not have absolute power in Pico Negro." Gabriel paused there, then sent a significant glance toward Lara. Her mother's lips pressed together, but she didn't say anything. It was clear enough that she knew exactly what he meant by his comment.

This exchange apparently ruffled Alessandro as well. He set down his glass of juice and stood, arms crossed. "What he isn't saying is that he wants me to aid him—that his so-called 'plan' will collapse around him if he isn't assured that I won't interfere."

"Well, of course you won't interfere," Teresa said, tone so matter-of-fact, it was clear that she hadn't expected anything else of her son. "You must do this for Lara…and for the rest of us as well. Weren't you telling me just the other day that you wished you could do something more to protect her?"

"Yes," Alessandro said, although the response was barely more than a mutter. Obviously, he wasn't too happy about having his own words used against him.

"Then it seems simple enough to me." She went over to her son then and laid a hand on his arm. "It doesn't sound as though Gabriel expects you to act directly against Vicénte. He simply doesn't want you to get in the way or use your gift to prevent him from using his own powers."

"That's exactly it," Gabriel said. "Anything else would be too risky. This fight is between Vicénte and me."

At the word "fight," some of the liveliness left Teresa's expression, as though she understood that he might have to remove his brother permanently if no compromise could be found. "It is terrible that it has come to this," she told him. "But you would not have been forced to this pass if your brother had led this clan in an honorable way."

True enough. The news that Vicénte had continued his search for dark, powerful artifacts was argument enough for his removal. If he had accepted his defeat when the grimoires were destroyed and had done his best to be a good *primus* to the Escobars, then Gabriel probably would have abandoned this quest. But it was painfully clear that his brother had no intention of doing anything of the sort.

"And the elders?" Alessandro asked then. "What of them?"

"They must be removed as well," Gabriel replied. "They are my brother's lackeys and nothing more—his servants, not servants of the clan itself."

"How good of you to think of everything," came a new voice, one Gabriel recognized at once.

It belonged to Raúl, the squatty, toad-faced elder, whom he had always hated.

A set of shadows filled the doorway—Vicénte in the middle, with Raúl and Elisa, the other elder, on either side of him. Vicénte's arms were crossed, and a gloating smile pulled at his mouth.

"Welcome home, little brother."

## 20

THE ENTIRE CONVERSATION AT TERESA'S house had been conducted in Spanish, and so Ava had sat quietly on her hard chair of carved wood, sipping from her glass of tamarind juice—which was quite good, both sour and sweet at the same time, and infinitely refreshing after her trek through the rainforest—and did her best not to look as left out as she felt. Logically, she knew it was more important for the Escobars to hash out their differences than it was for them to make allowances for the interloper by speaking English, but she still hated that she didn't quite know what was going on.

However, when she saw the three people standing in the doorway, saw the briefest flash of panic in Gabriel's eyes before it turned to a steely resolve, she knew exactly who they were—his older brother Vicénte, and a tall, severe-looking woman and ugly little man in plain, dark clothing...the clan elders, whose faces she recognized from Gabriel's memories.

She looked over at him, the air conditioning in the room only contributing to the icy chill of fear that spread through all her limbs, and the corners of his mouth lifted slowly.

"Hello, Vicénte," he said in English. "You are looking well."

Vicénte didn't bother to respond, only came farther into the room, the two elders flanking him. His eyes narrowed as he looked over the people who occupied the space, gaze resting on Ava at the end. It took all her effort to remain there in her chair, to not look away or try to smooth what she knew must be her hopelessly tangled hair, or make some other movement that would only betray her worry.

Then he smiled, but it wasn't the sort of smile she'd ever wanted to see directed at her. It was slow and lingering, and made her feel completely naked. "Who is she?" Vicénte asked, also in English. However, Ava had a feeling he wasn't speaking in that language to put her at ease, but more the exact opposite. He didn't want her to be left in ignorance of what he planned to do to all of them. "Someone you collected to help comfort you in your exile? She's very pretty."

"'She' has been of valuable help to me," Gabriel said, rising from his chair. "But otherwise, she is no concern of yours."

"On the contrary." Vicénte took another step toward them all, the two elders moving with him. He seemed utterly sure of himself—and of Alessandro, whom he glanced at briefly before returning his attention to Gabriel. That he took the null's loyalty for granted seemed obvious to Ava. "Every visitor to Pico Negro concerns me, especially one as lovely as she. But I will deal with her later. I am more interested as to why you are here, hiding in Teresa's home."

"I am not 'hiding.'" Gabriel met his brother's gaze squarely; aside from that initial moment of shock, he showed no sign of fear, gave absolutely no evidence that he wasn't completely ready for this confrontation. "I am having a conversation, no more."

"But it seems you have forgotten that you were banished, little brother. In case the meaning of that word isn't clear to you, it means you were never supposed to return here. I thought even you would be able to understand such a thing."

A glint flickered in his dark eyes as Gabriel faced his brother and *primus*. They were very nearly the same height, and Ava could see some similarities in their features, although Vicénte's were not quite as clearly cut, didn't have the same symmetry as Gabriel's. Those differences were enough to make Vicénte look almost brutish, with his heavier brow and jaw, although probably most women would find him attractive.

"Oh, but I had every reason to return, Vicénte. I wanted to show you that you couldn't defeat me as easily as you thought. I wanted you to know that you were not worthy to be *primus* of the Escobar clan."

That bold declaration made the *primus* laugh, but there wasn't any humor in the sound, only derision. Ava wished she hadn't been there to hear it—she knew if she possessed the sort of powers Gabriel did, she would have done her best to teleport the both of them far away from here, far from the danger Vicénte represented.

Unfortunately, her talent didn't seem to be of much use right now. Sure, she could look into the *primus's* mind—she sure as hell wasn't going to worry about her scruples when dealing with someone as horrible as he—but what good would that do? Maybe she could see what he planned to do next, but she'd still have to give Gabriel some kind of verbal warning about what she'd found, and that would only telegraph their moves to Vicénte and allow him to change his plans.

"Enough of this," said Raúl, the short, ugly elder. He waved a hand, and it was as though Ava had suddenly been nailed to her chair. She couldn't even lift her hands from her lap. For a moment, her breath caught in her throat, and she wondered if he'd stopped that, too, had somehow managed to paralyze even her body's autonomous functions.

But then she swallowed some air and realized she could still breathe and that her heart was still beating. Across from her, Teresa and Lara and Alessandro appeared similarly turned to stone, Lara frightened, Teresa resigned, as if she'd known Raúl would use this particular weapon in his arsenal. Alessandro, on the other hand, looked furious—or at least, as furious as someone who couldn't move any of his facial muscles could be. His black eyes snapped with dark fire.

"Let me go," he growled, proving that their magical paralysis didn't seem to affect vocal chords or tongues or mouths. "I haven't done anything."

"Yet," Vicénte responded with a smirk. "For here you were, conspiring with my brother."

"Listening to what he had to say."

"That is the same thing."

Teresa spoke then, sounding so calm, Ava wondered how the other woman had managed to keep her cool. Even though she realized this was merely the elder's magic holding her in place, panic seemed to curl in her belly, telling her that she needed to get out of here, needed to do something to break the bonds of the enchantment that currently held her immobile.

"You should take my son's words at face value," Teresa said. "Possibly you have forgotten, but his null power can affect all of you just as easily as it can affect anyone else. If he really was a traitor—if he really had any intention of helping Gabriel here—then you three would already have had your magic blocked. The fact that he hasn't done so should tell you where his loyalties lie."

This reasoned argument made Vicénte pause. He frowned as he looked down at the two elders who stood next to him, then rubbed his chin. "What do you think?"

Elisa, the female elder, was the one who answered. "Teresa speaks the truth. Alessandro does not need to move to use his gift—Raúl's powers would not stop him from using his own."

"Hmm." Vicénte glanced back over at Alessandro. "If you had no plan to betray me, then what were you doing listening to what my brother was telling you?"

"Gathering information, of course."

That explanation seemed to satisfy Vicénte, because he nodded at Raúl. Ava couldn't see that the elder did anything in particular, but suddenly, Alessandro was able to take a step forward. For a second, he looked clearly relieved, but then his face went nearly expressionless again.

"Free my mother and my sister as well," he said. "Unless you fear that my sister's gift for talking to animals or my mother's talent for growing things might be used against you somehow."

That comment earned him a chuckle from Vicénte and a contemptuous glance thrown in the two women's direction. "No, I suppose there isn't anything I need to fear from them." The barest of nods at Raúl, and Teresa and Lara were freed as well, both of them rising from their chairs, although they didn't move beyond that, didn't attempt to get any closer to any of the others in the room. Ava saw the wariness in their expressions and understood that they were willing to remain where they were for the time being.

"Free me," Gabriel said. Sweat stood out on his brow, despite the air-conditioned breeze that filled the room. As Ava watched, she saw him move one hand a fraction of an inch, although she could tell how difficult even that small movement was for him. He looked as if he was struggling against the gravity on a different, much larger planet. "Or are you such a coward that you can't bear to face me in a fair fight?"

"No, I don't think I'll do that." Vicénte shifted, gaze now traveling to Ava.

She swallowed but tried her hardest to stare back at him coldly. Even as she did so, she couldn't help but be horribly conscious of the way her damp tank top was sticking to her body. No, you couldn't really see anything except the outline of her bra, but—

"It might be good to bring some new blood into this clan," the *primus* went on. His tone sounded almost musing, and he came closer, so close that she could see the stubble on his chin, could smell a faint whiff of sweat from him. "Don't you think?"

"Leave her alone," Gabriel said, his voice even more strained. "This is between the two of us. She has nothing to do with any of it."

Vicénte only smiled. His teeth were very good, although one of the incisors was a bit crooked. "No, I would say she has a great deal to do with it, since it was only because of the help her clan gave you that your powers were restored. So, I think it only fair that I thank her personally for her inter-ference."

"Do whatever you want," Ava said, surprised she sounded so firm, so unconcerned. "I'm not afraid of you."

"Perhaps you should be," he replied, smile broadening. He reached out and took hold of her arm, grip so strong, she was sure it would leave bruises behind.

Gritting her teeth, she told herself, *Don't*

*wince…don't blink…don't let him know you're afraid….*

Teresa spoke up then. "Vicénte, surely that is not necessary—"

"Do not think to lecture me on what is or isn't necessary," he broke in, not even bothering to look back at her. "I would think you would be glad for me to transfer my attentions to someone other than your daughter."

A tremor went through Ava then, one she couldn't quite control. Out of the corner of her eye, she saw Gabriel's mouth turn down in a grimace, sweat dripping along the side of his face.

The next second, one of the large vases filled with tropical flowers went sailing through the air and smashed into the side of Raúl's head, shattering into a shower of pottery shards, shredded blooms flying everywhere. He staggered and fell to the floor with a heavy *thunk,* clearly knocked out.

At once, the invisible grip that had held Ava in place was gone, and she got up from her chair and took a hasty step backward, putting as much distance between herself and Vicénte as she could. The female elder—Elisa—let out a gasp of dismay at the sight of her compatriot unconscious, but almost at once, she raised her hands.

Ava couldn't help but flinch as she wondered what kind of attack the elder would throw at her. However, whatever Elisa had planned to do, it didn't seem to be working the way she intended, because she flinched and then sent a withering glare in Alessandro's direction.

"You dare?" she demanded.

"I do," he replied calmly. "I will not allow you to attack someone who cannot defend herself, especially a witch from a large, powerful clan. Don't you think they would try to seek vengeance if anything should happen to her?"

Vicénte scowled at the null. "You will pay for this, *cabron*. But I don't need my elders to protect me."

"Good," Gabriel said. He also rose from his chair. "Because it is time for you to defend yourself."

Ava couldn't see that he'd done anything in particular, except possibly raise his right hand a fraction of an inch, but Vicénte grimaced in pain and clutched his side, as if someone had just struck him there. It wasn't enough to stop him, though, because he lifted both hands and pushed toward Gabriel, who was hurled into the wall behind him with enough force that the tin mirror hanging there was knocked off its hook and fell to the ground.

Glass went everywhere, and the *primus* grinned. "There you are, little brother. Seven years of bad luck."

Gabriel shook his head, as if to clear it, and

smiled back at his brother. "Oh, I think the bad luck will be all yours."

In the next instant, Vicénte went flying backward, missing the window by bare inches. Even so, the wood frame splintered slightly as he struck it, and Teresa let out a little gasp. Even though it was obvious enough whose side she was on, it couldn't have been easy for her to stand there and watch the two brothers destroy her home.

And as much as Ava wished she could intervene, she knew there wasn't a damn thing she could do. Gabriel had told her he was stronger than his brother, but as she watched them trade magically driven blows, it looked to her as if they were fairly evenly matched. What if the unthinkable happened and Vicénte somehow managed to defeat his younger brother?

No, the universe wouldn't be so unfair. It just *couldn't*.

Alessandro stood to one side, grim-faced, but it appeared as though he didn't want to get involved any more than he already had, was content to let the Escobar brothers fight one another for the privilege of leading the clan. Judging by the warning glance he sent his mother and sister, it seemed he didn't want them to interfere, either.

On the floor, Raúl began to stir, moaning a little. The null sent his flat, dark gaze toward the elder, and he muttered an oath as he looked up at Elisa. She gave a very small nod, seeming to let him know that yes, their powers were being blocked.

Well, that was something. At least Alessandro was going to force the elders to remain on the sidelines as well, making this match-up a little more even. Maybe he'd known that was the only way the outcome wouldn't be questioned.

Because she really feared Gabriel and Vicénte were going to kill each other.

Gabriel sent the fireplace poker flying toward his brother, who ducked at the last minute rather than getting speared through the heart. In the next instant, the rug Gabriel was standing on jerked out from under his feet, sending him to his knees. Taking advantage of his momentary distraction, Vicénte picked up one of the empty chairs and broke it across his back. The chair splintered as Gabriel collapsed face down, and Ava let out a terrified gasp, taking a step forward even though she had no idea what she planned to do. Was he...?

But then his hand snaked out and grasped Vicénte by the ankle, dragging him down to the floor. It seemed that they had decided their magic was too evenly matched, and so they were going to do this the old-fashioned way. Or maybe they'd realized that flinging fireballs or lightning bolts at one another in such a confined space might create too much collateral damage. Teresa and Lara were flattened up against one wall, looking on in horror, but they, too, seemed to realize they couldn't do anything to interfere, had to let this struggle play out on its own.

Ava, however, wasn't about to abide by those rules of engagement. If a chance to help Gabriel presented itself, then that was what she would do. However, as she stared down at them while they wrestled on the floor, she wasn't sure how she could possibly intervene without risking serious injury. She wasn't a fighter. She read minds, and that was it.

*She read minds....*

Ever since her power had manifested, she'd worked very hard to not intrude on other people's thoughts, to make sure no one could see her talent as a threat. She hadn't always been successful, but that wasn't for lack of trying. And although she'd never believed she could use her gift as a weapon, she began to wonder whether that was entirely true.

"Stop it!" she cried out, even as Gabriel landed a decent-looking blow on his brother's jaw. "You're destroying Teresa's house!"

As she'd hoped, this plea seemed to get through the battle fog in her lover's brain. He didn't exactly release Vicénte, but he did pause and send her a befuddled look. "I'll fix it," he said.

"No…you…won't," the *primus* ground out. Already, a dark splotch was beginning to show on his jaw where Gabriel had punched him. "You'll be dead."

A strange, purple-edged white glow surrounded his hands. He wrapped them around Gabriel's head, and the glow covered his skull. A thin cry escaped his throat, his dark eyes frantic with pain as he writhed in his brother's grasp.

"I learned a few things from those books," Vicénte said, "before you burned them to ash. Some very good spells, tricks you couldn't possibly know. This is why you will lose."

The taste of sour fear rose in Ava's throat. Before she even realized what she was doing, she'd bolted toward the two brothers, reached out, and grasped Vicénte's hands, pulling them away from Gabriel so they touched her skull instead.

The pain was blinding, searing. A wail tore its way out of her, but she continued to grip the *primus* by the wrists, holding him in place.

And then…and then….

It was as if every thought, every memory he'd ever had came through to her via their contact. She saw every petty meanness, every harsh word, every act of unkindness. She saw his fist strike a pretty, heavily pregnant young woman in the face, saw her fall to the floor and cry out in agony. She saw him teasing and tormenting his unwanted half-brother, glad of the chance to cause pain to the interloper who should never have been born. Every insult, every cruel act, every moment he spent relishing the hurt he caused others. All these flowed into her, and she gritted her teeth as the darkness in Vicénte's soul threatened to over-whelm her.

But she would not drown in his hatred. Her gift granted her the ability to see into others…but she realized in a moment of blinding clarity that her ability was not a one-way street.

Ava pulled in a breath, gathered up everything she'd seen and heard and felt, and flung it back at Vicénte, showing him the depth of his malice, the emptiness of his soul, a heart that had no room in it for anyone but himself. She made him watch as his young wife died in childbirth because of him, made him see the fear in Lara's eyes when he turned his attentions to her…let him hear the whispers of the people of Pico Negro, who spoke behind his back of his cruelty and his mistreat-ment of those who were supposed to be his family, not his servants.

His dark eyes went wide, and he let go of her, slumping against the flat-weave wool rug that covered the tile floor. At once, the flow of images and voices and sensations stopped, but Ava knew that didn't matter now. They had done their work.

Feeling about a hundred years older than she had when she first entered the house, she slowly got to her feet. Gabriel pushed himself up from the floor as well and immediately came to her. "What...what did you do to him?" he asked, his expression a mixture of worry and wonder...and possibly relief.

"Nothing he didn't do to himself," she replied.

A pause, and then Gabriel gathered her into his arms, holding her close. That was better. With his arms around her, she could almost forget all the darkness she'd seen, all the hatred and vicious-ness and suffering.

Almost.

Silence, and then Alessandro spoke. "What should we do with them?" He glanced over at the two elders, who stood on the other side of the room, looking down in horror at Vicénte's limp form on the floor, at the way his wide eyes seemed to stare at oblivion.

Elisa drew herself up. "You will do nothing to us," she said. "We are this clan's elders, and we deserve your respect."

Gabriel didn't exactly let go of Ava, but he did loosen his embrace enough so he could face the elder who had just spoken. "You lost your right to our respect when you acted as my brother's lackeys. You are no longer this clan's elders." His gaze shifted toward Teresa, and he added, "I think it is time this clan had elders who will act in its best interests."

She sent him a surprised smile. Alessandro, however, didn't look all that impressed.

"Maybe," he allowed. "But what are you going to do with them?"

"No more than what they did to me." Now Gabriel did release Ava's hand, but only so he could step over to the null. "If I might borrow some of your gift?"

This request made Alessandro's brows furrow. "My gift?"

But then Gabriel took one of the null's hands and clasped it in his own, then reached out with the other to press his palm against Elisa's forehead. She let out a shocked cry and staggered backward, face pale.

"No—you can't—"

She didn't get any further than that before Gabriel turned to Raúl and did exactly the same thing. His swarthy face went pale, and his mouth twisted in anger.

"You dare—"

"I do," Gabriel said calmly. "I have. All I had to do was channel Alessandro's magic into you, driven by my power as *primus*. You are no more than ordinary folk now—I hope you can learn to do something more worthwhile with the rest of your lives. Now go!"

His eyes flashed fire, and the two elders fled the house. Watching all this, Ava couldn't help but be a little afraid of him, he looked so stern. This was truly a side of Gabriel she'd never seen before.

However, the tense moment faded as an odd hooting and howling erupted outside, followed by panicked-sounding exclamations in Spanish. He went to the window and let out a chuckle. Mystified, Ava followed him and looked outside, saw the two elders fleeing into the rainforest pursued by a band of angry, chittering monkeys. What the…?

From behind them, Lara spoke. Her voice was full of amusement as she said, "Vicénte seemed to think that my gift of speaking to animals was a joke…but who is having the last laugh now?"

And then, despite everything that had happened, despite Gabriel's brother sprawled unmoving on the floor, they all burst out laughing.

## 21

"HIS MIND IS GONE," PAZ SAID, TURNING away from where Vicénte lay blank-eyed in his bed, apparently noticing nothing of the world around him. "He breathes, his heart beats…but there is nothing left of him."

"Is it permanent?" Gabriel asked. He noticed how Ava's fingers had tightened around his as she stood there next to him, how she stared down at the floor and didn't seem to want to meet his—or the healer's—eyes. Did she blame herself? He knew she shouldn't. True, his brother wouldn't be in this condition if she hadn't turned her magical gift against him, but then again, it was his own cruelty magnified a thousandfold that had struck him down in the end.

Paz's plump shoulders lifted. She had been the Escobar clan's healer ever since he could remember, her once night-black hair now mostly gray. There seemed to be very little she didn't know about the human mind and body, so for her to be without an answer to his question seemed oddly unsettling.

"There has been no change for the past three days," she said after a long pause. "Of course, people have suffered brain injuries and not shown improvement for weeks or months or even years, but it seems to me that there is nothing here to even heal. I can make him comfortable, but we are not equipped here in Pico Negro to put him on a feeding tube, or to care for him the way someone in his condition should be cared for."

"Then what should we do?"

Her mouth tightened. It was clear that she did not much like the answer she was about to give him. "I think it would be best if he was sent to San Salvador, to a facility with the sort of equipment and medical staff who can properly look after him. I know it is not our way to put one of our own in the hands of nonmagical folk, but I don't see any other alternative."

This same solution had already been tickling the back of Gabriel's mind, so he was not overly surprised by Paz's suggestion. In a way, it would be the best thing for everyone involved. Yes, he was *primus* now—he'd felt the powers come to him at almost the same moment Vicénte's mind had snapped—but Pico Negro still felt unsettled despite the transfer of power that had taken place. With his brother safely removed to San Salvador and away from the village, they could all begin to heal.

Especially the woman who stood next to him now. Gabriel had done his best to reassure her that none of this was her fault, that Vicénte had brought this upon himself, but he wasn't sure whether Ava truly believed she was not responsible for his current condition. He'd also tried to tell her that her intervention had prevented him from having to shoulder the terrible burden of responsibility for his brother's death, although he feared she had only taken that burden on herself.

"Can you take care of that?" he asked, and Paz nodded.

"Of course. I will go down into San Matías today and make some phone calls."

Because cell phones didn't work in Pico Negro, all such arrangements would have to be handled in the nearby civilian village. Vicénte had owned a satellite phone—Gabriel had found it among his brother's effects—but no one yet had discovered the code that would unlock the device. Probably he would have to obtain another one in the near future if he didn't want to bother with a factory reset.

"Thank you, Paz."

She managed a very small smile, then murmured a goodbye to Ava and let herself out. The two of them remained where they were, Vicénte staring sightlessly at nothing from his bed a few feet away.

The sight still unnerved Gabriel—if nothing else, his brother had been a larger-than-life presence, and it was disturbing to see him reduced to such a shell, only a husk of the man he had once been—and so he took Ava by the hand and led her out of the room to the upstairs hallway. She bit her lip but didn't argue, only followed him to the spot he had chosen.

"You see?" Gabriel said. "It is going to be all right. Paz will handle everything, and then Vicénte will be taken someplace where he can be cared for around the clock."

A nod, although a very half-hearted one. "I suppose that is the best thing to do. I just—"

"Just what, my love?"

She summoned a ghost of a smile in response to the endearment. Even that small lift of her lips encouraged him, because she hadn't smiled very often since she turned his brother's magic on him and used it to strike him down.

"I just...how am I supposed to get past this?"

"By knowing you did the right thing." He kissed her, but gently, on the top of her head. "You more than anyone know what kind of person Vicénte was, what he would have done—to you, to Lara, to others outside this clan—if he hadn't been stopped. Because you were able to stop him more effectively than I ever could have, the Escobar clan has a chance to go forward without his influence, without the taint of dark magic to hold us back. Can't you see what you've done for all of us?"

A few seconds passed, and then a few more. Ava's big brown eyes stared up into his, searching for absolution, reassurance, love. All these things he would give her, and anything else she needed.

"I—I suppose so," she said at last. "I thought I knew what I was getting into when I came down here, but now…."

"Now?" he asked, fear striking at him. What if she decided she'd had more than she could take, that she needed to return to Santa Fe and leave all the terrible things she'd seen in El Salvador far behind her? His heart would break, and yet…and yet he knew he would understand. The life she'd lived before she came here couldn't possibly have prepared her for something like this.

She pulled in a breath, then reached up to touch his cheek. Softly, just a whisper of her fingers against his skin, but he was still able to sense the promise in that touch, the way she had begun to come back to herself. "Now I understand that sometimes it can be hard to get what you want."

Voice very quiet, he said, "What is it you want?"

"You," she replied without hesitation. "I want you. And that means being here in Pico Negro, and helping you guide this clan back toward the right-hand path. Even if it means living in this house," she added, with something close to but not quite a shudder.

Gabriel could understand her feelings. It was tradition for the Escobar *primus* to live in this house, the biggest and finest in the village, but it would probably be some time before they could cleanse the place of the dark residue Vicénte had left behind. "We will make it our house," he told her. "And in time, it will be our home."

"'Home,'" she repeated. "A home with you." The smile she sent him this time seemed much more genuine, and her hand crept into his again, fingers entwined with his. "I think I'll like that."

She sat on the bed in the room that was now theirs —a bed that Gabriel had brought in from San Salvador, since they'd both agreed they couldn't possibly sleep in the bed that had once been

Vicénte's—and stared down at the shiny new satellite phone she held in her hand. Both the bed and the satellite phone had appeared out of nowhere, although she guessed orders had been sent down to San Matías and had been quietly filled, just as they always had been. Ava might have suspected Gabriel of snapping his fingers and having them appear, except that he'd told her his gift of teleportation only worked on people, not inanimate objects.

Vicénte was safely installed in an expensive private room in a clinic in San Salvador, and the newly powerless former elders had disappeared into the rainforest and hadn't been heard from since. They were probably too mean to have perished in the wilderness; Ava guessed they must have found their way to the nearest civilian settlement and gone on from there. Whatever had happened to them, it was pretty obvious that the Escobars didn't need to worry about the man and woman who had once aided and abetted Vicénte in his reign of terror.

And now that those loose ends were tied up, she knew she had to tie up the loosest ends of all…the ones she'd left hanging back in Santa Fe. Yes, she'd told Tony where she was going and who she was going there with, but her family needed to know she was safe…and that the Escobar clan was no longer a threat. Six days had passed since she sneaked out of the house with Gabriel, and her parents had to be frantic.

So she typed in her mother's cell phone number and listened to it ring, wondering if she would even pick up. After all, she wouldn't have any idea who was calling…but maybe she'd recognize the foreign country code on the sat phone as something that shouldn't be ignored.

A small click, and then her mother's voice. "Who's calling, please?"

She sounded so brisk, so no-nonsense, that Ava hesitated for a second. Telling herself not to be a coward, she said, "Mom, it's Ava."

"Ava! Where are you? Are you okay?"

"I'm fine, Mom. I'm—I'm in El Salvador."

A pause. "With Gabriel."

"Yes. He—he's the new *primus* of the Escobar clan. Things are going to be much better now."

Was she saying that to her mother so she could reassure herself? Ava could already see changes occurring in the village—the elevation of Teresa and Paz's husband Luis to clan elders, the way people seemed to smile and laugh more—but was it enough? Could merely having a new *primus* be enough to bring them back from the darkness they'd dwelled in for so long?

It would have to be. Otherwise, what was the point in coming here in the first place?

"And you're sure you're all right."

"Yes, I'm sure. I—I want to be here."

A long pause. Then, "It's so far away, so different from what you're used to. Are you sure you know what you're getting yourself in to?"

The unspoken subtext, of course, was, *Do you really love this man enough to throw away your entire life?*

Only it wasn't throwing it away. Being here with Gabriel was discovering it all anew. Ava was still wrestling with what she had done to Vicénte, but, as Gabriel had pointed out more than once, it wasn't as though she'd created the darkness in him, had only forced him to see himself for what he truly was. In time, the shock would wear off, and she'd be able to move on. This morning, when she'd woken up next to Gabriel in their new bed, she'd found herself almost cheerful, looking forward to another day spent at his side, another day discovering what her new life here would be.

"I know what I'm doing, Mom," Ava said. "Maybe it's not what you would have chosen for me, but it's what I want. Gabriel is what I want. And it's not like you'll never see me again. We haven't really figured out what we're doing for a wedding yet—although I don't think we're going to wait too long—but of course you and Dad will come down here for that whenever it happens, won't you?"

"As if I would miss it," her mother replied,

adding with a chuckle, "especially since it's not as if we have to ask for permission to travel there."

No, that certainly wouldn't be an issue. Gabriel had already said her parents—and Tony and Cassandra—were welcome to visit any time they liked. Obviously, he wanted to do whatever he could to make sure Ava didn't feel as if she was exiled here, cut off from everyone she knew.

In a way, she supposed she was. But she'd already begun to make friends with Lara, although the girl's prickly brother seemed as standoffish as ever. Well, she supposed after feeling like something of an outcast for the past fifteen years, the null might be having a hard time trying to fit in. Anyway, Ava was starting to put down little soul roots, and she knew that soon enough, she'd have a hard time thinking of anywhere else as home.

"What about your house?" her mother asked next. "Or did you not even think about that?"

Of course, Ava had, although she still wasn't really sure what to do with the place. Part of her was tempted to just give it back to Tony, although he didn't have any more use for it than she did. "I'm not sure yet," she replied. "I guess just leave it for now—it's locked up tight, and I have auto-pay set up for all the utilities. Same with the landscapers."

"You can't just abandon it—"

"I won't. I'm not." Ava shifted the phone to

her other ear and went on, "I already warned Gabriel that I'd probably want to come back to Santa Fe to do some wedding shopping, so it seems like that would be a good time to take care of the house."

This explanation seemed to mollify her mother somewhat. "Well, if that's your plan—"

"It is." She hesitated. This was probably the time to come clean about her cousin Elena, still presumably hanging out at the La Fonda. On the other hand, why stir up trouble? Her mother hadn't said anything about the way Gabriel and Ava had busted Elena out of her house in Las Vegas, so maybe no one had yet made the connection. And since Ava had already told her cousin to go to Miranda when the ten days were up, she might as well let it slide for now. Besides, the last time they'd talked, it sounded as if Elena was having the time of her life.

*Pretty good rationalization there,* she told herself, but she knew she wasn't going to say anything. Her cousin was doing just fine for now, and would have a hell of a safety net for the day when she emerged from her five-star hotel and went to ask Miranda for help.

Ava heard footsteps on the stairs down the hall from the bedroom and guessed that Gabriel had returned from his meeting with Teresa and Luis. Good timing, because she didn't want to drag this out. Now her mother knew everything was fine, and had the promise of an upcoming wedding and a trip to El Salvador to cool the sting of her daughter's defection.

It could have been worse.

"I've got to go, Mom," she said. "But I'll call again soon. And I'll let you know when we're coming to Santa Fe for shopping."

"All right," her mother replied, sounding clearly reluctant to let her daughter go. "Take care…and send our love to Gabriel."

Those simple words were enough to bring a few stinging tears to Ava's eyes. A small gesture, but a sign that her mother was willing to accept Gabriel as part of their family. It was a beginning.

"I will. You take care, too."

She ended the call and looked up to see him standing at the entrance to the master bedroom. How handsome he looked, even in his faded cargo pants and a T-shirt that once might have been bright green but was now a washed-out avocado shade.

"Is everything all right?" he asked, then came over to her so he could bend down and kiss her cheek.

Oh, that felt so good, even when it was such a chaste little kiss. Her body thrilled at his nearness, and once again she felt a wave of happiness at the rightness of all this. Yes, no matter what anyone said, or anyone thought, she knew this was exactly where she was meant to be.

"Yes, Gabriel," she replied. "Everything is all right."

The Witches of Canyon Road series will conclude with Elena's story in *Haunted Hearts,* releasing in November 2019.

Broken

Forsaken

Forbidden

Awoken

Illuminated

Stolen

Forgotten

Driven

Unspoken

THE WATCHERS TRILOGY*

(Paranormal Romance)

Falling Dark

Dead of Night

Rising Dawn

THE SEDONA FILES*

(Paranormal Romance)

Bad Vibrations

Desert Hearts

Angel Fire

Star Crossed

Falling Angels

Enemy Mine

TALES OF THE LATTER KINGDOMS

(Fantasy Romance)

All Fall Down

Dragon Rose

Binding Spell

Ashes of Roses

One Thousand Nights

Threads of Gold

The Wolf of Harrow Hall

Moon Dance

The Song of the Thrush

THE GAIAN CONSORTIUM SERIES*

(Science Fiction Romance)

Beast (free prequel novella)

Blood Will Tell

Breath of Life

The Gaia Gambit

The Mandala Maneuver

The Titan Trap

The Zhore Deception

The Refugee Ruse

STANDALONE TITLES

Hearts on Fire

Sympathy for the Devil

Taking Dictation

Night Music

Golden Heart

* Indicates a completed series

# ABOUT THE AUTHOR

*USA Today* bestselling author Christine Pope has been writing stories ever since she commandeered her family's Smith-Corona typewriter back in grade school. Her work includes paranormal romance, fantasy romance, and science fiction/space opera romance. She makes her home in Arizona.

*Christine Pope on the Web:*
www.christinepope.com

facebook.com/ChristinePopeAuthor

twitter.com/ChristineJPope

pinterest.com/ChristineJPope